While the Coin is in the Air

KATE LAACK

Black Rose Writing | Texas

The author grants the final approval for this literary material.

First printing

This is a work of fiction. Names, characters, businesses, places, events, and incidents are either the products of the author's imagination or used in a fictitious manner. Any resemblance to actual persons, living or dead, or actual events is purely coincidental.

ISBN: 978-1-68513-568-3
PUBLISHED BY BLACK ROSE WRITING
www.blackrosewriting.com

Printed in the United States of America
Suggested Retail Price (SRP) $21.95

While the Coin is in the Air is printed in Minion Pro

*As a planet-friendly publisher, Black Rose Writing does its best to eliminate unnecessary waste to reduce paper usage and energy costs, while never compromising the reading experience. As a result, the final word count vs. page count may not meet common expectations.

Praise for
While the Coin is in the Air

"*While the Coin is in the Air* reminds us that we don't need non-stop, whirlwind action or melodramatic character conflicts to reel us in. The inner turmoil of this modern, relatable, complex young woman is more than enough to keep us enthralled and engaged right to the end. Five enthusiastic stars!"
–**Ruth F. Stevens, award-winning author of** *The South Bay Series*

"Kate Laack's *While the Coin is in the Air* has much to appeal to all readers: great scene-setting, fine writing, and believable characters."
–**Nancy Stancill, author of** *Deadly Secrets*

"Laack's brilliant novel addresses personal and professional issues faced by many women today in a page-turner full of memorable and likeable characters."
–**Diane Hawley Nagatomo, author of**
The Butterfly Café **and** *Finding Naomi*

"A women's fiction through and through. Laack's thought-provoking novel had me guessing and wondering until the final pages. A well-written and researched novel you won't soon forget."
–**Lucille Guarino, award-winning author of**
Elizabeth's Mountain **and** *Lunch Tales Suellen*

"When it comes to major life decisions, is it possible to toss a coin and let fate decide? Laack's story is relatable to women in all stages of life; an excellent book club choice."
–**Gail Ward Olmsted, best-selling author of** *Landscape of a Marriage*

For Josh– you are my great love story.

Dear Reader,

I'm not sure how this book will have found you. Maybe you picked it up off a bookstore shelf or stumbled across it online. Maybe a friend or family member recommended it, or perhaps you found it because you've either read my previous work, or I've convinced you to try this one. Regardless of how it came into your hands, however, I'd be remiss not to offer a word of insight and caution before you let it seep into your heart.

While I wholeheartedly believe this is a book for all women, I'm also keenly aware that this is not a book for all women *right now*. The themes of family planning, infertility, and unexpected pregnancy are difficult and personal topics. While I hope this story sheds light on the complicated experiences that millions of women endure, I also recognize that sometimes in the middle of those experiences, it's necessary to protect yourself. If it's best for you to stop right now, I only hope the knowledge that a story like this exists brings you the comfort of knowing that you're not alone and that there's a community of people who share your journey, your questions, your uncertainty, your heartache, and your decision…whatever that decision may be.

I am frequently asked if my writing is based on real people, and how much of myself winds up in my characters. I wrote this book fully aware that those questions were coming. Before you wonder about this author, however, consider the likelihood *you* already know someone in your own life, whether you've been trusted with their story or not, who has walked this path, asked these questions, harbored these doubts, and wondered how, in a world more connected than ever, this particular road is often walked alone.

I hope that this story starts conversations where they're ready to be had, provides healing and comfort to those who are ready to find it, and gives perspective to those to whom the answers and outcome came with merciful ease. Wherever you are on the journey, you are seen.

Best,
Kate Laack

"Whenever you're called on to make up your mind,
And you're hampered by not having any,
The best way to solve the dilemma, you'll find,
Is simply by spinning a penny.
No–not so that chance shall decide the affair
While you're passively standing there moping;
But the moment the penny is up in the air,
You suddenly know what you're hoping."

–Piet Hein

While the Coin is in the Air

Prologue

Harper guided her mother gently along the sun-dappled paths of the Northwestern University campus. It was a bright day, a warm day, tinged with the first hint of summer to come. Her parents had been in the city for a week while her mom underwent an experimental treatment at RUSH Medical Center. It was the first morning that Harper had seen any color in her mother's cheeks, and she seized the opportunity to bundle Helen up against the breeze off the lake and head toward campus and the mile-long trail along the water.

For a long while, they meandered in silence, taking in the sunshine and the technicolor landscape of brightly painted boulders studding the shoreline and sparkling with mist from the relentless pounding of the waves. As they reached the far end of the point, however, Helen stopped.

"So," she hung on the vowel as she had started so many conversations before. Her tone was casual, as if there was nothing unusual about the circumstances. "Where are you at with law school?"

"Mom," Harper protested.

"What?" Helen insisted. "I'm not allowed to ask about school? We can only talk about cancer?" She sighed. "You're still going to be a lawyer when I die."

Harper flinched. "I know. I just…" Her voice caught. "Can't we just enjoy the walk? The sunshine?"

They took a few paces in silence.

"All things being equal," Helen continued, "my vote would be Minnesota, and not just because it's closest to home–though it would be nice for your dad to have the support around. The man hasn't cooked himself a meal since the day we got married."

"Mom," Harper tried again.

"Of course, there's Northwestern." Helen pressed on despite the interruption. She spun in a slow circle, taking in the lakeshore campus. "I can see why you'd stay. And you know, George R. R. Martin is a notable alum. Your father loves 'Game of Thrones.'"

"Have you been Googling?"

"As for Cornell..."

Harper sighed. "I'm wait-listed at Cornell."

"I like the Ruth Bader Ginsberg connection," Helen persisted. "It's got a nice, feminist, liberal thing going for it."

"Feminist, liberal thing?" Harper asked, an unexpected chuckle escaping between the words. She rolled her eyes. "Mom? Are you ok?"

Helen stopped, peering at Harper from under the Northwestern baseball cap she had taken to wearing since surgical scarring and chemotherapy had claimed most of her hair. "No, I'm decidedly not," she said plainly. "I'm dying of brain cancer."

They stared at each other for a long moment. Her mom. The woman who had bandaged scraped knees and caught fireflies in jars, who taught her how to hem pants and make a perfect Manhattan, who took her to get her ears pierced and to her first R-rated movie, both at inappropriately young ages, was wasting away in front of her. They had known it for months. She had watched it for months. But in that moment, the blunt absurdity of it came bursting out as hysterical laughter.

They stood in the middle of the path, sunshine on their faces, bicyclists and joggers swerving and dodging around their maniacal display, heads tipped back, tears streaming down their cheeks, laughing at how much was wrong with life but how much was right in that moment. Only after they composed themselves, and the raucous guffaws turned to reserved chuckles, and they settled on a bench for Helen to catch her breath before walking back to the apartment, did Harper dare to turn the conversation back toward the decision she had been on the precipice of making for days.

"About law school," she began slowly.

Helen tipped her face toward the sun, her eyes closed. "Hmmm," she hummed contentedly. "Flip a coin,"

"What?" Harper asked, brow furrowed.

"A coin," her mother repeated. "Heads U of M, tails Northwestern." She opened her eyes and looked at Harper. "Unless you've already decided?"

"Not exactly," Harper admitted.

"Ok then," Helen insisted, digging into her purse. She held out a quarter. "Flip."

Harper stared at it. "Why?"

Helen shrugged. "Why not? What's it going to take to make up your mind?" She reached for Harper's hand, turned it over, and tipped the coin into her palm.

Harper shook her head. This was exactly the type of random, slightly bizarre idea her mother was infamous for running with. "I won't leave my law school decision up to the flip of a coin," she insisted.

"Oh, Harper," Helen chuckled. "Take a breath. You're always so serious. Besides, it doesn't matter which way the coin lands. What matters is how you feel about the result when you know it's coming. Now, do your dying mother a favor and flip the quarter."

"Fine," placated Harper, laying the coin heads up on the knuckle of her thumb.

"Heads U of M, tails Northwestern," Helen reminded.

"Sure," Harper sighed in agreement.

"One, two, three!"

Harper flicked the quarter into the air.

Heads. Tails. Heads. Tails.

She reached out with her right hand, caught it as it fell, and turned it over onto the back of her left hand, keeping it covered.

"What do you hope it is?" Helen leaned in.

"Mom," Harper started.

Helen gave a playful huff. "C'mon Harper, indulge me. What do you hope it is?" She pushed herself up straighter on the bench, and it broke Harper's heart to see her, even now in the clutches of a fatal disease, working to muster the excitement she felt the moment deserved. It made the words stick in Harper's throat.

"Neither," said Harper quietly. Her voice cracked as tears traced damp streaks down her cheeks.

Helen's eyes grew wide. "Oh, sweetheart." She slid down the bench and put a fragile arm around Harper's shoulders. "That's ok. We wait for Cornell."

"That's not what I mean," said Harper, shaking her head. She set the coin on the bench and reached for Helen's hand. "I'm going to defer." It came out as a hoarse whisper.

"Defer!?"

One glance at the look on her mother's crestfallen face, and Harper had to swallow hard around the growing lump in her throat. "For a year," she confirmed, forcing certainty back into her tone. "And then I'll reassess what makes the most sense. The admissions offices were very supportive of the decision…" She hesitated. "Given the circumstances."

"The circumstances?" Helen's shoulders fell. "You're going to wait to go to school until after I die?"

Though she was not wrong, Harper felt her mother's words like a punch in the gut. "Please don't say it like that," she whispered, voice cracking again. "We're going to make as many memories as we can with as much time as we have."

"And then?" The fatigue in her mother's voice was undeniable.

"And then," Harper said, steadying her tone, "I'll cross that bridge when I get to it."

Helen tipped back her head and closed her eyes again. She was silent for so long that Harper wondered if she had dozed off. The seagulls screamed overhead, diving at the white capped swells. A fishing boat idled past. A dog off leash came up the shoreline, treading bravely out onto the rocks, sniffing at the piles of seaweed washed ashore by the incessant waves.

"Just promise me one thing, Harper," Helen said, stronger than before. She pushed herself back up on the bench and looked hard at Harper, intensity and determination darkening her gaze. "Promise me you'll go."

"Go where?"

Helen waved a hand. "You know what I mean," she pressed. "Promise me that after the time we spend and the memories we make, when I'm gone, you'll go to school. You've made up your mind for now, and that's fine. Selfishly, I can live with being the reason you wait. But once I'm gone…"

Harper grabbed her mother's hand and squeezed. "I get it Mom," she assured her. "I promise. I'll go."

They looked out over the lake, the Chicago skyline cutting into the vast expanse of blue to their right, endless water and sky ahead, campus to their left.

"It's tails," Helen said placidly, looking down at the coin between them.

"What?"

"The quarter," Helen nodded. "Tails. Stay here. Northwestern."

Harper shook her head. "It doesn't matter."

Helen picked up the coin, turning it slowly to look at both sides, then laid it in Harper's lap. "Keep it," she murmured. "It will someday."

Part 1

Anything You Want to Be

12 Years Later

Chapter 1

At the tender age of six years old, Harper Andrews was told she could be anything she wanted to be, and like all children to whom the world has yet to reveal its hardships and heartache, she assumed that did, in fact, mean anything. She had no reason to believe otherwise. As a child, it's impossible to imagine the choices that will be made, the dreams that will be deferred, and the priorities that will change on the road to adulthood. Only much later would she learn that not only did opportunity and desire fail to exist in equal and abundant measure, but also that the great curse of growing up is having to fill a variety of roles that are as much an expectation as a desire.

Which was why, walking between the velvet ropes strung outside Indie Lime, she considered what her best friend, Maggie Evans, was doing tonight that much more incredible. Since they were kids growing up down the street from each other, Maggie had dreamed of opening her own restaurant. But unlike the vast majority of their friends and classmates who had taken drastically different paths than they once imagined, at age 33, after a relentless pursuit of mentors and investors, Maggie was on the precipice of doing exactly what she naively set her sights on decades earlier.

Harper looked up at the twisted green and yellow neon above the front door, bold in the falling autumn twilight. She chuckled–equal parts pride and disbelief.

"Name?" The host consulted the guest list with an air of authority. He wore a navy suit with a skinny, lime green tie that Harper knew Maggie had agonized over for a week.

Harper couldn't wipe the grin off her face as she responded, "Harper Andrews," fishing the invitation from her bag. The host reached for it, but Harper pulled away, holding it just beyond his grasp.

He raised an eyebrow. "Ma'am?"

"I'm sorry," Harper laughed. She looked at the card. "It's just...I was going to keep it." She fixed the man at the podium with an assured gaze. "It's not every day your best friend launches a restaurant in the heart of Chicago, you know?"

A corner of the man's mouth tugged upward. "Of course, Ms. Andrews," he nodded. "The rest of your party is already here. I'll show you to your table." He stepped from behind the podium and opened the front door with a dramatic flourish. "Welcome to Indie Lime," he proclaimed, motioning Harper into the dining room.

Despite knowing the gesture was designed for maximum impact, and having seen the space through various phases of design and remodel, Harper was not immune to the effect of walking into the restaurant full of diners for the first time.

A long bar stretched out in front of her, glowing under hundreds of small pendant lights with glass shades in every hue of green suspended at various lengths from the copper-plated ceiling above. The black-tiled wall beyond sparkled with liquor bottles and cut crystal tumblers, interrupted by a pair of swinging doors and a long, horizontal window that looked into a gleaming stainless-steel kitchen. Thin strips of teak, behind which warm backlighting glowed, accented the opposite walls, and tropical plants spaced along the front windows added a homey, comfortable vitality. Positioned thoughtfully around the space, two dozen round, white-clothed tables of various sizes, surrounded by chairs upholstered in supple, tan, calfskin–a custom choice over which, Harper knew, Maggie had also agonized–accommodated Indie Lime's opening night guests. The room vibrated with energy.

Harper swallowed hard, tears of pride pricking at the corners of her eyes.

"This way, please," the host indicated, moving Harper toward a four top table in the corner nearest the kitchen doors. The two men already seated looked up and pushed their chairs back, standing in unison as she approached.

"Thank you," Harper said to the host, who stepped away when he realized Harper had no immediate intention to sit.

"You made it!" exclaimed Seth Evans over the hum of the room. His sandy hair was swept neatly to the side, and his blue eyes sparkled with nervous excitement. Harper stepped around the table to meet his embrace, and as he opened his arms, she saw he had paired his black suit with an appropriately themed lime green tie.

"Cute," she said, nodding toward it as she stepped into the hug. "Congratulations. This is incredible."

"I know," Seth grinned widely.

Harper turned to the other man. "Hi," she said, a hint of flirtation making its way into the single syllable. She leaned in to press a kiss to her husband's darkly stubbled cheek.

Bryan Andrews slipped an arm around her waist. "Hi," he replied with a smile, turning to kiss her properly.

"Can you believe this?" She pulled back to take in the entire space. "It's actually happening."

"It's happening," Bryan agreed, pulling out her chair.

As Harper slid into her seat, her attention shifted to the long window through which she could watch the commotion of the kitchen. She waited anxiously to see a flash of Maggie's familiar, dark, curly ponytail bobbing among the bustling white chef's coats.

Their waiter arrived at the table. "Good evening." He filled Harper's water glass. "On behalf of Head Chef Maggie Evans and the entire team, welcome to Indie Lime." Harper's heart swelled at hearing her best friend's name announced so officially. "In honor of the opening, Chef is presenting a prix fixe menu focusing on her Caribbean roots and signature fusion flavors. Appetizers will arrive shortly. In the meantime, can I start anyone with a cocktail?"

Harper glanced to the bar where three bartenders in dark denim aprons mixed drinks with precise and fluid movements.

"What does Chef recommend?" she asked. A tiny thrill coursed through her at the privilege of being able to refer to Maggie by her formal title.

The waiter smiled and referenced his notepad. "The classic mojito."

Harper glanced between Bryan and Seth, nodding. "Three of those."

"With your top-shelf rum," added Bryan. Harper glanced at him in confusion. They already knew Maggie had curated one of the most extensive, and expensive, selections of Caribbean rums in Chicago.

The waiter offered an amused smile. "Sir, we have over 80 varieties of rum available, at least 74 of which are considered top shelf, six of which are over 100 dollars a pour, and one that, if it were available privately, would retail for over 10,000 dollars a bottle."

Seth shrugged. "In that case, just make it Bacardi."

"Very good." The waiter nodded and set off toward the bar.

Harper smirked. "Now you're testing the waitstaff?"

"Not at all," Bryan insisted. "I just wanted to hear him say it. It's impressive."

"The whole thing is impressive," agreed Harper, eyes sweeping the room and picking out recognizable faces in the gathering. Maggie's parents were seated, separately, near the bar. Next to her mother, her Bahamian grandmother, wrapped in a stunning blue and yellow dress that flowed around her like sun-drenched waves, held court with their waiter. A few tables over, seated with his new wife and stepson, Maggie's father scrolled on his phone while sipping, what Harper guessed to be, the most expensive rum and Coke he had ever ordered. There was a table of tittering young professionals that Harper knew to be friends of Maggie's from culinary school and a woman with an updo of intricately woven braids Harper recognized from photographs as the mentor who had offered Maggie her first sous chef position at a five-star restaurant. The woman watched the kitchen window intently, and

Harper felt a sudden jolt of nerves along with excitement for her friend. The space was beautiful, and the atmosphere was exhilarating, but Maggie still had to cook.

The waiter returned with the tray of cocktails and a promise that their food would arrive presently.

"To an incredible night," Seth offered, holding up his glass. "One of many more to come at Indie Lime."

Bryan smiled. "To sharing it together."

"And to Maggie," Harper added, raising her glass to the other two.

"Cheers," Seth proclaimed. He closed his eyes as he took the first sip and sighed in satisfaction. "So, Bryan, how's tenured life?"

The conversation drifted to the inner workings of academia. At 36, Bryan had recently earned the distinction of being one of the youngest professors to earn tenure at Lancaster University's School of Environmental Sustainability. Seth worked as the dean of students in a STEM-driven charter high school downtown. Their friendship had formed easily over a shared passion for data, technology, and education. That their girlfriends, and eventual wives, also happened to be best friends would end up being just one of the many things they had in common.

Without Maggie among them tonight, however, Harper embraced her place as the third wheel and turned her attention back to the kitchen window. Her leg bounced anxiously under the table as she waited for the first plates to make their appearance. She wondered how Maggie felt, moments from sending her first dishes, months of preparation coming down to this moment. She hoped that, whatever the storm of emotions, Maggie would take a moment and savor it. Harper had once known the thrill of standing on the edge of achievement, of accomplishing the very thing she had worked hardest for. Hers slipped away, but even now, the dull ache of regret remained. She wanted so much more for her friend.

An excited murmur rippled through the dining room as a line of waitstaff trailed from the kitchen bearing trays of white ceramic plates.

"Tonight," their waiter laid the first plate in front of Harper, "we begin with a fried conch croquette, pickled pineapple tartar sauce and a lime infused chili oil." The dish was beautifully presented with tiny vesicles of lime arranged among artistic dots and swirls of oil on which the croquettes were staged. Harper glanced around the room, wondering if it would be distasteful to take pictures and seeking anyone who might have thought to do the same. "Enjoy," the waiter bowed slightly to the table as he departed.

There was a moment of eager, nervous hesitancy as Harper, Bryan, and Seth exchanged glances before picking up their silverware and taking the first bites. A collective sigh of relief settled among them. As hoped, the food was indescribably good.

The meal continued, a stream of colorful, flavorful, beautiful dishes from which Harper was certain she could not choose a favorite. Mussels in a rich coconut curry sauce. Hearty white fish in a lime and potato broth. Roasted oxtail served in the style of osso bucco. A savory plantain lasagna. When the small, perfectly proportioned dish of Chantilly cream with a chilled, tropical fruit reduction was placed before her, Harper realized Maggie had thoughtfully curated the meal to the last bite. She was neither uncomfortably full, nor lacking for any substance, flavor, texture or spice. She laid the tiny dessert spoon next to her empty dish and sighed with contentment.

"Wow," she breathed.

Bryan squeezed her knee under the table. "She did it."

"Yes, she did," Seth agreed in a distracted voice, his attention on the kitchen window where Maggie was now clearly visible and speaking to the host.

Harper fought the urge to wave and call out to her friend. Then Maggie disappeared from the window, and the host moved to the center of the room.

"Ladies and gentlemen!" he announced. The buzz of conversation quieted, and for the first time, the noises of the kitchen–the clanging of pots and the clattering of dishes–filled the space. Then, they too died away. The host smoothed a hand over his tie, holding the room in a suspended moment of anticipation. "May I introduce, Chef de Cuisine, Maggie Evans!" He gestured broadly to the kitchen doors as Maggie stepped out, white chef coat buttoned high on her shoulder, lime green apron tied at her waist, and tight black curls pulled back from her face where she wore a confident, yet humble smile. The dining room burst into applause, diners rising to their feet as Maggie nodded in gratitude and recognition.

Harper glanced at Seth and found him watching with tears in his eyes. Her own throat tightened. Maggie began a lap of the room, stopping at tables to make introductions and accept congratulations. Her father gave her a gentle, yet awkward, hug, while his wife merely nodded and patted Maggie's hand where it rested on the back of her chair. Her grandmother overwhelmed her, holding Maggie's olive face in her dark hands and booming praise and adulations in a thick accent for all the surrounding tables to overhear. Harper knew it meant the world to Maggie that her grandma had made the trip; she had been the first one to let her get near a stove when her family visited the islands each summer.

Maggie shook hands around the far side of the room, stopping briefly for selfies with her culinary school friends and a lingering hug with her restaurateur mentor. Then, she turned to the table in the corner nearest the kitchen doors and, with a smile that suddenly bordered on shy, walked into the waiting arms of her husband and best friends.

"Oh my God!" Harper exclaimed, pulling her in. "I'm so proud of you. You absolutely crushed it."

"Outstanding," confirmed Bryan. "Really Maggie, it's beyond words."

"How do you feel?" asked Seth, admiration glowing in his eyes.

Maggie took a slow breath, blowing it out dramatically as she looked around the room. "Unreal," she said simply. "It's been an incredible night."

Seth draped an arm over her shoulders and pressed a kiss to her temple. "You're going to have lots of incredible nights."

Waitstaff circled the dining room with flutes of champagne, and Harper accepted the glass offered to her. The bubbles rose like flecks of glitter in the dim light, giving a magical, ethereal quality to the final act of the evening.

"Speech!" called an overzealous guest from the bar.

"Speech!" Scattered voices picked up the call across the dining room.

Maggie smiled reluctantly before stepping out from under Seth's arm.

"First, tonight I want to thank my waitstaff and the team behind the bar. They are the face and the pulse of Indie Lime and are the finest at what they do."

A polite smattering of applause punctuated the room.

"Next, to my team in the kitchen." Maggie glanced at the long window where half a dozen chefs now lined up, champagne glasses in hand. "If the staff out here is the face, then my crew back there is the heart and soul. Thank you for making my passion your own."

More enthusiastic applause as a few of the chefs at the window waved and nodded at Maggie's acknowledgement.

"And finally," she continued, "to my family, who has supported this ambition longer than anyone. To my mentors and teachers, who have taken the time to honor me with their wisdom and advice. And to my husband, Seth, who is the best and only partner I can imagine on this journey." Seth wiped at his eyes, and Maggie smiled back at him as she raised her glass. "Thank you all for sharing at my table. Cheers!"

"Cheers!" The response rumbled around the room as glassware tinkled together. A small crowd surged forward to further inundate Maggie and Seth with praise and congratulations.

Harper took Bryan's hand, stepping back from the table to give their friends some breathing room.

"Some night, huh?" She turned to face him, looking up into familiar green eyes framed in dark-rimmed glasses.

"I'd say," Bryan smiled and leaned down to kiss the crease in between her eyebrows. "Did you always believe that she'd do it?"

"Always," Harper confirmed immediately. "It was never a question for her."

Bryan nodded slowly. "It shows." He watched over Harper's shoulder as their friends continued to greet the doting dinner guests. Then his eyes slid back to Harper, and he smiled affectionately. "I'll go pull the car around for you," he offered. "I'm sure you want to catch her for just another minute if you can."

Harper squeezed his hand as he stepped away. "Thank you," she said, turning around to face the crush of people still surrounding Maggie. While Harper didn't need a throng of people fawning over her best friend as confirmation, there was no denying Maggie was an absolute triumph. Tonight was the culmination of years of hard work, preparation, and sacrifice. Harper was honored to be a part of it.

She caught Maggie's eye through a gap in the crowd, prompting Maggie to disentangle herself from two men in pinstripes and beg off another two conversations in passing as she moved toward Harper.

"Thanks for being here," she said, and for the first time, Harper heard the edge of exhaustion in her voice.

"Are you kidding?" Harper smiled. "We wouldn't have missed this for the world. Can you believe you did it?"

Maggie shrugged, noncommittal. "Yes, and no," she admitted. "I mean, of course I was going to do it, but it still feels like a dream."

"Enjoy every single second," Harper said, stepping forward for a hug. They held each other, years of history seeping into the embrace. When she pulled away, Harper noticed a sheen in Maggie's eyes that she knew matched her own. "Bryan's bringing the car around. Lunch Monday?"

Maggie started to protest, but Harper interrupted. "I know you don't open until five, and you need to eat regardless of everything else going on. Your team can run prep without you for an hour, can't they? At least let me buy you someone else's cooking."

"It won't be as good," Maggie smirked.

"It never has been," Harper smiled back. "Now the rest of Chicago knows, too."

"Maggie!" Seth called behind them. "*Bon Appétit* would like a word."

Maggie turned to Harper; her brown eyes stretched as wide as her grin. "I better go." She pulled Harper into a quick hug. "Monday. It's a date. Love you." She turned, immediately swallowed back into the waiting crowd.

The waitstaff scurried to clear tables as Harper worked her way around the edge of the dining room, stopping briefly to kiss Maggie's mom and grandmother on both cheeks. At the door, she looked back a final time. Maggie talked animatedly to a reporter taking notes. It was a glorious night, but that success needed to sustain, and again, Harper felt the smallest pang of nerves for her friend.

Nerves…and something else. Harper looked away, thanking the host who held the door as she stepped out onto the sidewalk.

A deep chill had settled over the darkened streets, and as the door closed behind her, and the hum and bustle of the restaurant faded away, Harper felt like she stepped from a dream world back into a cold reality. The breeze cut easily through her satin blouse, and she wrapped her arms around her chest, hugging them to herself, trying hard not to focus on the feeling that needled her uncomfortably.

Bryan rolled up to the curb in their black Subaru, and Harper hurried toward the car, eager to leave the cold and her wandering thoughts behind. She was thrilled for Maggie. Proud of Maggie. Excited for Maggie. Anxious, yes, but only because she cared so much that her best friend succeed. So why, she wondered, as she slid into the passenger seat and took one last glance through the glowing front windows of Indie Lime, was the emotion now growing in her chest no longer one of adoration, but jealousy?

Chapter 2

Unlike the crowds of young professionals that flocked from their small college towns to urban hubs like Chicago after graduation and dreamed of high-rise condos and bustling downtown living, Harper had found herself in Chicago by accident. Not initially. She spent her undergraduate years at Northwestern–a cookie cutter, 4.0-student-body-president-two-sport-athlete-band-and-choir-overachiever type– and after four years she felt like a native. She had not spent her time on campus lingering in her dorm room or at the student union, but immersed herself in big city life. By the time she graduated, she had discovered her favorite parks, favorite restaurants, and favorite bars in her favorite neighborhoods.

Her pre-law studies had been a grind, a double major in philosophy and political science, and her professors were more likely to call her stubbornly determined than academically gifted. But on paper, her A's were the same as everyone else's, and when it came to law school, the real equalizer was the LSAT, the admission exam required of all applicants. Harper had prepared for months, hoping to score above 170 and make herself a competitive applicant for a top 20 program. Ultimately, her 168 was both a disappointment and a relief. Though she missed her own mark, she was still highly qualified by other's measure. When it came time to ask for letters of recommendation, there was unanimous agreement that she had the grit and potential to be successful. As Harper visited schools and applied to programs, it seemed possible, even likely, that she might leave Chicago after graduation.

Then her dad called three weeks into the fall semester to say that he had finally convinced her mother to see someone about her chronic migraines.

At first, Harper hardly considered that bad news was possible. But two weeks later, when the doctor ordered additional tests, she couldn't ignore her suspicions that something more was wrong. Her mom reassured her that she was fine and asked animatedly about her applications, voicing a preference for a Midwest school that might keep her closer to their suburban Minnesota home. When her dad suggested she come home to visit at midterm, however, the gravity of the situation set in. And when her sister in Duluth texted to ask why Helen might have requested she come home at the same time, Harper began to assume the worst.

The sisters went home to the news.

Glioblastoma.

A word Harper knew only as a rare, complicated, and fatal diagnosis from *Grey's Anatomy*. There would be surgery and chemotherapy, but no cure. The doctors gave Helen a year.

Of all the things that were difficult about her mom's diagnosis, Harper did not consider her decision to defer law school high on the list. Not that it didn't hurt, but that hurt is relative. After Helen passed and Harper stumbled through the stupor of pain and grief that came with losing a parent, she sought a comfortable familiarity and routine that she knew beginning a stressful and competitive academic program would not provide. She offered to move back to Minnesota, but her father refused, gently prodding her back toward the aspirations she had put on hold. He had, no doubt, hoped the city might inspire her back to those old ambitions.

But the longer she stayed in Chicago, the more comfortable she became in her new routines, gradually adjusting her mark of success from how many floors the elevator climbed before dropping her at an imagined Manhattan law office, to how many blocks she had to walk from her favorite yoga studio, or preferred Trader Joe's, to her apartment. Classic and familiar comforts. That was Harper's Chicago. When she met Bryan–Lancaster University's handsome, charismatic wunderkind–the final piece fell into place. The city was home.

Which is why, even now, years later, she would often skip the cab on her way home from Sunday evening yoga class to wander the nine blocks to her apartment. Dusk fell around her, and a brisk wind cut along 55th Street, prompting her to nestle into her scarf. Traffic was thin, just the comfortable hum of the neighborhood. Kids wrapped in puffer coats played football down the alley. Week old jack-o'-lanterns wilted on porch stoops. An ambitious jogger in fleece lined spandex bounded toward the park. Mrs. Copperton walked her ornery, toothless bichon frise. Harper took it all in. Content.

True, the little one-bedroom apartment over DiAngelo's Corner Mart paled in comparison to the new lofts being built around the corner, and you could hear the "L" train screech just a few blocks away, but she had built this life for herself out of the ashes of her own heartbreak and tragedy, and she felt lucky it was hers. The windows of the apartment glowed in the settling indigo twilight. White Christmas bulbs, a festive touch year-round, winked along the edges of the curtain. Harper smiled as she swiped her keycard and headed upstairs.

Frank Sinatra seeped into the hallway as she turned her key in the lock, and she opened the door to candlelight, bellowing music, and Bryan in an apron at the stove.

"Hey!" Harper called over the music.

Bryan turned, a sheepish grin on his face. "Hey you." He set down the spoon and met her at the door, kissing her quickly as he helped her out of her coat.

"You cooked?" Harper asked, surprised.

"I did," Bryan confirmed, hanging the coat in the closet and returning for a more enthusiastic kiss. He tasted tart, like merlot. Harper pulled back with a wry smile.

"And you opened the wine without me."

Bryan glanced over his shoulder. "Just now. Maggie says red wine is crucial to a red sauce."

"I see." Harper slid from his arms and crossed into the kitchen. Two pots steamed on the stove, one full of boiling pasta, the other a simmering marinara. She picked up the spoon and dipped it into the sauce. "This is good," she confirmed. "Fantastic even."

Bryan laughed. "The wine is actually for the chef, not the sauce. Can I pour you a glass?"

"I'll shower first." She stepped from the stove, trailing a hand along his arm as she passed. She was to the bedroom door before she thought to stop and ask. "Bryan? What's the occasion?"

"Do I need an occasion to spoil my wife?" he asked with forced casualness. It did not, Harper noticed with some amusement, mask the nervous excitement in his tone. Bryan was attentive, helped around the house, and was, by every definition, an excellent husband. But even by his standards, this was definitely not ordinary Sunday night behavior.

She showered, changed into leggings and a navy tunic sweater, and checked herself over in the bathroom mirror before returning to the kitchen. She swiped the last smudges of mascara from under her eyes, pulling gently at the skin in the corners and assessing how the tiny wrinkles stretched and returned. Her whole life she was told she looked like her dad. Same angled nose. Same freckles that darkened in the sun. Same hazel eyes and strawberry blonde waves. But, if a well-regimented skin routine started at age nineteen and followed meticulously every night since could help it, she would not have his crow's-feet. Plates and silverware clattered in the background, and Harper smiled at her reflection before turning off the light and heading back to the kitchen.

Bryan had pushed their bistro set to the living room under the window framed in the fairy lights. The lamps were dimmed. The candlelight flickered. He set down two glasses of wine and gestured for Harper to take her seat. She watched him assemble plates in the kitchen, humming along to Sinatra, straining the pasta, spooning the sauce over the noodles. He grated fresh parmesan and minced parsley and basil, his movements unpracticed yet careful. Harper smiled, catching his eye as he carried the dishes to the table.

"What?" he asked.

Harper shook her head. "You're adorable. This looks amazing."

Bryan smiled. "It's no Indie Lime," he deflected.

Harper rolled her eyes, ignoring the small pang of envy that flared at the mention of the restaurant. It had lessened, but not dissipated, in the days since the opening, and Harper remained unsettled at her inability to brush it aside.

They fell into comfortable conversation, Harper's curiosity of Bryan's intentions lessening as the meal continued with routine weekend normalcy. The food was good, and despite knowing that she would be up early for work, the wine flowed. As she reached for the bottle a third time, it occurred to her that Bryan was probably hoping to get lucky. She smirked.

"What's funny?" Bryan asked softly.

"Nothing," Harper sighed. She leaned forward, elbows on the table. "Thank you for dinner."

Bryan leaned in and took her hands. "You're welcome." He hesitated for a moment, and his thumb skimmed over her palm. "You know," he started, tentatively. "I wanted to talk to you about something tonight."

Harper's curiosity piqued, and she looked between the flickering candles and the empty wine bottle. "You don't say," she chuckled.

He shifted in his chair. "I wasn't exactly trying to be subtle." He pulled a folded paper from his back pocket and smoothed out the creases as he laid the page on the table between them. "I want to know how you feel about this?"

Harper reached for the paper. A real estate listing. The stone townhouse sat back from the sidewalk behind a short, wrought-iron fence and neatly landscaped row of hedges and perennials. The tall windows were trimmed in black, and the house number was set in stained glass in the transom window above the craftsman front door.

Her heartbeat skipped at her husband's insinuation, and she looked up, catching her surprised expression reflected in his glasses.

"What is it?" she asked, attempting levity.

"What do you think it is?" Bryan responded. His eyes sparkled with excitement and candlelight. "It's a house."

"I can see it's a house," Harper chuckled nervously.

The house was gorgeous. Just off Nichols Park in an area they loved. The price was high, but not out of reach given the money they had already saved for a down payment. The colorfully worded description from the realtor checked many of the boxes on Harper's would-have-been wish list. It was nearly impossible to keep from getting swept up in Bryan's excitement. Even so, Harper forced herself to think rationally.

"I don't know what to say. It's beautiful. Everything we talked about one day. But…" She looked up, meeting her husband's eyes. "Why now? We're comfortable here. We don't need to spend the money. There's no rush…" She watched Bryan's Adam's apple bob as he swallowed hard. Something about it made her lose her train of thought.

Bryan nodded slowly. "It's just, I started thinking after the restaurant opening, we're at that point in our lives when we can do the big things. We're settled. I have tenure. You're in a stable position at the firm. I want us to have a place that's ours. Really ours. For us, and one day…" He hesitated. The room was still and silent, and Harper wondered when the music had stopped. "One day for our family."

A hard pit settled in Harper's stomach. It had been six months since they last talked about children. Six months since she had stopped tracking cycles, counting days, or following any kind of schedule or plan to try for a pregnancy. Before that had been sixth months of Clomid pills prescribed by her general practitioner after Harper admitted at her annual physical that she and Bryan had been trying, unsuccessfully, for just shy of a year. Her doctor had made it sound easy. Harper didn't have any underlying health concerns, at least nothing of interest to family medicine. Her cycles were regular, mostly.

With any luck, the pills would be just the boost her body needed to help the pieces fall into place.

Except they didn't.

Somewhere along the way, as the months ticked by and the pregnancy tests came back negative, trying for a baby became less something they were doing and more something they were enduring. Harper found it easier to disassociate than face repeated disappointment; by the time the pills ran out, she was nearly numb to it.

Harper had never been desperate about children, not in the way she knew some women panicked over their biological clock or perceived 'perfect' timelines. Bryan agreed to take a break before re-involving the doctors. They both knew they would come back to the conversation when the time was right, but Harper found herself genuinely surprised that Bryan believed that the right time was now.

She let the paper drift from her hand onto the table. "I know it's been a while since we talked about kids, but…"

Bryan shook his head. "Not but. I'm ready to take a step, Harper. Any step."

"A house is a pretty enormous step," Harper said with a nervous laugh. "More of a giant leap, don't you think?"

Bryan picked up the listing. "So, let's leap. I'm ready for something." He gazed at her, eyes smoldering in the candlelight, and Harper felt the same magnetic draw she always did when Bryan was open and excited and ready to draw her a picture of their future. It was part of the reason it had been so incredibly easy to fall in love with him. "Aren't you?"

"Aren't I what?" she whispered.

"Ready?"

Harper thought again of the pinprick of jealousy she felt at leaving Indie Lime. She *was* ready for something, though she wasn't entirely certain what it was. She nodded, a near involuntary response.

"Is that a yes?" Bryan asked, hope dripping from every word.

"It's a…we-can-talk-about-it," she offered, not entirely certain where that particular conversation might lead.

Bryan beamed, undeterred, pushing back from the table to carry the plates into the kitchen. He called to the smart speaker on the counter, and music burst back into the room as he started the dishes.

Harper took her glass of wine to the couch and pulled a blanket into her lap. Despite her suspicions about Bryan's ulterior motives, she had not expected the evening to take the turn that it did. She glanced around the living room. When they moved in, she never imagined they would be here forever, but she had loved it on site. The exposed brick walls. The fireplace, long out of commission, stacked with birch logs and studded with tea lights. The copper fixtures in the kitchen. The wood beams overhead. The sound of the hot water running through the radiator pipes.

The townhouse on the park–with its three bedrooms and walk-in closets and trey ceilings and hardwood floors–was everything she thought she wanted in whatever phase of life came next. An uncomfortable feeling of time passing and future uncertainty rolled through her. It was a family, she had imagined, that would move them into a house like that someday. A family that had yet to come.

"Whatcha thinking about?" Bryan asked, coming up behind her. Harper jumped. "Whoa, sorry," he laughed, kissing the top of her head.

Harper shrugged and pulled the blanket tighter around her waist. "I'd say you gave me *plenty* to think about tonight."

"Hmm," Bryan murmured against her hair. "Relax," he whispered. "We're just starting a conversation. I'm going to take a shower."

Harper watched him cross to the bedroom, waiting until he was around the corner before pulling out her phone to text Maggie.

Harper: Bryan wants to buy a house.

She knew there would be no response, or if there was, then not for hours. Now that Indie Lime was up and running, Maggie was running non-stop with it. While Harper had continued to send Maggie daily texts and messages of encouragement, she had yet to receive more than a few quick words or an emoji from Maggie since opening night. It was one of many adjustments she would have to get used to in this season of friendship.

She heard the water stop in the bathroom, and she stood up, making her way around the room, blowing out candles, and unplugging the fairy lights. She rinsed out her wineglass, folded her blanket over the end of the couch, and threaded the chain lock on the front door. Heading back toward the bedroom, she paused briefly, looking around the darkened room. It had been home for seven years, the only home Bryan and Harper had ever known together. For seven years, she had made her place here. Belonged here. It was enough.

But now, looking at the shadowed forms of her familiar furniture and possessions, Harper unexpectedly considered that this was a home she had never expected to make, in a place she had never expected to stay, with a man she would have never met had things only played out the way they were *supposed* to. The thought made her stomach hurt, but she couldn't help but feel that maybe, like Bryan, she was ready for something more, too.

Chapter 3

Horowitz, Walsh, and Pickett comprised the twenty-third through thirty-second floors of Falstaff Tower. Just off La Salle, with views of the Chicago River to the west and Grant Park to the east, the building was all silver steel and shining glass in the wilted sunlight of the November morning. Fractals of frost etched the windows of the lower floors where warmth from the pavement, passing cars, and hurried foot traffic was able to condense and freeze in complicated spiderwebs. Two giant revolving doors pushed pockets of cold air into the lobby in regular intervals, and a janitor stood nearby, mop bucket at the ready, to wipe away the incessant trail of grime tracked toward the bank of elevators on the other side of the tiled entry.

Harper flashed her employee ID at the security turnstiles before filing into the crowded, chestnut-paneled elevator compartment. Cramped against the back wall, she fished her favorite black stilettos from her bag, inadvertently elbowing the man pressed in next to her. His bushy, gray eyebrows furrowed, and Harper offered an apologetic smile as she slid out of her trusty New Balance trainers and into the heels. The added height brought her eye level with the man, and he turned away with a "humpf."

The elevator climbed, doors opening and closing, depositing employees and executives at their offices and suites. The crowd thinned, and by the time they reached the twentieth floor, Harper was alone with just a pair of attorneys she recognized from acquisitions and Tate Bishop, fellow paralegal. Tate leaned lazily against the silver rail that ringed the elevator compartment, dapper in a three-piece, gray wool suit.

He whistled through his teeth. "Looking good this morning, Andrews. Good weekend?" His British accent was clipped, yet not unfriendly.

Harper smiled. "Great, and yours?"

Tate shrugged. "Passable. My family was over."

"They came to Chicago?" Harper asked with pleasant surprise. Tate was quintessentially British–elite, aristocratic, British high society to be precise–and Harper had a hard time imagining his upscale British family popping over for an autumn stroll up Michigan Avenue in tweeds and tartans.

"No, New York. Would you believe my sister missed fashion week this year? Turns out a proper job with real responsibilities wasn't as easy to ditch as uni."

"Imagine that. Still, it was nice of you to fly out to see them."

"They're family," Tate shrugged. "I wouldn't miss a chance to see my baby sister, even though my father made me fly commercial."

"Poor thing." Harper rolled her eyes. "So how was...*not* fashion week?"

Tate gave her a placating smile. "Dismal. We visited two showrooms after which she tired of the whole thing, and we spent the rest of the day ordering room service and drinking champagne while watching carriages trek through the rain in Central Park out the window of our suite at the Plaza."

"Well, good to know you didn't leave any of the pretentiousness we all know and love behind in Manhattan."

"You love me, Andrews?" Tate teased with a grin. He slid around the compartment, moving next to Harper and throwing an arm over her shoulders. "I've always suspected, but it's good you've made your feelings known."

Harper felt the eyes of the other two attorneys dart their direction and shrugged out from under Tate's arm. They had been this way since they came into the firm together twelve years ago. Tate, swaggering, arrogant, loose with both his humor and his manners, lest the occasion called for the strict, social discipline ingrained in him during years of boarding school. Harper, self-assured, tolerant, unthreatened. It helped that Tate was incredibly efficient at what he did and unapologetically uninterested in dating anyone as "averagely American" as Harper. When she started seeing Bryan, she noticed how tense he would get when she talked about office dynamics and cases she was assigned to work with Tate. After the two met at the annual firm Christmas party, that tension had vanished. Bryan thought he was a bit of an ass, painfully pretentious, and "British to a fault." Not a threat.

The doors slid open on the twenty-eighth floor, and Harper pushed herself from the wall and stepped into the marble-tiled corridor. Already the office was buzzing with busyness, everyone working on paperwork that had persisted through the weekend and cases they were being pushed to wrap up before the end of the year. Harper loved the hum of it. Tate hurried after her, shouldering past the two attorneys and sticking his arm between the sliding doors before they could close.

"Hang on, Andrews," he called.

Harper laughed but didn't turn around as Tate tripped over himself to catch up. She nodded at murmured greetings as she made her way through the maze of cubicles to her tiny office on the perimeter of the room. It wasn't much. One glass wall looked out over the cubes. A modest window provided a view of urban sprawl; a jade plant sat on the sill. A few sepia-tone prints of city landmarks bordered by thick white mattes and sleek black frames hung on a gray-blue wall. A wedding photo, Newton's cradle, and large glass paperweight flecked with gold sat on the front of her desk, and the wall behind it featured floor-to-ceiling bookshelves stacked with tomes of case law and neat piles of file folders. Polished and professional, just how she left it Friday night. Just how she liked it.

She dropped her bag on the black leather chair under the window and moved to hang her coat on the hook by the door just as Tate loped into the frame. He glanced around the room.

"Homey as always," he teased.

Harper scoffed and went to her desk. "Don't you have work to do?"

"Yes, but," Tate glanced over his shoulder before stepping into the room and lowering his voice. "First, I brought you a present." He perched on the arm of the chair beneath the window; hints of a smile pulled at the corners of his mouth.

"What?" Harper leaned back and folded her arms. Tate glanced out the glass wall before rising from the chair and closing the door. He turned to face her with a toothy grin. Harper arched an eyebrow. "Ok, you've got my attention."

Tate flicked a business card from the breast pocket of his suit coat and passed it over the desk with a dramatic flourish. Harper took the card. It was trimmed in a thin, black border with a gold monogram embossed in the upper left-hand corner and serifed text centered on an ivory background. Along the bottom edge, someone had scrawled *2:30 ET–Monday* with a blue fountain pen. Harper looked up.

"What's this?"

"That," Tate said, giddy smile still plastered on his face, "is your ticket to an interview with Pollard Frank this afternoon."

Harper laughed out loud. "Pollard Frank is enormous...and in New York..."

"And London," Tate interrupted with a wink.

Harper laughed again. "Tate, I'm not interviewing at Pollard Frank. Why would Pollard Frank even *want* to interview me?"

"Us," Tate clarified. "Pollard Frank wants to interview *us*. My father's office switched counsel back home, and he stopped in to make a few stateside connections with the New York office over the weekend." He gestured at the card. "Harold Turner is a senior partner and *very* interested to hear from two paralegal stars looking to leave Chicago."

Harper sighed. "I get it. It's a favor. Your dad's a VIP account, and they owe him one." Tate's smile fell by a fraction. "Which is great for you, Tate. Really. It's all about who you know, so..."

Tate shook his head. "Don't make this about my parent's money, Andrews. Or do. Who cares? My dad knows people, and you know me.

Six degrees of separation and all that bullocks. He wants to have a conversation. And I said, if they're really looking for the cream of the crop, they need to talk to my associate. She's the superstar. The absolute best person to have on your side heading into a legal scrap."

"Why would you do that?" Harper sighed.

"Because you are!" Tate burst. "C'mon! We've been talking about what comes next since we came in together."

Harper shook her head. She held the card back out to Tate. "I *talked* about it when we came in together," she clarified. "That was twelve years ago. I settled down, got married, and made my home here."

"Your mom died," Tate added quietly.

Harper's hazel eyes flashed.

"Don't be an asshole."

Tate held up his hands. "I'm sorry."

"Now *you've* been talking about it," Harper went on. "What's Bryan going to do in New York?"

"He's a weatherman," Tate scoffed. "There's weather in New York."

"He's a tenured professor of climatology and a private environmental impact consultant."

"Whatever." Tate waved the comment away. "There are schools and businesses in New York, too."

"There are law firms in Chicago," Harper insisted. "We work at one, remember? A good one."

Tate deflated. "I thought you'd be more excited about this. You're good, Andrews. Better than Horowitz, Walsh, and Pickett."

Harper pulled a file folder toward her with a sigh. "I like it here Tate. You did too a week ago."

Tate considered her. "Wait. Why are you blowing this off? Didn't you just support six years of Bryan working toward tenure? He's always supported your work, too. It's your turn. I don't even think this would surprise him."

Harper dropped her pen and looked at Tate in disbelief. "You don't think expressing a sudden desire to move across the country would surprise my husband?"

"I don't think it would surprise him you want more than this." Tate gestured around the office, and the incessant niggle of discontent that had plagued Harper for days twinged again.

"He wants to buy a house."

Tate laughed, a relieved chuckle. "Buy a house in New York."

Harper looked up from the documents. "That's not how it works, Tate!" she burst in frustration. "He wants a life here, and I…"

Tate held up a hand, waving the rest of the sentence away. "Is that what you want?"

Harper took a deep, deliberate breath, but did not respond.

Tate set a finger on the card where Harper had left it on the corner of the desk and slid it back toward her. "Do yourself a favor," he said quietly, "and take the phone call just in case." He threw her a withering smile at her before turning around and leaving the office.

Harper turned back to the file folder, trying to lose herself in the minutiae of a complex legal transaction. It was not uncommon for Tate to be aspirational, talking about moving back to London or breaking out of the Chicago office. In fact, when they first met, Harper had been a bit surprised Tate ended up in Chicago at all. Sure, Horowitz, Walsh, and Pickett was a well-known and respected firm that boasted additional offices in San Francisco, Austin, and Toronto, but it seemed an odd landing spot for the Englishman, especially given his family's extensive connections.

It was during their first year, over one-too-many gin and tonics, that Harper got the full story. Tate's father had pulled lots of strings. Strings to get his son into the best boarding schools. Strings that, had he stayed in Britain, would certainly have landed him at Oxford or Cambridge–no, not or. It would have been Oxford. Tate's father was an Oxford man. But Tate had his sights set on the States, and, as a proud Englishman, his father refused to call in a favor at any of the American "Ivies." Tate had laughed. He was quite certain that, "as a proud Englishman," his father didn't have any favors to call in at Harvard or Yale or anywhere else.

So, Tate had looked at the list of top American universities, skipped the east coast Ivy league schools so as not to tempt his father into withholding tuition money, and landed on Stanford or the University of Chicago. Chicago was a shorter flight home, a top ten undergraduate program and a top five law school. It was difficult for even his father to argue with the logic of his choice, outside of the fact that it wasn't Oxford.

But unfortunately for Tate, when it came time for law school, it turned out his father didn't hold any sway over the LSAT either. Though a decent student, Tate was not a good test taker, and despite months of preparation and sitting the test three times, his scores never climbed above the median, let alone crack the upper echelon needed for a top law program. His father told him it was time to come home and start working in the family's real estate empire. But Tate was defiant. He found the paralegal job at Horowitz, Walsh, and Pickett himself, and he had earned every bit of praise on his own merits ever since.

Until now, Harper thought, pulling the card toward her. Now that he had proven his mettle, he would be the prodigal son returned. She could picture him, navy suit, wing-tipped shoes, strolling up Lexington Avenue with a styrofoam cup of coffee in hand from a cart on the corner. She once pictured herself there, too. She would work a hundred hours a week and come home to a tiny studio apartment in a soon-to-be-trendy neighborhood. She would date a financier, artist, lawyer, or advertising exec and walk through Central Park and form strong opinions about bagels, pizza, and New Jersey. It had been a vibrant daydream, on the precipice of reality. And then her mom got sick.

She and Bryan had never seriously talked about leaving the city together, though there had been one moment when Bryan was settling in as an assistant professor that a larger, west coast university had made him an enticing offer. Harper would have to jump firms, but she was already a standout at Horowitz, Walsh, and Pickett. There were plenty of big firms looking for solid paralegal support, and she would have glittering recommendations to supplement an otherwise limited resume. "Why not?" she said with a smile and a shrug one night when Bryan had asked if she would ever consider leaving Chicago.

Then they got married and found the apartment in Hyde Park. Bryan began to research and publish, moving him onto the tenure track. He consulted with startups in the city for both for fun and some extra cash. They got comfortable. As time passed, the idea of leaving did too, though certainly, had she asked for them, the references from the office would have remained impeccable.

Harper picked up the card and rubbed her thumb over the thick, linen-textured paper. A week earlier, she would have tossed it in her trashcan and gone back to work without a second thought. So why, she wondered, did she suddenly feel an undeniable desire to take the call?

Chapter 4

"So, your work husband wants you to move to New York, and your actual husband wants to put down roots and buy a house in Chicago," Maggie chortled between bites of gyro a few hours later.

Harper shook her head, taking a sip of iced coffee. "What am I going to do, Maggie?"

"Do? What do you mean? This is between you and Bryan. Tate doesn't really get a vote here." Maggie took another bite, nodding slowly as she chewed. "I might not get a vote either, but seeing as I just tangibly tied myself to this city, I'd also prefer that you stayed. So, let's forget about New York." When Harper didn't answer, Maggie set down her sandwich and raised an eyebrow. "Unless you don't want to," she said with surprise. "Do you? Want to?"

Harper shrugged. "It's not something I was looking to do. I wouldn't have thought it was seriously an option."

"It's *not* seriously an option, Harper."

"Why not?" Harper asked with a touch of defiance. "Everyone else got their chance. Bryan earned tenure. You just opened the restaurant. Seth is all but running his school." She looked away. "I'm sick of feeling left behind." A small wave of relief rippled through her for having put words to her lingering envy.

Maggie leaned back in her chair, eyes wide. "Are you kidding? You're a star at the firm."

Harper looked away.

"No one's leaving you behind," Maggie added gently. "Besides, this is Tate we're talking about. I mean, I get wanting more. He dropped this in your lap unexpectedly, and I'll admit it's at least interesting. You're processing in real time. But when have you ever let Tate have the last word about anything, let alone where you should take a job and move?" She reached across the table and snagged a fry from Harper's basket. "You know I'm your biggest fan, but please tell me you're not really considering this?"

Harper threw her head back and groaned. "I don't know. Not moving. Just the meeting."

"Then you might as well consider all of it. The move. Bryan. Saying no to the house."

Maggie's phone chirped, and she glanced at the screen.

"Fan mail?" Harper teased. Maggie's picture had run on the front page of the city section of the Chicago Tribune that morning.

"It's been a lot," Maggie said, blowing out a deep breath. "Everyone wants to hitch their wagon to a shooting star."

"Shooting stars flare out," Harper said pointedly. "Everyone wants to hitch their wagon to a sure thing."

Maggie ignored the compliment, returning the text before looking back to Harper. "What are you going to do about the interview?"

Harper stood and wound her scarf into a decorative twist around her neck. "I can take a call without deciding, can't I?"

Maggie looked skeptical. "Ok, but are you going to tell Bryan?"

Harper, reaching for her purse, stopped. "Before?"

"Um, yeah. I'd think you'd let your husband know before you took a job interview across the country. Besides, have you ever *not* told Bryan something?"

Harper considered. "No."

Maggie nodded. "Ok, so call him. Talk it over. You don't need me to tell you this. C'mon. Relax. Think." She offered a one-armed hug. "And good luck."

Harper smiled. "It's just a phone call. Nothing official."

Maggie pulled back with a small frown. "I meant with Bryan."

"Right." Harper grimaced, embarrassed. "I'll call him on my walk back."

The walk from Greektown back to the office was short, and Harper knew she should place the call right away to catch Bryan in between classes. However, as she marched back toward the tower, she repeatedly stopped herself from pushing the buttons. There was something about telling her husband that legitimized the idea of leaving in a way she wasn't quite ready to commit to. There wasn't any reason to get Bryan worked up over something that likely would not happen. Maggie was right. It wasn't seriously an option. Still, she wondered briefly why, if the call really was nothing, she felt the need to conjure so many excuses. Then she was pushing through the revolving doors and heading back toward the gleaming elevators packed full from the returning lunch crowd, and her moment of privacy had passed.

As the elevator climbed, she glanced at her watch. 1:00pm. Her heart fluttered. Still time to back out and pretend she didn't care. Let Tate go to New York or back to London. She would miss their friendly banter. He had been a fixture of her entire time at the firm. But things changed. He wanted something different, and Harper didn't blame him.

The doors opened to the hum of the twenty-eighth floor, and Harper wound her way to her office. She sagged into her chair, elbows dropping onto the desk as she caught her head in her hands. Maggie was right. Forget the call. Tate could have all the conversations that he wanted, but she couldn't imagine uprooting her entire life at this point. He didn't get a vote.

Her cell phone lit up on her desk.

Tate: Back from lunch? Don't let Maggie talk you out of this. She has Indie Lime now. What do you have?

An uninvited current of resentment rippled through her. She sighed and shook her head in her hands.

"This is a terrible idea," she muttered to herself, pushing back from her desk.

"Then let me stop you before you start," a clipped voice announced from the doorway. Harper's head shot up. There, leaning against the doorframe, stood Candace Walsh, resplendent in an expertly tailored, forest green pants suit. Harper stood up quickly, embarrassed.

"Candace, I didn't hear you at the door."

Candace waved a hand casually and stepped into the office. An enormous diamond on her left hand winked in the fluorescent light. "No matter, I only just arrived." She glanced around the office, looking for a place to sit.

"Oh, allow me." Harper leapt from behind the desk to move her coat where she had hastily thrown it over the armchair. "Have a seat," she gestured, heart pounding.

Despite having worked for Candace on numerous cases, there was something about her that Harper had always found disarming. She was incredibly intelligent, unfailingly kind, and had been nothing but fair, respectful, and gracious about Harper's work and responsibilities. But none of that changed the fact that, as a named partner, she was also more important than just about anyone in any room she entered. Candace was as good a boss as Harper could have asked for, had Candace actually been her boss. Candace was something more like her boss's boss's boss. She terrified her, yet Harper revered her. She was everything Harper had once wanted to be and a big reason she originally applied to Horowitz, Walsh, and Pickett.

Candace swung her column of pin-straight, black hair over her shoulder as she settled into the seat next to the window. Harper returned to her desk. "What can I do for you?" she asked.

Candace smiled, fingering a jade leaf on the windowsill. "Relax, Harper. I'm not bearing bad news. Why does everyone down here assume the sky is falling when I show up? Did you have a good weekend?"

Harper laughed once, nervously. "I did." She fidgeted with her fingers. "Um, you?" she asked before the silence could stretch uncomfortably.

Candace fluttered a hand as if to brush away the question. "Fine," she said shortly. "Family. Work. Everyone's busy and spread around, so we try to spend a little more time together on the weekends when we're all back in the city."

Harper nodded slowly in reply. She had a hard time imagining Candace Walsh anywhere but the office, let alone relaxed and casual with family.

"Anyway," Candace went on, her tone shifting, "I'm obviously not here to make small talk." She crossed her legs and leaned back in the chair, hands folded on her knees.

Harper's heart skipped. "Ok," she said, forcing her tone to remain calm.

Candace smiled. "I'm sure you're familiar with the firm's scholastic endowment," she said casually. "A novelty at a firm of our size and caliber, really. There's no need to offer tuition reimbursement as an incentive when there's a long list of applicants for every summer internship and entry level associate position." She picked a piece of lint from the sleeve of her blazer. It was more than blustery showboating, Harper knew. Candace was assured of her firm's place in the legal landscape.

"For years, we've considered absorbing the designated funds back into the operating budget," she continued, fixing her gaze on Harper. "But Lyle Pickett is quite fond of it. He's got a real soft spot for an underdog."

"I see," Harper said, unsure of where this conversation was going and how she was expected to respond.

"Some of the partners have even come to call it the 'Pickett Prize,'" Candace said, rolling her eyes. "Not that the man needs his ego stroked, but he *has* been its champion."

Harper chewed the inside of her bottom lip. "It's very generous that he's kept it going," she said finally, just to have something to add to the conversation.

"It is," Candace agreed. "It's also why I'm here, Harper." She leaned forward, a twinkle in her eye.

Harper's brow furrowed. "I don't follow."

"We used to allow any incoming law student to apply, but a few years ago," Candace smiled, "we decided to only award scholarship funds to non-traditional students. Single mothers. Retired teachers starting second careers. Veterans. That kind of thing. It significantly shrunk the applicant pool and really allowed us to focus on a unique niche of the next iteration of legal talent."

Harper nodded slowly, still not comprehending.

"Which is where you come in," Candace said, as if all the dots should have magically connected.

"I'm sorry?" Harper sputtered.

Candace clutched her hands together, elbows on her knees, and looked hard at Harper. "I know you don't need me to tell you any of this because you've already applied for a Pickett Prize."

Harper's cheeks flushed, and she let out an embarrassed laugh. "I'm not sure…"

Candace held up a hand. "I've read your application. You were Harper Davis then. Looking forward to law school at the University of Minnesota or Northwestern or…" Candace hesitated, raising an eyebrow.

"Cornell," Harper whispered, throat tight. When she started at Horowitz, Walsh, and Pickett, she momentarily wondered if anyone she worked with would have seen the application. After a few months of relative anonymity as a new paralegal, however, any lingering apprehension had vanished. She had all but forgotten about it until this moment.

Candace nodded. "Admittedly," she continued, "I can't say I remember your application when it came through the first time. It could be I wasn't part of the committee that year. And it's lived deep in a file cabinet somewhere ever since. Only this summer, when Lyle wanted to run an audit of former applicants to find out where they had graduated from and what firms they had landed at, did your name reappear. And to realize that you were working here…" Candace stopped and smiled, and it moved Harper to see both kindness and sadness in the expression. "So, I have to ask," she said cautiously. "What happened, Harper?"

Harper took a deep breath. This was not where she had foreseen the afternoon heading. "I, um," she hesitated, considering if there was any reason to avoid the truth. If Candace had really reviewed her application from twelve years ago, then she already knew at least part of the answer. Harper's essay had detailed the challenges of her mother's diagnosis. "My mom got sick," she admitted. "And it didn't feel like a good time to leave. So, I deferred and started working here."

"And then?" Candace asked gently.

Harper looked away. She fiddled with the etched clasp of her watch band. "A year passed, and she hadn't…" She trailed off. "I couldn't leave knowing she had just weeks left." Harper paused, but Candace did not interject. "After things settled back down, I thought about starting the application process again, but my heart wasn't in it. Plus, I was already good at my work here. Really good," she reiterated, eyes snapping back to Candace. She was touched to find sympathy written plainly across her face. "I like my job," Harper continued. "So, one year turned into two. Eventually, I met Bryan, and my priorities changed."

"And now?" Candace prompted.

"Now?" Harper asked. She stopped from rushing to confess Bryan's house aspirations and Tate's waiting phone conversation. "Now, it seems too late."

"Not at all," Candance scoffed. "That's what I came to tell you, Harper. Lyle was so tickled to learn that one of his applicants had magically found her way into the firm that he put forth your application for reconsideration."

"But I'm not a law student," Harper laughed in disbelief.

Candace sighed. "I know, and the scholarship committee will have some follow-up questions for you given it's been over a decade since you first applied. But if you ever considered still giving law school a chance, this could be an amazing opportunity."

Harper froze. An expectant silence hung between the two women. When she finally brought herself to respond, her voice seemed far away, like she was listening to someone else have the conversation. "What are you asking me?"

Candace leaned in. "I want to know if you have any interest in law school? Because if you do, I'd like to help, and if not, I'd like to talk you into it before Lyle Pickett comes down here to offer you a scholarship."

"That's insane."

"Hardly," Candace insisted. "You would have to apply somewhere in the city, and would continue to work as a paralegal until the term started. Then you'd intern here over the summer while you were taking classes. You'd owe the firm at least three years as an associate once you passed the bar. It's doable. This is what you wanted, right? I mean, *before*?"

"*Wanted*, sure," Harper choked. "But now, I don't know."

"I understand," Candace smiled. "Think about it. You've got Bryan to consider as well. Talk it through. The term won't start until next fall, and the committee won't decide for months. Lyle will, no doubt, reach out with some additional questions before that. I just wanted you to be ready when he asked."

Harper's heart crawled into her throat. "Thanks," she managed.

"Well then," Candace pushed herself up from the chair, perching neatly on nude Louboutin stilettos, "I'll let you get back to it." She moved to the door, then stopped. "I do hope you'll consider it." Her tone was warm. "You're an asset here as a paralegal, but if you've got bigger ambitions," she smiled, "there's room here for those too."

Harper watched through the glass wall of her office as Candace crossed the maze of cubicles back toward the elevator doors. Heads turned and people ducked out of her way in deference as she passed, yet she had a kind word and smile for anyone who looked for one. Candace Walsh was a female icon in the Chicago legal world, and if she believed Harper should consider Pickett's potential offer, that meant something. It was a vote of confidence that was impossible for Harper to ignore. Her heart continued to hammer.

She opened the slim drawer in the center of her desk, shifting notepads and loose pens around until she found her mother's quarter taped to the bottom of the drawer. She stared at the dull, silver circle. It had been twelve years since she flipped that coin. Twelve years since she promised her mom she would go. Twelve years since Helen had pressed the quarter into Harper's hand and said that someday it would matter.

She would never have guessed that *someday* was still an option.

"Andrews!" Two offices down, Tate leaned out his door, gesturing animatedly at his watch. "Are you coming? Three minutes?"

She shuffled the stack of files on her desk, still mostly untouched, into a wire basket on the bookshelf behind her.

Heads. Tails. Heads. Tails.

A phone call with Pollard Frank was no more bizarre and unexpected than a potential scholarship to law school, was it?

Mind made up, she rushed from her office, aiming for something akin to Candace's confident stride.

Chapter 5

"How was your day?" Bryan asked. He leaned casually against the kitchen counter and twirled his fork through a bowl of leftover spaghetti.

"Fine," Harper huffed, dropping an armload of files onto the small table next to the front door. They wobbled precariously. Between her mind wandering through the morning and losing an hour to New York and Pollard Frank that afternoon, she was woefully behind, and it was only Monday.

Bryan moved to catch the tower of documents before it toppled. "That good, huh?" he asked, sizing up the stack. He moved half the pile to the coffee table.

Harper sighed. "It was alright." She hung her coat in the front closet, then turned to face her husband. "Busy. Overwhelming." Both true, though incomplete, assessments.

Bryan raised an eyebrow as he moved toward her. "Anything I can do to help?"

She leaned into him, allowing herself to be enveloped in his arms. Her head tucked into his shoulder, and she breathed in the familiar comforts of home: cedar and tea tree soap. "I'm better now," she murmured. "What about you? How was your day?"

"Good," Bryan said. Harper felt his voice rumble in his chest as he held her. "I..." He lingered on the vowel, and Harper looked up expectantly.

"You what?" she asked.

Bryan smiled, a small grin that Harper could tell masked a greater excitement. "I don't want to add to your overwhelm," he said slowly. He loosened himself from their embrace and led Harper toward the couch. "But I called the agent for the listing on Nichols Park today, just out of curiosity. There's already been a lot of interest." He took her hands. "She's had a dozen showings and has a full schedule tomorrow. She expects multiple offers."

Harper's stomach twinged, though whether in relief or regret she was not entirely sure. "It's ok," she said, aiming for indifference. "In this market, we should have expected that. There will be other houses." She watched Bryan's shoulders fall.

"True," he said, his tone even despite his eager expression. "But in this market, we're also going to have to be ready to move quickly. I made us an appointment to see it tomorrow morning, and I've got a call into Mike at the bank to run some mortgage numbers so that we can be ready with pre-approval."

Harper blew out a breath.

"Hypothetically," he added, his expression suddenly sheepish.

"Bryan…" Harper started. The unidentified twinge grew into a rising panic. "We've barely even talked about…"

Bryan moved closer to her on the couch. "I know." The listing lay on the coffee table, and his eyes shifted to it. "It's fast. It might not even matter. Maybe it's already sold. But let's just go look at it, see how it feels to picture a life there." His eyes searched hers.

To picture a life there was to picture the future. To picture the future was to wrestle with the present. And Harper couldn't ignore the present reality that, had everything worked out the way they had planned it, they would be more than casually browsing homes. They would be urgently debating the need for more space and seeking something with a family-friendly backyard and room for a nursery.

Present reality was also her conversation with Candace, and Harper couldn't imagine saying no to touring a house only to turn the discussion to her visiting law schools instead.

"Of course," Harper sighed. "Yes, let's go see it."

Bryan beamed. "You want me to heat you up some spaghetti?" he asked, crossing back to the kitchen for his bowl. "I put it in the oven instead of the microwave. It's supposed to keep the noodles from drying out, and…"

Harper reached for the first file on the stack, thinking to lose herself in a train of legal thought as Bryan went on about reheating the pasta and various other trivial facts about cooking leftovers. There was, apparently, a repeat offender on campus notorious for reheating fish and various fibrous green vegetables in the science department staff lounge. His chatter, though banal, was comforting, and Harper knocked out annotations on three briefs in the time it took Bryan to return with a bowl of pasta and a glass of wine. She pushed her paperwork aside and touched her glass to his with a soft clink as he reclaimed his place on the couch.

Bryan nodded toward the stack of files on the coffee table. "Do you want to talk about *that*?" he asked.

Harper shook her head, shoveling a forkful of pasta into her mouth to avoid having to comment. She would tell Bryan about the scholarship and Pollard Frank, but she just couldn't figure out how to start. *Hey, so I know we're looking at a house tomorrow, but how would you feel about moving to New York?* It was the first time in their entire relationship she could remember feeling absolutely tongue-tied.

Not that moving to New York was an option worth considering, or even an option *to* consider. The call with Pollard Frank had been far less formal than Tate had suggested. It was not an interview. Pollard Frank wasn't even hiring. Harold Turner, the friend of Tate's father, might look at some staffing changes next spring when new associates were hired and there was general movement around the firm. A lot of the conversation had been pleasantries, getting acquainted with each other, and gentle posturing by Harold to work a wealthy client's potential business heir. Still, at the end of the call when he suggested that they all stay in touch and to stop by the office if they happened to be in New York, it felt genuine.

For his part, Tate had been ecstatic, thought they had both completely crushed it, and was certain they would pack their offices by May.

The Candace Walsh conversation had been something else entirely. An offer that would keep them in Chicago, keep her at the firm, and keep the house on the table for Bryan while complicating just about everything else they considered part of their five-year plan. It was a long shot, but not impossible. She chewed and swallowed another bite of spaghetti before plucking up the nerve to broach the subject.

"Have you ever wondered if you're doing what you'll do for the rest of your life?" she asked.

Bryan's head tipped in confusion. "What do you mean?"

Harper picked at her spaghetti. "Like, you're tenured, but not even forty yet. Are you doing what you always want to do, or do you think someday you'll want to look for a bigger pond?"

Bryan set his bowl on the table and rested his elbows on his knees. He looked sideways at her and shrugged. "I don't know," he admitted. "I obviously feel confident enough where I am to look at houses. Getting tenure was everything I worked for, everything we sacrificed for. I mean, I've been doing school for so long, I don't know if I know how to do anything but academia."

"You consult," Harper offered.

"Sure," Bryan agreed. "But my passion is in the lab. Research. My students." He looked around the room before his eyes settled back on Harper. "My schedule is better now with tenure. Less stress and more security. I'm in a good place." He smiled at her and reached for his bowl again. "Why do you ask?"

Harper took a deep breath. "Candace Walsh came to see me today," she admitted.

"Ok." Bryan slowed his chewing.

"Apparently, Lyle Pickett uncovered my scholarship application from years ago during an audit of former applicants, and he was amused I'd wound up at the firm despite not having received a scholarship."

Bryan raised an eyebrow. "Don't tell me she came down to make some comment about how you were a paralegal? There are some really pretentious…"

"That's the thing," Harper interrupted. "Lyle was interested in my application *because* I'm a paralegal at the firm. The endowment is now used exclusively for non-traditional students, and while I didn't catch anyone's attention twelve years ago, for some inexplicable reason, he now feels like I'm this novel, underdog story."

Bryan's hand stopped, fork halfway to his mouth. "Are you telling me the firm wants to send you to law school?"

Harper looked away with a nervous laugh. "I mean, no. Candace just came to tell me Lyle had moved my name into consideration."

The fork clattered into Bryan's bowl. "And you told her?"

"I didn't tell her anything," Harper admitted. "It was a courtesy visit. She was just giving me a heads up."

"A heads up?" Bryan laughed in disbelief. "A heads up about whether you should start applying to law schools?"

Harper bit her bottom lip and shrugged. "Well, yes."

"That's absurd." Bryan tipped his head back and laughed.

"Is it?"

Bryan's laughter died instantly. "Isn't it?" he asked, with cautious confusion. When Harper didn't respond, his eyes went wide. "You're honestly thinking about this."

"Maybe," Harper hedged, her voice catching. In truth, it was almost all she had been thinking about it since Candace left her office. It both thrilled and terrified her.

Bryan slid the length of the couch to reach her. "I didn't realize that was something you still wanted. You haven't talked about law school in years."

"I know." Harper instinctively reached for Bryan's hand. "I didn't really consider it an option anymore. It's just…" She looked down at their joined hands. "It felt good to be told someone still thought I was good enough. You got tenure, and Maggie's got the restaurant, and I'm just here. Going through the motions. Waiting for the next thing to happen. Wondering if it ever will."

Bryan leaned in, and Harper dropped her head onto his shoulder. They sat quietly, the unspoken truth stretching between them. Things *should* have happened by now, but it hadn't been the office they were waiting for.

"Ok," Bryan said, breaking the silence. "I guess I'll ask the million-dollar question. Do you want to go to law school?"

"I don't know," Harper said with a moan. "We made different plans, and now we're looking at houses." She looked up into his sea glass eyes. "I don't want to give those things up. But I gave up law school once before, too. I never thought I'd have to pass on the chance again."

Bryan took off his glasses and rubbed his nose where the pads pinched the bridge. "We can take some time to figure it out. I'll call the agent first thing tomorrow and cancel the showing."

"Don't," replied Harper. "Even if I was going to consider it, I'd owe the firm years after I graduated. We're not going anywhere. It's just a showing. You said yourself the house might already be sold. It doesn't hurt to look. Just," she swallowed hard, "like it wouldn't hurt to have a conversation with Lyle Pickett if he comes to my office to talk about law school?"

Bryan held her gaze, his expression unreadable. "Ok," he finally offered, nodding. He looked at the files scattered across the coffee table and sighed. "But Harper, we've got to figure this out. I need to know what you want. Whatever it is."

Harper leaned forward and kissed him. "I want you."

Bryan rolled his eyes, but Harper felt the trace of a smile on his lips when he kissed her back. "You know what I mean," he murmured.

"Yeah," Harper agreed. "I know."

He took her bowl to the kitchen and returned with the wine bottle. "How long will you be?"

Harper shrugged. "A couple hours."

Bryan topped off her glass and set the bottle carefully amidst the papers and folders. "I'll be waiting." He smiled softly at her and turned toward the bedroom. A minute later, Harper heard the soft murmuring of the television.

Tucked into the cozy corner of her couch, the work flowed easily. She moved through the folders methodically, reviewing and flagging documents for signatures, breezing through two previous mergers looking for language that might apply to a third acquisition, and browsing a thick financial report that Candace had handed her as Harper had been waiting for the elevator to go home. She finished the stack on the coffee table, refilled her wineglass, and carried it back to the entry to retrieve the rest of the files from the table. She shuffled the pile clumsily, trying to tuck it against her hip with one hand without sloshing the wine in the other. The mail beneath the folders fell to the floor.

Harper sighed and awkwardly carried the stack to the living room where she left it with the wine before returning to the mess in the hall. An array of bills and credit card offers sprawled across the floor along with a magazine for Bryan, a Victoria's Secret coupon for Harper, an invitation to an early holiday party, and a postcard, printed on thick, glossy cardstock. A color photograph on the front featured a man and woman in coordinating cable knit sweaters, swinging a small girl in cream tights and a corduroy jumper between them. A technicolor of autumn leaves swirled in the background, against which a scripted message in black, embossed text read: *The future doesn't wait!*

Harper stared at the picture, her heartbeat skipping uncomfortably the way it always did when she thought about the family that they had, thus far, been denied. She flipped the card over. Her full name and address were printed on a label stuck crookedly to the right side of the card. Where the stamp should have been was a prepaid business postage box. There was no personal message, though a generic paragraph about calling a toll-free number for information about whole life insurance was styled in a font meant to mimic handwriting.

She sighed, perturbed to have been frazzled by a piece of junk mail. Pushing herself off the floor, she walked the postcard and the credit card offers to the kitchen garbage can. They fell into the bag in a heap, photo up, the faces of the happy family beaming back at her.

Harper stared at the little girl, unable to close the lid, haunted by the simple, generic message. Her future was waiting, but what future was *she* waiting for?

Chapter 6

The listing agent introduced herself as Rachelle and was very tall, very blonde, and spoke to Harper and Bryan as if she was reciting from the first draft of a scripted Netflix real estate show that never made it out of the writer's room. Her forced laughter came out in high-pitched bursts that echoed down the hardwood hallways. She had an annoying penchant for laying a hand on Bryan's arm to emphasize an impressive feature or strong selling point. Harper had never met a realtor who seemed as much a liability to her listing as this one, for in the twenty minutes they had been in the house, the realtor was the only thing that Harper could find to dislike.

The home enchanted from the moment the front door opened. A welcoming entryway gave way to a staircase on the right, railed with a dark mahogany banister wrapped in bushy Christmas garlands twinkling with tiny white lights. Hardwood floors stretched into a comfortable living space, a gleaming kitchen of stainless-steel appliances and sleek marble countertops, a breakfast nook looking out over a tiny backyard garden, and a small first-floor sunroom. Though premature for mid-November, a handsome Douglas Fir sat tucked into the corner of the living room blocking a wall of built-in bookshelves that the irksome realtor explained were cherry and original to the house. The tree, Harper noticed, was artificial, yet the first floor smelled of fresh pine and cinnamon.

Upstairs, the hall opened to three well-appointed bedrooms, and Harper flinched only slightly at the minimally veiled suggestion that they could easily transition one into a nursery. Bryan did not comment, but he reached for Harper's hand as they followed down the hallway toward the primary suite at the front of the house that overlooked the park and featured an ensuite and a walk-in closet over which Harper swooned.

It was easy to imagine the life that Bryan had pictured here. The patter of little feet rushing up and down the stairs. Sleepy breakfasts around the kitchen island, cartoons murmuring in the background. A playhouse in the tiny backyard. Saturday picnics in the park. Part of Harper, undeniably, ached for it.

Yet, she also took one look at the smallest bedroom overlooking the backyard and imagined it richly wallpapered, with a stately desk in the corner and stacks of case law and leather-bound classics piled on the bookshelves. There she could sit in an overstuffed armchair under a warm pool of lamplight, early on a Sunday morning before Bryan was awake, and sneak in a few hours of work.

It bothered her that she struggled to imagine these two visions of their future overlapping. Nevertheless, she could not deny that, in either version, the house would set a beautiful backdrop. As she kissed Bryan and slid from the passenger seat in front of her office, she agreed to meet him for lunch to finalize a decision and a potential offer.

In the meantime, there was plenty of work to keep her busy, especially if she wanted to prove herself an asset worthy of the partners' attention and investment. She dropped last night's stack of files unceremoniously on the chair in the corner, already lost in thought about which briefs to file first and how to best manage the four additional binders of materials that had been delivered to her office, part of the financial records Candace had asked her to review. She opened the first, revealing neatly labeled records stretching back over the past year. Harper sighed, looking over the other materials. No small task. That the work was for Candace, however, made it both top priority and, strangely, more exhilarating. She dug in.

The hours crept along. Though normally diligent, Harper went over every line an extra time. She told herself she was just being cautious, ensuring her very best work a day after receiving a big vote of confidence from a named partner. However, in truth, she was double checking for her own mistakes. Her mind wandered from the house, to law school, to babies, to the scholarship, to Lyle Pickett, to Candace Walsh–all of which invariably prompted Harper to refocus and double back over the last few lines to make sure she had not missed some egregious error.

She was nearly through the first binder when there was a soft knock on the glass wall of her office. Harper looked up to find Tate, jacket off and shirt sleeves rolled up, watching her with casual curiosity. She leaned back in her chair and waved him in.

"Anything good?" he asked, nodding to the pile on the desk.

"Urban City Apparel," Harper replied, clicking her pen against the cover of the binder.

Tate raised an eyebrow. "The merger? That's Candace Walsh's case."

"It's not a merger; it's a sale. They're being bought out."

Tate nodded approvingly and gave a low whistle. "Brilliant. I didn't know you were on it."

"I wouldn't say I'm *on* anything. Candace just handed me the financials last night on my way out the door. She asked for a review." She watched Tate fidget with the Newton's cradle on the front of the desk. He sent the metal balls ricocheting into each other. Their rhythmic ticking filled the silence between them, and she realized he was stalling. "What do you need?" she prompted.

Tate stuffed his hands in his pockets and rocked back on his heels. "Well, um…" he started.

Harper couldn't remember the last time she had seen him lost for words at the office. "What's wrong?" she asked, trying to imagine what part of Tate's perfectly curated world could have come undone to unsettle him.

His mouth pulled into a thin line. "I just got an email from Pollard Frank," he said. "Harold Turner was impressed with our conversation yesterday and wanted to follow up."

Harper's stomach flip-flopped. "I thought they wouldn't be making any staffing moves until the spring," she said.

"I thought the same," Tate admitted. "But he asked for a call this afternoon."

A small laugh escaped Harper. It was one thing to take yesterday's phone call on whim, kick the hypothetical can down the road a few months, and then politely decline on the off chance that an offer came through. It was entirely something else to follow up less than 24 hours later.

"What's funny?" Tate asked.

Harper shook her head. "Nothing. It's just, I'm not going to take another call with Pollard Frank, Tate. I shouldn't have taken the first call yesterday. Curiosity got the best of me." She pointed a finger at him. "Plus, you were so damn excited about it; I couldn't say no. But Bryan's serious about wanting to stay in the city, and so am I. We actually looked at a house this morning." Tate looked away, his eyes shifting around the room to avoid Harper's. "What?" she asked, suddenly aware of the tension in the room.

"They didn't ask for both of us," he admitted quietly. "I'm sorry, Andrews," he added. His gaze flickered back to meet hers.

Harper's chest tightened. "Did they say why?"

"You just said you wanted to stay put."

"Tate!" Harper interrupted. It was one thing to know she shouldn't have taken the call. It was another to have taken the call and been found wanting. "Did they say why?" she asked again, insistent.

"No," Tate admitted. "They merely asked for a private conversation."

"Got it," Harper said, opening the binder on her desk and reviewing the next page of data.

"Andrews," said Tate, gently.

Harper immediately found she preferred his normal, arrogant swagger to his sympathy. "It's fine," she insisted, laying down her pen. "It's done. Like I said, I'm serious about staying here." She looked back at the page.

Tate watched her cautiously for a moment. "Right," he said finally. "Well, I'm relieved you feel that way." His tone was clipped and even again. "I just wanted you to hear it from me."

"Thanks," Harper said, not looking up. It was foolish, she knew, to feel jilted over a job she had no desire or intention of accepting. But it still stung to feel overlooked. As Tate took a step toward the door, however, she felt the faintest obligation to bite back her pride.

"Congratulations, Tate," she offered as genuinely as she could. "I know what it means to you. It won't be the same when you leave."

"Blimey, Andrews. Don't go soft on me now," he teased, rolling his eyes.

Harper smiled. "I would never." She waved a hand in dismissal. "Now, close the door on your way out."

Tate gave her a mocking salute. "Aye, aye." The door swung closed quietly behind him.

Harper picked up her pen and returned to the binder, more determined than ever to show Candace she was worth every penny.

•   •   •

An hour later, a cutting wind whipped along the avenue, nipping at Harper's exposed nose and cheeks so that she was raw and pink by the time she finished the four short blocks between her office and Milton's Tavern. A welcoming burst of warm air and friendly conversation greeted her when she pushed through the doors, and the blood rushed back to her fingers and toes as she unwound her scarf and pulled off her mittens. A popcorn machine in the corner fired up, perfuming the air with salt and butter, and the jovial mix of laughter and rattling glassware tinkled above the general din.

"Harper!"

She heard Bryan's voice rise above the noise, scanned the room, and found him tucked into a corner booth, already nursing an Irish coffee. His dark hair was mussed from his stocking cap, and he ran a hand over it haplessly as he smiled and waved her over. She slid out of her coat as she approached the table and cozied in next to him on the bench. Bryan kissed her as she leaned into him, and he draped an arm over her shoulders, melting the last of her chill.

The quick walk to the restaurant had been all the more time she needed to talk herself into buying the house. Everything they wanted was there: the neighborhood, the craftsman details, the extra space. Yes, it was pricey, and true, the possibility of law school introduced some undeniable indecision about the future she wanted within its four walls. But these factors unnecessarily complicated an otherwise straightforward decision. Faced with possibilities and potential changes, the townhouse was a place they could call home for whatever the next phase of their life was going to bring.

Of course, she was not too proud to admit that a small part of her instantly latched onto the house to soothe the sting of Harold Turner leaving her out of the follow-up conversation with Pollard Frank. Let Tate have New York. She didn't want it. She wanted Nichols Park.

By the time she and Bryan finished exchanging pleasantries about their mornings, and the waiter returned with her iced tea and taken their lunch order, Harper was positively bursting to tell him.

"About the house," Bryan finally opened the conversation. He paused and took a sip of his coffee.

Harper seized the opportunity.

"Let's do it," she exclaimed.

Bryan raised an eyebrow.

"I mean it," she continued. "I know I hesitated the other night. I wasn't expecting it, and I didn't know how to react. But seeing it today, you were right. I can imagine our life there."

Bryan set down his mug, his eyes dropping from Harper's. "I didn't think you'd warm up to the idea so quickly."

Harper shrugged. "You were sold already. I just had to catch up."

Bryan turned his coffee cup in his hands and sighed. "I kind of wish you hadn't. I figured you wouldn't mind so much that we didn't..." He paused.

"We didn't get it?" Harper finished, less a question than a small hope that she might be wrong.

Bryan nodded. "Rachelle called about an hour after I got to campus. A buyer made a full cash offer 30,000 dollars over asking."

"She's a terrible realtor," Harper scoffed, taking a sip of her tea.

"Apparently not," Bryan chuckled.

Harper rolled her eyes. "She didn't annoy you, even a little?"

"Oh, she was obnoxious in every sense of the word," Bryan agreed, reaching for Harper's hand under the table. "And who stages a house for Christmas knowing full well it'll be sold before Thanksgiving?" He laughed weakly. "I'm sorry I got your hopes up."

"Don't be." Harper squeezed his hand. "We can look for something else."

Bryan smiled tightly and sipped his coffee. "About that," he said. His thumb traced a slow circle on the back of Harper's hand, a habit she knew he absentmindedly fell into when he was nervous. She laid her free hand on top of his.

"What's up?"

He bit his bottom lip and looked away. "I want to ask you something," he said finally.

Harper released his hand and began drawing lines in the condensation on the outside of her glass. "Again?" she asked with a small laugh that didn't quite mask her sudden uneasiness. "Your last question has us looking at houses."

"I know, and I know we have a lot of things to consider at the moment." Bryan took a determined breath and met Harper's eyes. "I just wondered, when you walked through that house today, if you could see us there with a family?"

Harper drew a sharp breath. The bells over the door jingled, filling the brief silence, and the cool draft that swept through the dining room raised the hairs on the back of her neck.

"Of course I can," she offered. It wasn't untrue, but she suddenly felt guilty for having pictured an entirely different future there as well. "Why do you ask?"

"Honestly, because we haven't talked about kids in months, and now with law school suddenly back on the table…"

"We don't know that I'm going to law school." Harper interrupted.

"It's a possibility though," Bryan replied with a shrug. "And I just wondered if it changed things?"

"Where is this coming from?" Harper asked, deflecting the question as her defenses unexpectedly rose.

Bryan sighed. "Do you remember Jamie Donovan, the postdoctoral fellow we have working in environmental physics?"

"Sure."

"Well, I caught him in the lounge this morning. He just came back from paternity leave. They had a little boy. He said they'd been trying for over two years, and then it took three cycles of IVF, but they worked with a great clinic here in the city, and he highly recommended the staff." He trailed off and reached for his coffee cup. Harper knew he was waiting to gauge her reaction, and she fought to remain impassive.

"We really only tried for eighteen months," she said, her throat tight. "It wasn't two years."

"Even so," Bryan pressed gently, "most medical advice says if it hasn't happened after a year to consult someone."

"I know. We did, remember? I don't need you to mansplain fertility to me," Harper snapped more harshly than she intended. She caught herself, closed her eyes, and swallowed hard. They did not fight, especially in public, but she couldn't believe that he had finally decided to revisit this conversation somewhere with an audience.

They may not have been *trying* the last six months, but they had done nothing to prevent a pregnancy either. Intentions aside, she knew those months counted in the timeline of their struggle, and Harper suddenly realized that, despite not having taken a single precaution, if it happened now it would come as a shock to find herself pregnant. She took a calming breath. When she looked back at Bryan, he met her gaze with a sad smile.

"I'm not mansplaining anything," he insisted calmly. "I know we took a break, and I think we both needed it. And I know you might not be ready to come back to this conversation yet, so I'm not asking you for anything. But I'm going to get myself tested again," he explained.

"You really think something has changed?"

Bryan shrugged. "I hope not. But if we have a problem, I want to know if I'm a part of it."

"And if you're not?" Harper struggled to keep her voice even. "Then what? Then I'm the problem?"

The waiter crossed the dining room toward their table, and Harper forced a smile and a curt thank you as two burgers were placed in front of them.

"I didn't say you were a problem," Bryan said quietly as the waiter retreated. "I didn't mean to imply it either. I just meant that I'd like to think about trying again. And I want to be proactive." He placed a business card on the table between them. Navy blue lettering on a background swirled in seafoam green waves. "I made myself an appointment."

Harper nibbled a French fry, stalling. She had no argument for why Bryan shouldn't test himself, and no explanation for the panic that had set in at the thought of visiting the clinic for her own consultation. Bryan was right. They had tried without success, and if they were serious about continuing to try, she should agree with, even welcome, Bryan's willingness to seek additional counsel. A more insecure man might have raised an objection to the suggestion that his *contribution* was anything less than grade A certified genetic material. Here her husband was volunteering that his might not be.

"I can't believe you told Jamie we're trying to get pregnant," she said finally.

Bryan shrugged. "We told Maggie and Seth."

"That's Maggie and Seth."

Bryan bit into his burger. He watched Harper as he chewed. "Did you tell Tate?"

Harper picked at another French fry. "Absolutely not," she scoffed. She had told no one else. Not her sister; not her dad; and definitely not anyone at the office. It was too awkward and private to bring up in casual conversation. Why announce the decision to have copious amounts of intentionally scheduled sex?

"Well, I'm sorry. For what it's worth, I actually found it helpful to hear another perspective." Bryan took another bite of his burger.

Harper followed suit to avoid having to think of something more to say. She was, by nature, an information gatherer. Her job was, in large part, seeking and organizing and double-checking facts. The simple fact now was that Bryan was right. If they were serious about having a baby, it was time to get some additional information. Bryan was obviously serious. He was secure in his job. They were secure in their relationship. He was ready. She had yet to decide if the nervous churning in her stomach was a product of her not being in the same place, or a recognition that, if it was time to see a doctor, something could, in fact, be wrong.

She wiped her mouth with a paper napkin. "Back to houses," she offered, aiming to diffuse a bit of the quiet tension that had settled over the meal. "If the market is moving that fast, maybe we should consider an agent?"

Bryan chewed and swallowed. "Or maybe we should wait."

"Wait!?" Harper blurted. A few nearby diners glanced toward their corner table, and Harper flushed in embarrassment. "Why?" she added in a strained whisper.

Bryan bunched his napkin and tossed it in his empty basket before shifting in the booth to face Harper directly. "Jamie and his wife took out a loan against their house for their IVF cycles. If we've got the money sitting in the bank right now, maybe it makes sense to keep it there until we're sure how we want to use it. Maybe that *is* a house. Maybe it's the clinic. Or maybe," he reached over and squeezed her knee, "you'll decide you want some of that money for law school books and a new laptop."

Harper scoffed, noncommittal, but the thought needled her desire.

"I'm just saying," Bryan continued, "I think it makes sense to pull back for a second, get all the facts straight, and figure out which way we're headed."

There was no accusation in his tone, but Harper still felt defensive. She could not, however, deny his logic.

"You're right," she whispered, surprised by the depth of her disappointment at moving the house to the back burner. It had been a welcome momentary distraction.

Bryan ate a fry out of Harper's basket. "I didn't realize you'd take it so hard. I honestly thought you were just placating me this morning."

"It's fine." Harper pushed the basket toward him. "I just got swept up in it."

Bryan smiled. "Well, let me try to make it up to you." He reached for his coat on the bench next to him, fishing in the pocket. "I made a quick stop on the way to campus this morning." He handed her a glossy brochure, folded in half. "Open it," he prompted.

Harper unfolded the paper, wary of further surprises. It took her a moment to figure out what she was looking at.

"You were so willing to go see the house and jump into my version of the future; it's only fair that I take the plunge into yours too," he explained. "I want us to have *all* the facts. I don't want you to always wonder about what you might have given up."

Not knowing what to say, Harper leaned forward and kissed Bryan instead.

"Is that a smile?" he teased, pulling away.

Harper nodded, looking back at the page: a checklist for admission to Northwestern University's Pritzker School of Law. She laid it on the table next to the business card for the clinic. Looking between them, she was careful not to let her smile falter, but the knot in her stomach tightened.

Chapter 7

"Hello?!" Harper called, stepping into the darkened dining room of Indie Lime. Stacks of chairs sat against the wall nearest the bar, and the tables were piled two high, table top to table top. A floor polisher sat, unplugged, in the middle of the room. "Maggie?!" Harper called again. She could see the lights on in the kitchen through the cutout used to pass dishes to the front of house.

"Kitchen," came a faint reply.

Harper moved toward it.

Though the opening had been a wild success, and Indie Lime had booked several exclusive holiday parties to further showcase the menu and create a buzz around the restaurant, Maggie continued to spend every spare moment cooking, tasting, working with staff, meeting with vendors, and apparently–Harper stepped around the polisher–buffing the floors. She couldn't help but admire the single-minded focus with which Maggie had pursued every detail of the restaurant. Harper craved that kind of clarity and focus about her own future. So, as there was no pulling her best friend away from life in the kitchen, Harper had offered to spend her Saturday morning helping with whatever Maggie wanted in exchange for face-to-face conversation and heartfelt advice. She pushed through the swinging door and found the kitchen empty.

"Hello?!" she hollered, setting two cardboard cups of coffee on the nearest counter. The kitchen was shining stainless, impeccably clean and polished, with racks of cookware and knives mounted to the walls, and an enormous gas range flanked by ovens on one side and a deep fryer on the other. Harper smiled, overwhelmed with pride over what her best friend had created.

"Hi," said Maggie, walking out of the cooler with a clear storage bin of lemons. Her black curls were stuffed under a colorful bandana, and she wore her white chef's coat unbuttoned over a gray t-shirt. She set the box on the countertop next to the coffee cups as Harper slid one toward her. "Thanks," she said, taking a sip.

Harper lifted her own cup. "You're welcome. Also, have I told you lately how amazing this is?" She spun a quick circle, taking in the entire space. "Seriously, Maggie, the place looks incredible."

"It does, doesn't it?" Maggie glowed. "Though the floors are driving me crazy. People drag their feet, and track in rocks and pebbles, and scuff and shuffle."

"I didn't even notice," Harper admitted, glancing out the kitchen window.

Maggie took another sip. "Well, I did, and critics will." She lifted the lid on the box of fruit, rotating the lemons, testing for soft spots, and removing the offenders before counting what remained and making an entry on a small, touchscreen tablet.

"Can I help?" Harper offered.

"Obviously," Maggie replied, returning the lemons to the cooler and reappearing with a crate of mangoes. "Pull out anything you wouldn't buy for yourself," she instructed, disappearing back into the cooler and coming out with strawberries a moment later. She sifted through the tray. "Ok," she said after a moment. "Catch me up."

Harper tossed a mango toward the compost bin. She had already been giving one-sided play-by-plays via unanswered text messages about the house showing and the potential scholarship; she wasn't even sure what needed rehashing.

"Well, for starters, New York is completely off the table," she said with an edge that made Maggie glance up in surprise.

"Be serious. It was never on the table. You're miffed because Tate got something you didn't."

"Fine," Harper said, holding up another mango. "And before you start, I know that's petty."

"You're allowed to be petty." Maggie shuffled through the berries. "Though I *did* warn you to leave it alone."

"You did," admitted Harper, returning the lid to the box. "Which is why I promise to take your advice under better consideration next time. So, I'm listening. What would you do about," she waved a hand in a flapping, swirling motion, "everything?"

Maggie stacked the tray of strawberries on the box of mangos and walked both into the cooler. This time, she reappeared empty-handed. She picked up her coffee cup and eased onto her elbows, leaning across the countertop. "So, here's my question." Her brown eyes fixed on Harper. "Why the sudden need for a change? The house? Law school? The move that was never actually going to be a move?" She looked at Harper expectantly. "What gives?"

Harper shrugged. "It's all kind of dropping in my lap at once. And I know I could just ignore it and go on with life as it is, but…" She sipped her coffee, stalling. "I can't shake the feeling that it's time."

"Time for what?"

"Something. Anything. I didn't think there would ever be a reason to consider law school again. I didn't even know I wanted to," she admitted. "Mom died, and it just didn't make sense to go back to school, you know? I was behind my classmates, and I would have had to start my applications over."

"You were grieving," Maggie added sympathetically.

Harper spun her coffee cup between her palms. "But now what's my excuse? It's too late? I'm too old?"

"You don't need an excuse, Harper." Maggie insisted. "You're allowed to change your mind. Nothing says you *have* to still want it. It was twelve years ago."

"But what if I do…want it?"

"Well," Maggie considered a moment, "then my original question stands. Why now? Is it really just because Candace suddenly brought up the opportunity of the scholarship, or is this about something else?"

Harper sighed and looked away.

"Ok," Maggie leaned in. "You're my best friend, so I'm going to ask the question you're not supposed to ask. It's been months since you've said anything about it, so how does starting a family factor into this? Because I know you, and I can't imagine it hasn't crossed your mind that this is a massive change of plans." Maggie let the silence hang between them for a moment. "I'm not trying to pry; you just seemed pretty sure about the direction things were heading before all this other stuff came up."

Even after decades of friendship, it still caught Harper off guard sometimes when Maggie so easily saw through her. It did not, however, make the question any easier to answer.

They had been through a lot. Awkward middle school years and first boyfriends. Harper's mom's death and Maggie's parents' divorce. Two weddings. Their friendship had formed during years of living down the street from each other as kids, and had survived their subsequent moves to college and Maggie's training around the country. They covered so many milestones that Harper took for granted that their paths had remained so neatly in sync. Which was why, when she and Bryan had shared the news that they were going to start trying for a baby, the weighty glance that passed between Maggie and Seth had come as a complete surprise. Whatever imaginings Harper had of walking strollers side by side along the lakeshore with Maggie instantly vanished as Maggie met their baby news with the revelation that she and Seth had decided not to have children.

In her initial shock, Harper had embarrassingly failed to meet Maggie's decision with the same enthusiasm and acceptance she had expected of her own announcement. In hindsight, however, she should have seen it coming. Maggie had never fawned over babies or talked much about having a family at all. Her parents' divorce made her skeptical of marriage, and the late hours of dinner service were far from conducive to traditional family life. Her relationship with Seth had come as a pleasant surprise, and that he dutifully followed her from place to place through her years of sous chef training before coming to Chicago, sealed the deal between them.

Maggie had patiently reiterated that her dream was a restaurant, an ambition requiring time, money, and flexibility complicated by a family. Seth's work as the dean of students already left him worried enough about kids without adding a few of their own to the equation. They lived comfortably for the two of them, but were not so comfortable that the added expenses of childcare, health insurance, and endless diapers would go unnoticed in their household budget. To say nothing of the fact that, as a mixed-race couple, they frequently wrestled with navigating a cultural, social, and political minefield. Forget introducing a child into that chaos.

Selfishly, Harper wanted to change their minds. Though after Bryan pointed out on the way home that she was taking a surprisingly close-minded view of the thing, and playfully accused her of being the traditionalist in the group, she dropped it.

As a result, Harper treaded lightly into all future conversations about family planning, and when they began the fertility drugs, she stopped talking about it at all. It seemed too private and personal, even with their closest friends, and she worried they might judge her choice as she had inadvertently judged theirs.

But more than judgment, Maggie's words now needled at a truth she was ashamed to admit even to herself. She *hadn't* been sure. Not when she and Bryan decided it was time to start trying. Not after she finished the last packet of birth control. Not when she preemptively bought a bottle of prenatal vitamins, which she let sit on the counter for two weeks before finally plucking up the courage to break the seal and start taking one with her morning coffee. Not after the first negative pregnancy test, or the second, or the fifth. Her reasons for wanting a family amounted to a general desire, a certainty that she desired that family with Bryan, and a leap of faith that–when the moment came, and the test was positive, and everyone around her was celebrating, and she had an impending deadline of forty weeks before a new little person arrived in her world–she would find the rest of the certainty that she lacked.

She tried to ignore it, putting off conversations that might have brought her comfort in hopes that not naming the fear would somehow help it fade away instead. Certainly, some level of wavering was normal with a decision of such magnitude. And, if things went like they were supposed to, a pregnancy would force her to assuage her doubts. Thus, Harper had channeled her energy, misgivings and all, into those early, procreative efforts.

But as time went on, and the test never flashed positive, the enthusiasm with which she had embarked on trying, gradually ebbed to an effort that certainly could have proved effective, though was far from rigorously regimented. Harper's nerves eased not because she had grown confident in the decision, but because the decision had yet to prove life-changing.

And now, the possibility of law school was giving her the chance to go back and second guess every choice that had brought them this far. She knew what to expect from law school in a way that she would never know what to expect from children, and there was some comfort in that, especially as the next step to family likely started in a sterilized exam room. But Harper also couldn't stop the guilt that her sudden change in priorities was in direct odds with Bryan's renewed sense of urgency.

"Bryan wants to go to a fertility clinic," she finally offered quietly.

Maggie's brow furrowed. "Why?"

"Because we've been trying, and it's obviously not working. Even with the medication, we still haven't…"

"You went on meds?" Maggie asked, concern plain on her face.

Harper peeled the sticker off her coffee cup. "Six months ago, and still nothing. Bryan's worried something might be wrong. He's getting himself tested again."

"Again? And you?"

Harper shook her head. "I haven't made an appointment."

Maggie dragged a stool over to the counter and sat down. Her dark eyes fixed on Harper. "I meant, are you worried that something is wrong?"

"A little," Harper admitted. "If everything is fine, then it should have happened, right?"

"Maybe." Maggie admitted. "Or maybe they'll tell you everything *is* fine and you just need more time. Or a vacation. Isn't that a thing? Get a nice hotel, and turn off your phones, and order room service, and just relax and let it happen?"

Harper bristled. "It's been two years, Maggie. We've done relaxed, stressed, quick, drawn out, at home, on vacation, in every position suggested for higher rates of conception."

"Too much information," Maggie laughed.

"I know you and Seth have never sullied your exceptional sex life with the forced intimacy of attempted procreation," she teased with a sigh. "Believe it or not, it's not roses and romance all the time."

A corner of Maggie's mouth twitched. "Well, have you tried whips and handcuffs instead?"

They laughed, and the tightness in Harper's chest eased slightly. She tossed her empty cup into the bin next to the door. "When did you know for sure?" she asked.

"Know what?" Maggie walked her own cup over to the trash.

"That you wanted the restaurant more than anything else?"

Maggie considered. "I don't think I want the restaurant more than *anything* else."

"More than kids," Harper pressed.

Maggie shook her head. "It's not that simple. I guess I never thought of it as a direct trade off. There are chefs who are moms, just like there are lawyers who are moms. People make that work." She returned to the stool. "For me, I just didn't want to have to compromise my time with either one. I wanted to feel like I was all-in on something."

Harper chewed her bottom lip. "When Mom got sick, I went all-in on family," she admitted. "And I've been all-in ever since then. Giving up school. Staying in the Midwest. Getting married. Supporting Bryan's tenure. Starting a family of my own."

"That's not a bad thing."

"No," agreed Harper. "But now, suddenly, law school feels exciting and interesting, and a baby feels…" She paused.

"Feels like what?" Maggie asked, curiosity wrinkling her forehead.

Harper shrugged. "Inevitable. I think I'm resigned to that being the next phase of adulthood."

"Resigned?" Maggie shot Harper a loaded glance. "What a charming way to bring a baby into the world."

"And there we've arrived at the crux of my ennui," Harper professed dramatically.

"The crux of your ennui?" Maggie smiled. "Simmer down, Jane Austen." She stood up, dragged the stool back to the side of the kitchen, and moved next to Harper on the other side of the counter. She held her by the shoulders at arms-length. "You're one of the smartest people I know, and I know you'll make whatever decision makes the most sense for you and Bryan. But since I know you're looking for advice, here it is: I don't think there's a wrong choice. Law school was your dream. Having a family is a worthy pursuit. Doing them both at the same time sounds like insanity to me, but is totally badass if that's what you want."

Harper sighed. "So, if you were me, you'd go after the scholarship?"

Maggie shook her head. "Girl, what kind of question is that? That is not what I said. I'm not even a lawyer, and I know you can't lead a witness that way."

"You're not a witness," Harper laughed.

"Are you kidding?" Maggie said, folding her arms across her chest. "I've witnessed almost three decades of your life." Her expression softened. "You want to know what I'd do if I was you? Fine. I'd give myself permission to choose what I want. And then, I'd give myself permission to not give two shits about what other people think about it. Because people *will* have opinions." Maggie's cell phone dinged, and she fished it from her pants pocket and glanced at the screen. "Case in point," she muttered under her breath.

"Everything ok?" Harper asked.

The smile Maggie offered in return did not reach her eyes. "Yeah. No big deal." She tapped out a quick reply, then set the phone on the counter, screen down. She glanced up at Harper. "Make a choice. Don't just resign yourself to a version of your life you're not actually interested in."

"That's good advice," Harper said quietly.

Maggie nodded once in affirmation. "You're welcome. Now, can we please trade an existential problem for a practical one?"

"Go ahead," Harper chuckled.

Maggie's expression melted to one of hope mixed with desperation.

"Seeing as Chicago Cuisine Magazine is now on the guest list tonight, please tell me you know something about how to buff a floor?"

Chapter 8

Candace Walsh's office claimed one corner of the thirty-second floor of Falstaff Tower. A large, glass top desk sat in front of two walls of nearly floor-to-ceiling windows that looked out over the Chicago skyline, which abruptly gave way to the steel gray of Lake Michigan and a stormy, late November sky. A sideboard against the wall held a few personal effects, a crystal decanter filled with honey-colored liquor, two framed black and white photographs, and a swirling, silver statue attached to an engraved wood base that Harper guessed was some type of award. Candace's university diplomas were framed on the wall above: Syracuse for undergrad; Columbia Law. Like Harper's own office, much of the remaining wall was glass, revealing the hallway happenings of the rest of the floor and the workspace of her personal assistant, Greta.

It had been Greta who showed Harper to one of the tawny upholstered chairs around a low table in the center of the office when she arrived that morning to deliver the summary report on the binders of Urban City Apparel's financial records. Candace, Greta explained, was finishing an early deposition in the conference room next door, and had specifically requested Harper to wait. Harper's palms grew sweaty, and she lay the file of her work on the table before she could leave behind conspicuous fingerprint stains on the clean, cream folder. Greta offered coffee before returning to her desk. With her back to the only non-transparent wall in the room, Harper had the uncomfortable sensation of being trapped in a fishbowl.

She could hear the steady hum of conversation on the other side of the wall and wondered as to the specifics of the deposition. It was unlikely related to the documents she had been poring over. When Candace first passed them off, Harper assumed there must be some layer of nuance or wrinkle of intrigue she was being tested to parse through. But though Harper wasn't particularly interested in mergers and acquisitions, she had seen many and understood enough about them to know that Urban City Apparel would be a straightforward, low-drama sale. It hadn't required any deep diving, or extensive research, or cross-referencing past sales, or following money to offshore accounts. It merely required time, and exacting attention to detail, to ensure it remained as easy in reality as it appeared on paper.

The murmurs from the neighboring room swelled, and Harper heard chairs scrape back from the table. She glanced out the glass wall at Greta, who looked toward the conference room before glancing at Harper and giving a quick nod. A moment later, Candace strode into view, gold jewelry sparkling against an eggplant-colored shift dress. Harper could not hear the brief words she exchanged with Greta as she walked by, but she turned to Harper and smiled warmly as she pushed through the door.

"Sorry to make you wait," she said.

"It's no problem." Harper stood up quickly. There were very few people who *wouldn't* wait for Candace Walsh. "Here's the overview of the financials you requested." Her palms were sweating again, and she picked up the file folder as delicately as possible.

"Sit," Candace insisted, taking the folder from Harper and moving to one of the other arm chairs. She paged through the documents, skimming the work. "This is good," she murmured, more to herself than Harper. "Everything seems like it's in good shape."

"Yeah," Harper agreed with more enthusiasm than a niche, alternative textile, clothing brand sale warranted. "This one should be pretty straightforward."

Candace looked up, amusement dancing in her eyes. "I would hope so," she said. "It would look bad for me if it wasn't, given my vested interest."

Harper's smile faltered. "Oh?" she asked. She had spent days on the files and was confident in her work. But even though Candace had given her the assignment, Harper hadn't detected a personal connection between the two.

"My stepson, Mark, is one of the founders," explained Candace, her tone non-judgmental. "He and his college roommate first wrote the plan as part of a business project at Duke."

Harper remembered Mark Archer's name on some of the file documents. For professional reasons, Candace had obviously decided not to take her husband's name, but now Harper tried to remember if she might have heard it at the holiday party or in conversation around the office. It hadn't been her job to recognize the relation, but she still felt foolish for having missed the detail. She stole a quick glance at the black and white photos on the sideboard. The two boys in the first photo were young, dark-haired, in matching polo shirts and seersucker shorts. They stood barefoot in the sand, arms around each other, waves and horizon hazy in the background.

She presumed the other photo was more recent. A family snapshot taken at some wedding or formal event. Candace in a floor-length, sequined gown. Her husband, broad shouldered, six inches taller, to her left, his arm around her waist. The boys, now grown men, crowded in on her right. They wore their bows undone and draped around their necks, and their shirt sleeves were rolled up. For stepsons they looked, Harper thought, remarkably like Candace.

Candace's eyes followed Harper's. "That's Mark on the far right," she nodded toward the frame.

"I didn't realize," Harper started, turning back to Candace.

Candace waved a hand. "I didn't mean you to. I was going to do the paperwork myself, but Mark didn't want any favors. He considered hiring a different firm entirely." Candace chuckled. "Which was, obviously, just insulting. I promised him I'd keep things quiet around the office."

"You're not handling the sale?" asked Harper.

"As you said, the financials are in order, and it's a relatively straightforward acquisition. Of course, I'm overseeing things, but heaven forbid the evil stepmother swoop in and be of any actual assistance. I'm passing parts off to make sure everyone stays comfortable."

Harper looked away awkwardly. "I have a hard time imagining anyone calling you an evil stepmother."

"Oh, I've been called much worse. Mostly at the firm." Candace laughed. "Every step-parent in the world is the villain at one point or the other. Every biological parent too, for that matter. Do you have kids?"

Harper's jaw flexed. "Not yet," she managed, trying to sound indifferent.

"Well, take your time," Candace sighed. "I met John after I'd been made a partner. Part of me was relieved that Mark and Dominick were part of the package and already had a mother." She glanced at the photo. "It made it easier to stay at work, keep the hours I did. Less stepping on toes." Her attention snapped back to Harper. "Sorry," she said with a light laugh. "You don't need to hear any of this." She stood and moved to her desk. "I didn't ask you to wait so we could talk about Mark or Urban City."

"You didn't?" Harper asked, debating whether she was meant to follow Candace to the desk. She stood just as Candace turned back with a file folder.

"No, no, sit," Candace insisted, returning to her own chair. She laid the folder on the table between them. "The scholarship committee reconvened earlier this week to consider its list of semi-finalists."

Harper's heart fell. Lyle Pickett had not been down to talk to her. "I see."

"Relax, Harper." Candace leaned back in her chair, crossing her legs at the ankle. "It's not bad news. You are, however, behind. Some of the other applicants already have early admission decisions in hand."

Harper swallowed uncomfortably. "I've started looking at Northwestern," she offered, a stretch considering it was Bryan who acquired the application information.

Candace nodded. "Which is great, but there are a few practicalities to tackle before that." She reached for the file folder and glanced at the top page. "Your LSAT score was good. A 168 paired with your grades, your body of work here, and the recommendations you'll have would get you a look somewhere."

"Thank you," Harper interjected, relaxing slightly for the first time in the conversation.

"The problem," Candace flipped to the next page in the folder, "is that your test score has expired."

The small bubble of hope that buoyed Harper's spirits burst.

"You're saying I'd have to retake the test?" she asked. She remembered studying for the exam years earlier, the massive books of test prep materials, the timed practice sessions her senior seminar advisor held in the political science office, the sleepless nights poring over logic diagrams and word problems. It had been months of preparation, followed by three and a half hours of grueling test taking, and three weeks of sweating it out while she waited for results. She wasn't keen to jump back into it. "When?" she asked, trepidation clear in her tone.

"The next test date is the middle of January. Registration closes December 1st."

"That's next week," Harper exhaled in a rush. "That gives me less than two months to prepare."

"Yes," Candace confirmed, voice light. "But don't sound so demoralized. You're hardly starting from scratch. You use most of the test skills in your work here every day."

"I should start asking the associates to send their briefs over as analytical grouping setups," said Harper, her voice strained.

Candace chuckled. "You did it once, and you've had a lot more practical practice since then. Reading comprehension. Legalese. Your experience here is probably worth an extra two or three points on your score." Candace leaned forward. "The test is merely a hoop to jump through. If it intimidates you, so be it, but it shouldn't discourage you. We're only having this conversation because I believe that you have the potential to be successful." Candace flipped back to the front page of the folder. "In fact," she went on, "I'm willing to bet on it."

"Excuse me?" Harper asked.

Candace slid an envelope from under a paper clip on the inside of the folder and passed it to Harper. "This check should cover your test registration fee."

Harper stared down at her name showing through the cellophane window on the front of the envelope. It was one thing for Candace to swing by her office with a kind word and vote of confidence, but it was another thing entirely to be handed a check and expected to perform on an exam she hadn't studied for in over a decade.

"Is something the matter?" Candace asked, returning the folder to the table.

"Um, no, thank you," Harper managed. "I appreciate your encouragement, really. It's just a lot to take in. When we last talked, it all seemed so hypothetical, and now I'm holding a check and talking about taking the LSAT. I haven't even spoken with Lyle yet, and…"

Candace held up a hand. "Don't worry about talking to Lyle," she insisted. "I'm going to oversee your application and make sure you wind up our top choice."

"Why?" asked Harper automatically. She knew her work was good. She was often requested among the associates and had assisted on plenty of notable cases, but she had never had Candace's, or any other partner's, undivided attention this way. "I don't mean to sound ungrateful. I just thought, well, you said Lyle was the one with the interest in having an internal applicant considered among the finalists."

"He is," Candace said slowly. "The difference between us is that I'm specifically interested in that applicant being you."

Harper looked down at the envelope again. "I don't understand," she admitted, overwhelmed. "Why me?"

Candace leaned back in the chair and smiled. "If you're worried I'm handing you something you don't deserve, you shouldn't be," Candace assured her. "I'd have vouched for you based on your work at the firm alone. But when I read your essay, it admittedly got personal for me."

"Your mother?" Harper asked, treading carefully back into the personal territory of a named partner.

Candace shook her head. "Grandmother."

"I'm sorry," Harper offered.

Candace waved a hand. "It was a long time ago. She lived with us. Helped raise me. She passed the week of my bar exam."

"I can't imagine." Harper wondered how much sympathy was appropriate to offer in the current circumstance.

Candace looked at her intently. "Sure, you can. You were just willing to do what I wasn't."

Harper froze. "I'm not sure I follow."

"You gave up your plans for your mom," Candace said, admiration clear in her tone. "I barely gave up 24 hours to go home for the funeral. I actually studied in the pew while my parents stood in the reception line." She shook her head, as if in disbelief at the memory. "My parents blamed my behavior on the grief, but it was selfishness more than anything. As a result, I got what I wanted. You didn't. But you made a nobler decision. I'd like to help you reclaim the opportunity."

Harper could not imagine a more surprising conversation or personal revelation with the woman she had admired since walking in on the first day. "Candace, that's incredibly…"

"Ridiculous?" Candace chimed in. "I'm sure it sounds that way. Sentimentality isn't worth much in this business."

"I was going to say generous," Harper finished.

Candace smiled. "There's something else you should know," she admitted.

Harper's heart skipped uncomfortably.

"Lyle Pickett has recruited a second applicant from the staff."

A deep vee formed between Harper's eyebrows. She had considered that Candace's enthusiasm may not be matched by all members of the committee, but she had also assumed she would hold Lyle Pickett's interest beyond the first round of scrutiny. If he no longer considered her the best applicant, so be it. But this seemed more like he was actively working against her.

"In fact," Candace went on, "you could say that this has come down to a two-horse race." She leveled her gaze at Harper. "I told you that the scholarship is essentially a vanity project for Lyle, which is why he was keen to make it a friendly wager. His top-pick versus mine. An in-house competition between two of Horowitz, Walsh, and Pickett's homegrown, paralegal stars."

The color drained from Harper's face. "Who's the other candidate?"

Before Candace could answer, the door across the hallway opened, and Lyle Pickett stepped out of a private conference room followed closely by Tate Bishop. Harper watched as Lyle laughed and slapped Tate on the back, moving him toward the elevators at the end of the hall. As they crossed in front of Candace's glass wall, Tate's eyes locked on Harper's. He had been aloof in the days since his conversation with Pollard Frank, which Harper assumed was out of consideration for her feelings. Holding his gaze, Harper realized it was shrewdness and not courtesy that had kept him away.

"Excuse me one moment," she said to Candace, leaving the envelope on the table and rising from her chair. She pushed through the office door as the elevator chimed its arrival. Tate and Lyle shook hands as the elevator doors slid open.

"Hold the door!" she called down the hallway.

Lyle glanced briefly in Harper's direction before turning down the hall toward his own corner office. But Tate waited, slipping his hands into his pockets awkwardly as Harper approached.

"I'm sorry," he mumbled, turning briefly to make sure Pickett was out of earshot. "I swear I didn't know that phone call would have anything to do with Horowitz, Walsh, and Pickett."

"It shouldn't have." Harper closed her eyes and took a deep breath. "How the hell did this happen?"

Tate's shoulders were up around his ears, and for the first time, Harper could imagine what he must have looked like as a chastised student standing in front of the headmaster at his upper-crust boarding school. "Listen, Pickett only called me after Harold Turner called him."

"And let me guess," Harper hissed. "Your father called them both?"

A muscle in Tate's jaw twitched. "Keep my father out of it. His business is with Pollard Frank. This happened because Turner happened to call Pickett for a professional conversation. As I understand it, he mentioned both our names. That's when Lyle mentioned you may be off the job market by spring, given you were up for scholarship consideration." He folded his arms. "Which you failed to mention, by the way, when coming up with all your excuses not to consider New York. Here I thought it was about a bloody house."

Harper's voice rose. "I didn't even know about the scholarship yet when you brought that business card into my office."

"Well, you did by the time you were on the phone call," replied Tate.

"It didn't matter," protested Harper. "You wanted New York. I already told you I didn't want to go."

Tate cocked an eyebrow. "I brought you onto that call because I meant it when I said you were the best colleague to be considered. Pollard Frank could have offered you the job, and I would have been stuck here. But I welcomed that competition, even if it hurt me. If you really just wanted me to take it…"

"That's not fair," Harper interrupted. "You all but begged me to take that call with you. You wanted us to go together."

Tate laughed, a hard chuckle. "And since when have I been able to force you into doing anything? You were curious. Fine. But now, so am I." The elevator doors began to close, and he pulled a hand quickly from his pocket to stop them. He stepped into the lift. "Turner was genuinely impressed with you on the call. You're good, Andrews. Everyone knows it. It's not like you're going to make this easy on me. It's not like it's a sure thing."

Harper stepped toward the elevator, holding out a hand as the doors slid closed again. "Tate, please." It came out as a weak, whispered plea that she instantly wished she could take back.

Tate gave her a small, pitying smile. "Good luck, Andrews," he said, leaning forward to punch the buttons.

Harper pulled back her hand, and the doors closed between them.

She stared at her distorted reflection in the elevator doors for a long time. Tate was right. He had invited her on the call to his potential detriment, and she hadn't shared with him what Candace had come to her office to discuss. But it wasn't because she was hoarding the information for herself; it was because she was afraid. She had wanted it once before, and it had slipped away. She was afraid to want it again. Afraid to recommit, only to lose the opportunity to someone younger, brighter, more ambitious. Afraid that, if she admitted out loud how strongly she was considering it, there would be no talking herself back out of it. Afraid of how prioritizing law school at the same moment her husband was prioritizing having a family would interrupt the synergy that had always existed between them. She had been wrestling with it for days.

Heads. Tails. Heads. Tails.

As she marched back to the office, however, her fear gave way to something else. Not exactly courage, but determination. Yes, this would be a big change. No, she didn't know what it meant for the idea of growing their family. Yes, the idea of preparing for the LSAT and filling out applications again was daunting. But she wanted it, and she was willing to fight for it.

She pushed back through the glass office door to find Candace sitting behind her desk, a pair of gold-framed readers perched on her nose. Harper strode over to the chairs. The check still lay on the table between them, and her hands trembled as she reached for it.

"I take it this means you're interested?" Candace asked coyly.

Harper turned and faced her boss, finally feeling the full weight of the opportunity she would give up if she walked away now.

"I'm more than interested," she confirmed. "I'm all-in."

Chapter 9

The certainty with which she left Candace Walsh's office had all but dissipated by the time Harper stood on the curb in front of her apartment. She had practiced her speech to Bryan the entire way home. They had time. He was only just tenured and could continue to invest in research and publication. She had already given up the dream once and didn't know if she could stomach doing it again.

She stared up at the glowing square of the living room window and let out a heavy sigh. Committing to her choice hadn't made her immune to, what she imagined would be, Bryan's immense disappointment. True, he found her the application list, and true, he was the one who said they should have all the information, but there was a difference between information gathering and decision making. And Harper had essentially decided on the spot without talking it all the way through with the one other person who deserved to have his opinion considered.

They so rarely disagreed that she had a hard time imagining his response. He was so rarely confrontational she had a hard time imagining him being anything but supportive. Still, this wasn't a friendly debate about where to get takeout or which family to spend the holidays with. It wasn't even their momentary disagreement over whether to buy a house, which had amicably resolved in the span of a meal. This was their future family. Harper knew it was different. Her pulse quickened as she swiped herself into the building and climbed the stairs to her front door.

Energetic conversation met her as she turned the knob and stepped into their small entryway. Seized with a sudden jolt of panic, she scrambled to remember what dinner or event she had overlooked amidst the drama at work. A moment later, her heart rate steadied as she saw it was just Bryan and Seth in the living room, though she still couldn't recall if they planned to be together or not. She glanced reflexively for Maggie before realizing that she would be at Indie Lime. Harper's spirits sank.

Still, Seth provided a welcome buffer to the forthcoming conversation racing through her mind.

"Hey," she called, trying to split the difference between pleasant surprise and expectant welcome. "Sorry I'm late."

Seth shook his head. "You're not. I dropped in unannounced."

"Oh?" Harper said, surprise clear this time. "What gives?"

"I was actually in the area." Seth shrugged. "Thought I'd hit up Bryan for a beer." He clanked the neck of his glass bottle against Bryan's.

Harper slid out of her coat. "Everything ok?"

"Great," Seth said with an awkward laugh. "Busy. I'm in that stretch between the holidays everyone at school *loves*, and you know Maggie. She'd sleep at the restaurant these days if I'd let her."

"Definitely worth a beer," Bryan said, swigging from his bottle.

Harper couldn't shake the feeling that there was something uncomfortably forced about the conversation now that she had joined in. It wasn't necessarily weird to find Seth and Bryan in the apartment having a beer after work, but it wasn't particularly common either. The charter school was in Bridgeport. The restaurant was even further north, just off the Loop. Yet, Seth said he was in the area, meaning he likely left school early. Something didn't add up, though when she heard their voices walking in, the conversation had been normal and lively. She decided not to interlope any longer to figure it out.

"Well, you guys enjoy," she said, dropping a kiss onto Bryan's cheek as she crossed the living room. "I'm going to change." As she closed the bedroom door behind her, she heard the murmurings of conversation return. She paused a moment before moving to the bathroom. There was a quick burst of laughter. Harper wasn't sure what to make of it. She unlocked her phone and texted Maggie.

Lots to share when you have time. Good luck tonight! Miss you.

She knew any reply would come long after she was asleep, and she set the ringer to silent before dropping it onto the charging pad.

She tried to let the warm water of the shower relax away some of the tension from the afternoon. The mood on the twenty-eighth floor felt dramatically different now that she and Tate had been made competitors. By the time she returned to her office, after accepting the check from Candace and promising to register for the test before she left that evening, it seemed everyone in the cubicles knew about the scholarship and the wager between Candace and Lyle.

At first, Harper assumed Tate told as many people as possible, stroking his ego in the process. However, she was surprised to find that after their confrontation at the elevator, he stayed in his office, the door closed, making a point to interact with as few other paralegals and associates as possible. Only as she registered for her test did she remember what Tate once drunkenly confided about his own scores. He would have the same accelerated timeline to retake the test, and he had never been competitive as an applicant to one of the prestigious schools in the city. Arrogant British swagger aside, Harper had to wonder if Tate was just as afraid of appearing the fool as she was.

She stopped the water, wrapped her hair in a towel, and shrugged into her bathrobe, stepping into the steam filled room.

Bryan appeared in the doorway behind her.

"Hi," he said warmly, snaking an arm around her waist. He moved the collar of the robe to the side and lowered his lips to the exposed skin, kissing along the top of her shoulder. Goosebumps broke out over Harper's arms.

"Hi," she said with a light laugh. "How was Seth?"

Bryan's breath was warm on her neck as his kisses rose higher.

"Seth's great," he said flatly, not stopping.

"What was he doing in Hyde Park?" Harper asked, attempting to both satisfy her curiosity and not lose her head as Bryan moved up to nip at her earlobe.

"I don't want to talk about Seth right now," Bryan whispered, mouth at her ear.

Harper shivered and spun around to face him. "Me either." Bryan leaned forward, and Harper forced herself to put a hand on his chest to stop him. "But I need to talk to you about something."

"It can wait," Bryan said, trying to press past the hand.

Harper held firm. "I don't think it can," she insisted.

Bryan pulled back, his expression melting from desire to concern.

"Are you ok?" he asked.

"Yeah," Harper said with a deep breath. "I'm fine. I just had a..." She hesitated, forcing herself to meet her husband's eyes. Deep emerald flecks sparkled in the bathroom light. "...really interesting day at work."

Bryan cocked an eyebrow. "You've been having a few of those recently," he admitted.

"Yeah," Harper said again. "Can we go sit down?"

Bryan leaned in and kissed her forehead with an exasperated sigh.

"If I let you put your sweatpants on, you'll never take them back off for me."

"Not true," Harper teased, hesitating just a moment too long. She ran a hand over his dark stubble.

"Fine," he huffed overdramatically. "I'll meet you in the living room."

By the time she made it to the couch in her oversized Northwestern hoodie and a pair of black sweatpants, Bryan had two glasses of wine on the coffee table and a frozen pizza baking in the oven. Harper tucked into her favorite corner of the couch, and Bryan pulled her feet into his lap. His thumb pressed into the ball of her foot where she balanced in her heels all day. Harper closed her eyes and moaned.

Bryan chuckled. "Are you sure this can't wait?"

"You just put a pizza in the oven," Harper murmured, opening her eyes.

"I can be very efficient," Bryan assured her with a wink.

"Be that as it may," she made herself continue, "I've got to tell you something."

"Tell me something," Bryan said.

It hurt Harper to know that she might be about to hurt him. She took a deep breath. "I was in Candace Walsh's office today," she started.

Bryan shook his head, a knowing smirk on his face. "Why is she at the start of all your work drama these days?"

"It's not drama," Harper insisted, knowing very well that's exactly what Candace and Lyle had started. "I turned in my financial assessment of Urban City Apparel, which turned out to be her stepson's company."

"Did you find something?" asked Bryan, taking a sip of wine.

"No." Harper raised her own glass. "It's nothing like that. While I was there, we got to talking about the scholarship again." She took a long sip, gauging Bryan's reaction. He was frustratingly impassive. "So, it turns out I'm on the shortlist, with just one other applicant."

Something flickered behind Bryan's eyes. "That's great," he said with what sounded like genuine sincerity.

Harper took another drink. "Kind of," she continued. "I'm behind on the application process, and my LSAT score has expired. I have to be ready for the test again on January 13th, and, realistically, I'll need at least a 168 to be a strong applicant."

Bryan shifted on the couch to face her properly. He set his wineglass on the coffee table, lost in thought. "Ok," he said finally. "So, I guess it's time to talk about how serious you are about this."

Harper looked away. "Really serious," she admitted quietly.

"Oh?"

She looked up at Bryan and sighed. "I haven't told you all of it yet."

His brow furrowed. "There's more?"

She confessed everything then: Tate originally offering the interview in New York; the phone call with Pollard Frank; Lyle Pickett recruiting Tate as the firm's other internal applicant, a sure favor from his father care of Harold Turner; Candace and Lyle's wager; having registered for the exam that evening before leaving the office. Bryan did not interrupt, and remained quiet a long moment after she finished.

"Ok," he finally replied with a heavy exhale.

"Are you mad?" Harper asked, setting her wineglass on the coffee table and sliding toward him on the couch.

"Not mad," Bryan replied slowly. "A little disappointed, I guess. I thought this would be more of a conversation." The oven timer chimed in the kitchen, and he rose to attend to the pizza.

"I know," Harper said, swiveling to face him. She swallowed hard to clear the growing lump in her throat. "It's just, I didn't know I wanted this as badly as I do until I realized I could lose it again. To Tate, of all people."

"So, I have to ask," said Bryan, returning to the couch and setting two plates on the coffee table. "Is this really what you want, or is this more about what you don't want Tate to have?"

"I gave this up once," Harper snapped more sharply than she intended. She blew out a breath and lowered her voice. "Is it not fair to pause before deciding to give it up again?"

"It's fair," Bryan agreed. "I was the one who told you to explore whether this was something you really wanted, remember?" He sighed. "I want you to go after the things that are important to you, Harper. I really do. The only thing that bothers me is that I'm not really hearing you say this is what you want. I'm hearing you say you *don't* want to lose the opportunity again, and I'm hearing you say you *don't* want Tate to take your spot." He paused, but Harper did not have a reply. "So, is this what you want, really?"

Harper hesitated. "I don't know," she whispered, finally.

"How can you not know?" Bryan said with an exasperated laugh.

"I don't know," Harper said again, voice rising. "Probably the same way that you want to buy a house one day and then completely change course and want a baby the next." She regretted her tone immediately. Bryan merely shook his head.

"That's not fair," he said calmly. "What I want hasn't changed. A future with you. A family with you."

Harper swallowed hard. "You don't think I still want that? A future with you?"

Bryan reached for her hand. "That's not what I meant, and you know it," he insisted. "But I can't help but think that if you felt the same urge for a family as I do, it would at least be more of a question in your mind as to how we make this work."

Harper rubbed at the furrow between her eyebrows. "Look, I'm sorry. I'm sure it feels like I'm saying no to you and our family. But I'm not. Not forever. Just for now. Putting things on hold doesn't mean the conversation is over. I don't want the conversation to be over."

Bryan looked away, clearly considering his next words. "So then, is this the conversation in which you want to hear that my test results came back today?"

Harper's heart skipped a beat. "They did?" Bryan nodded and reached for his glass on the table. "I didn't realize you had already gone in." Nervous adrenaline coursed through her, overwhelming the soft buzz from the wine. "You didn't say anything."

Bryan shrugged. "I didn't think it was that big of a deal. It wasn't like I expected you to come hold my hand."

"I know what the test is," Harper laughed stiffly. "And it would not have been your hand that needed holding." She swallowed hard, fighting against a rising tide of anxious curiosity. "What did they say?"

"Same as last time," Bryan said, reaching for his cell phone and swiping through his email. "Count, concentration, and motility all within normal ranges." He scrolled down as he continued reading. "Morphology slightly above normal ranges. Numbers are consistent and stable when compared to previous testing."

"Remind me what morphology is?" asked Harper.

"Irregularly shaped. I've got some weirdos." The tiniest grin pulled at the corners of his mouth. "Long story short, they should be able to get the job done."

"Great," said Harper, guilt rising. It was impossible not to feel like they had reached an impasse, and she couldn't ignore the nagging realization that if Bryan was ok, then any potential problems were likely her own. She bit into a slice of pizza to avoid a more elaborate response, and an uneasy silence stretched between them–a first in as long as she could remember.

"You know, these are the moments my mom used to say we should flip a coin," she said, changing tactics the way Helen often had to break the quiet uneasiness.

"Should I go get a quarter?" Bryan asked.

Harper heard the slightest bite of sarcasm in his tone. She set her empty plate on the coffee table.

"I'm sorry," she said. "When I was in Candace's office today, it was like I could feel the coin in the air. And when she said it was between Tate and me, I knew which way I wanted it to land." She squeezed his hand. "I have to do this. It feels right. Does that make any sense?"

"Hm," Bryan murmured, a resigned exhale through his nose. "Yeah, it does, because I had the same feeling about starting a family with you."

Harper felt the prick of tears. "At the clinic?" she asked, throat tight.

Bryan shook his head. "No," he admitted. "Tonight. Talking with Seth."

Harper's curiosity prickled. She had all but forgotten the evening started with Seth in the living room. "Why?" she asked.

Bryan looked at her, and Harper was certain she had never seen quite that mix of sadness and excitement in his expression before. "You should call Maggie in the morning," he said.

The hairs on the back of Harper's neck stood up. "Why?" she asked again. "Bryan, what's going on?"

"You should hear it from her," he insisted, looking away.

"Bryan!" Harper pressed. "Is she ok?"

Bryan ran a hand over his stubble as he turned back to Harper. "They're expecting."

Harper could not stop the gasp that escaped her. Her heart flip-flopped.

Heads. Tails. Heads. Tails.

Her coin, it seemed, was still in the air.

Part 2

Anything it Takes

Chapter 10

Lakeview Fertility Clinic was on the fourth floor of a glass high rise four blocks off Lake Shore Drive. The waiting room was modern, with comfortably appointed furniture in variegated white and gray upholstery. Reading materials ranging from *People* magazine to the *New England Journal of Medicine* lay in neat stacks on end tables, and abstract, water-centric landscapes in teals and blues covered three of the walls. The fourth, into which the reception desk was built, displayed framed photographs of the families that the clinic had most recently helped to grow.

The first time Harper arrived at the clinic, the wall had taken her aback as she wondered if someday, she and Bryan would pose for a picture that would hang in this gallery. Part of her ached to, even if she still struggled to imagine it. Now, she hardly noticed it. She rushed from her office an hour before she would normally leave, fighting the traffic heading uptown in order to make a 4:30 appointment. Sleet slapped at the car, landing in icy splotches along the windshield and threatening to turn into the first snow of the season at any moment.

The intensity with which baby fever had gripped Harper after she learned that Seth and Maggie were expecting was matched only by the intensity with which she had been certain she could beat out Tate Bishop for the firm scholarship just hours before. She had called the clinic the next morning to make an appointment, grown immediately frustrated that she would have to wait three weeks, then dug out the dusty box of ovulation test strips from the bottom drawer of the bathroom vanity in a renewed effort to work toward conception.

It was not lost on her that the decision was entirely impulsive, and she half expected Bryan to question her motivations. If he thought she was in it for the wrong reasons, however, he never mentioned it, only briefly inquiring whether their redoubled efforts toward parenthood changed anything about law school.

Harper could not bring herself to renege on her commitment to Candace to prepare for the LSAT, however. It was more than a sense of obligation. She still *wanted* to take the test. And so, while she waited for a lab tech to come and take vials of blood at her first appointment, she worked from an enormous volume of test preparation questions that she now lugged with her everywhere. It was the object of both amusement and scorn at the office. Those colleagues with whom Harper had always been friendly offered words of encouragement and advice when they saw her pouring over it in between depositions or during lunch in the office kitchen. Meanwhile, those who worked to curry favor with Lyle made no effort to hide their mocking whispers as they sidled past her table. If Tate was preparing for the exam at the office, he was not making an open show of it, though it was rumored that Lyle was taking a personal interest in his preparation.

The book lay open in her lap now as she waited for one of the nurses in seafoam green scrubs to call her back to the exam rooms. Around her, women waited in various stages of pregnancy. Some had other children with them. Some propped their phones or e-readers on the roundness of their bellies. None of them looked like they just stepped out of corporate America. Harper avoided eye contact and stared down at the logic problem on the page–a mixed setup, one of several types of reasoning exercises that appeared on the test. She had started to think of her own life in terms of these setups. Just making this appointment had been an exercise in logistical problem solving.

Harper is arranging seven appointments on her calendar–deposition 1, deposition 2, discovery research, client interview 1, court appearance, lunch with Bryan, and fertility clinic. The appointments must all happen in five days between Monday and Friday, with at least one event per day, and must follow these guidelines:

- *Deposition 2 must happen immediately before the court appearance.*
- *Discovery research must be scheduled somewhere before the court appearance, but cannot happen Monday morning.*
- *Client interview 1 and lunch with Bryan must happen on the same day.*
- *Fertility clinic must happen Monday or Tuesday (or else she'll be out of sync with her cycle)*
- *Deposition 1 must occur Monday or Friday.*

She had fit this appointment in Tuesday afternoon with the assurance of the scheduler that it was a straightforward consultation, Harper's first time actually meeting with Dr. Amy Bluffton, and there would be no reason to think she wouldn't be able to return to the office later if needed.

Harper scratched out a small diagram in the margin of the prep book and began to work through the setup, a situation involving the correct order of paintings on the wall of an art gallery. She was through labeling the first two rules with the appropriate numbers and letters when the woman two seats over cleared her throat. Harper glanced up. The woman smiled. She had straight, mousey hair that was pushed back in an elastic headband, and her baby bump stretched under her fleece jacket, testing the resilience of the zipper.

"Trying for your first?" the woman asked.

Harper glanced in both directions, hoping this horrendous opening line wasn't meant for her. No one else in the clinic was remotely interested in, or close enough to, the woman to be the target of the conversation.

"Yes," she said tightly, returning her gaze to the page and adding the next set of conditions to the diagram.

"This will be our third," the woman persisted. "We've used the clinic for all three." Harper looked up again to find the woman smiling warmly at her. "IVF," she offered as further explanation. "Dr. Bluffton and her team are wonderful. You're in excellent hands."

"Great," Harper said with a forced smile.

"With our first," the woman went on, uninvited, "we tried for two years. On our own, initially, of course. Then medication. That was before we came here. My primary care doctor did his best, but endometriosis wasn't really his specialty, you know?"

There was a slight lisp to her pronunciation, and when she smiled, Harper saw she was wearing clear aligners over her teeth. Harper guessed she was no older than twenty-seven. That she was on baby number three after two years of infertility struggles and an untold number of IVF treatments was a timeline Harper could not comprehend.

"What about you?" The woman asked.

Despite Harper's recent interest in the clinic, she was not yet comfortable with the language around treatment and appointments and "her journey" as the nurse called it during her very first visit. Nor was she comfortable with others' willingness to share every detail of their experiences. She understood her own fertility on an academic level, if not an individual one. It felt, somehow, too personal, like requiring some kind of intervention to accomplish what millions of other couples achieved all by themselves was a character flaw rather than a medical diagnosis. Hell, Maggie and Seth managed it by accident despite active efforts to avoid it.

She was definitely not going to share this intensely personal part of her life with a random stranger in the waiting room of the clinic.

"I'm just here to follow up," she offered vaguely. "And trying to get some work done." She raised the book slightly off her lap and nodded toward it. The other woman glanced at the cover.

"Wow," she said. "Law school. Good for you. I can't imagine being in school when I had my first. The sleepless nights and cluster feedings, whew. For two months she'd only sleep if I was holding her. I'd go a week without a shower. I'm so envious of moms who can do it all."

A familiar pang of anxiety twinged in Harper's stomach. She was resolute in pushing forward on both fronts, but that determination could not assuage every doubt.

"Kara Grobbert?" a nurse called from the door next to the reception desk.

The woman gave Harper a final smile. "Good luck to you," she said as she pushed herself awkwardly from the chair. "It'll be so worth it."

Harper looked back to the logic setup but couldn't focus on the conditions or the diagram. Admittedly, coming to the clinic often made her feel like a fraud. Looking around the waiting room, she knew some women had been there for years, waiting, hoping, praying, begging for a baby that had yet to come. She could never admit to these women that it had taken her best friend's undesired pregnancy to bring her here.

Which was also part of the reason she wouldn't give up on law school. She was hedging her bets. If the results at the clinic were discouraging, the scholarship could act as a consolation prize. Or if she faltered on the test, or Tate somehow won the day, the excitement and expectation of a baby would be a welcome distraction. But Kara Grobbert's words touched on a reality Harper was still reckoning with. She wasn't sure if she could be a mom that did it all, or even that she wanted to be. If both came to pass, well, then she just didn't know.

Consequently, she had also started feeling self-conscious at the office, where everyone believed her to be wholeheartedly invested in her work and her competition with Tate. On the days she left early for appointments, she half expected Candace to appear at her door demanding to know what else could be taking precedence over the firm. She would remind herself that Candace had a family, and hadn't even flinched at the suggestion of children when talking about her stepsons, but Harper was still torn between two separate paths, like she was constantly jumping between different versions of her life.

She scratched in the final sets of letters and numbers where they fit in the diagram just as the side door opened and a nurse called her name.

Harper looked up, and the nurse smiled, holding the door open a little wider. Stuffing her pencil in the spine of the book to hold her place, Harper switched her brain into would-be-mom mode and hurried to follow the nurse to the exam room.

Dr. Amy Bluffton was petite and close to fifty. Uneven streaks of gray ran randomly through her loose ponytail. She wore the same seafoam green scrubs as the rest of her staff, white Nike sneakers, a pair of electric blue reading glasses when considering Harper's chart, and 'Notorious RBG' earrings. Harper liked her instantly.

"Any changes since your last visit?" Dr. Bluffton asked, clicking through the test results.

"No," Harper confirmed.

"Pain during sex?"

"No."

"Irregular bleeding?"

"No."

"And no known history of fertility issues?"

"No, my sister has twins."

Dr. Bluffton looked up and over the top of her glasses. "And they were conceived naturally, without intervention?"

Harper hesitated.

"Twins can be more common as a result of fertility treatment," Dr. Bluffton elaborated.

"Right," Harper said slowly. "I guess I never had a reason to ask. She never mentioned anything."

Dr. Bluffton made a note in the chart. "Is there a history of twins in your family?"

"No."

"Well, that doesn't necessarily mean anything. If you have the opportunity, you might ask, just for perspective. What about your mom?"

Harper shifted in her chair. "She passed away twelve years ago."

Dr. Bluffton turned away from the screen to face Harper. "I'm sorry," she said gently. "It says that here in your chart, of course. I meant," she removed the reading glasses, "did she ever mention anything about struggles with conceiving?"

The blood rose to Harper's cheeks at the thought of her parents being intimate. Her mother had been liberal in discussing sex with the girls. In high school, no topic had been off limits, though Harper often shied away from plenty of conversations that Helen had started against her daughters' wishes. But despite her openness, there had never been any talk of infertility. Plenty of conversations on how to avoid pregnancy. Not a single one about what to do when you couldn't seem to make it work.

"Um, no," Harper said quickly.

"Hm," Dr. Bluffton chuckled knowingly to herself as she turned back to the computer and made a note. "No one wants to think about mom and dad getting it on. Ok, Harper," she said, spinning the chair away from the screen. "Let's talk about where you're at. I think we can confidently rule out several factors. Your bloodwork came back normal, and your ultrasound showed nothing of immediate concern. Your partner's tests are also within the desired ranges."

"Ok," Harper said plainly. She was, at once, relieved and disappointed. It was encouraging to hear that there were no major concerns, yet finding something of concern may have led to quicker answers and options.

"The goal is to create the optimal environment for conception. We have a number of medications we can use to stimulate ovulation, and we'll give you a precise timeline for you and your husband to schedule intercourse accordingly." She opened a drawer in the computer desk and pulled out a blank paper calendar. She glanced at her watch for the date and labeled the remaining days and weeks. "So, let's estimate your next cycle starts here." She circled one of the calendar boxes. "Then, starting on day three, you'll take three tablets of Letrozole." She placed a checkmark in the corresponding box. "And you'll continue through day seven." She looked up. "So far, so good?"

Harper nodded.

"Great," Dr. Bluffton continued. "You'll likely ovulate around day thirteen, but we want to make sure we catch the window. That's why, starting on day ten, you'll have intercourse." She drew a smiley face in the calendar box. "And then you'll continue to have intercourse every other day through day seventeen or eighteen." She glanced at Harper. "Some online armchair physicians will tell you every day is better. Husbands seem to find those links a lot. And, of course, if your preference is more frequent, it won't hurt the process." She shook her head. "But every other day is plenty to be effective."

"Good to know," Harper forced a small laugh. The plan sounded easy enough, not all that different from what they had already tried, which perhaps explained why she wasn't immediately overwhelmed with hope and optimism of its eventual success. "So, what would our next steps be after a round of the drugs?"

"In a best-case scenario, a positive pregnancy test," Dr. Bluffton said confidently. "But don't be surprised if it takes more than one cycle. We're improving the odds, not guaranteeing them. We can do ultrasounds confirming follicle growth and trigger shots to stimulate ovulation. Of course, we can always talk about IUI or IVF, too. Let's get through this first cycle and see what happens, and I'd like to get you scheduled for an HSG to ensure there are no blockages."

Harper's mind was swimming in acronyms. "An HSG?"

"A hysterosalpingogram," Dr. Bluffton explained. "It's an x-ray of your uterus where we insert dye that allows us to view whether the fallopian tubes are open."

"And if they're not?" Harper asked, nerves tingling with apprehension.

"We'll see where the blockages are on the x-ray and from there decide a course of treatment. Surgery used to be a common option, though I find the invasiveness and risk not worth the potential tradeoff."

"Sounds," Harper started, entirely unsure how it sounded. "Informative," she decided.

Dr. Bluffton laughed. "I don't think I've ever heard it described quite *that* way before. I'll be straight with you; it's not particularly comfortable, but it is incredibly helpful in ruling out contributing factors. We can schedule it with this cycle," she nodded toward the calendar. She wrote a small HSG in the corner of the box corresponding with day five and drew an arrow pointing through day ten. "Anywhere in that range should be fine. You can make the appointment before you leave if you'd like. They'll ask you to call back and confirm when your cycle starts."

"Ok," said Harper, voice small.

Dr. Bluffton clicked around the computer screen, inputting prescription information and talking about timelines and potential side effects. Harper looked down at her hands and did her best to concentrate as her mind involuntarily organized the information into a logic setup.

Patient X must start a 28-day course of Drug A before starting a five-day course of Drug B. At least three days must pass between the end of Drug A and the start of Drug B. Cramping, hot flashes, and anxiety are common for at least five days after patients finish Drug A. An HSG may be ordered on any day five through ten while taking Drug B. Cramping and anxiety are also common side effects of the HSG. Given these conditions, which of the following scenarios can be reasonably assumed...

Dr. Bluffton closed out the medical chart and turned to Harper, leaning an elbow on the desk. "Any questions for me?"

Harper's attention snapped back to the doctor. "Um, well," she fumbled, embarrassed to have been so easily distracted.

"That's alright," Dr. Bluffton encouraged. "No one wants to ask, but everyone wonders. What are my odds? When will it happen?" She leaned back in the desk chair. "I never make promises," she admitted. "But I like your chances, Harper. This is straightforward. For right now, take your meds. Follow the calendar." She slid the paper across the desk. "I'll see you after the new year for your imaging appointment."

"Thank you," said Harper. She wondered what it meant that she hadn't been thinking to ask about the odds.

Dr. Bluffton rose from her desk chair, tucking her reading glasses into the chest pocket of her scrubs. "Happy holidays," she said warmly. "See you soon." The door latched with a sharp click behind her.

Harper stood and collected her things, snugging the belt of her peacoat tight at the waist and twisting her scarf around her neck. She was relieved to hear Dr. Bluffton's frank assessment of her situation. She had steps to follow, boxes to check, a timeline to which to adhere. These were the terms under which Harper worked every day. The doctor had assured nothing, and yet had been reassuring. Following the signage back toward the lobby, Harper dutifully reported to the desk to schedule her next appointment. The receptionist seemed unsurprised when Harper referenced the paper calendar in response to a question about preferred dates. She stared at her screen.

"Hm," she mused. "That's a popular week. Everyone's just coming back from the holidays. I could do," she looked up, "Friday, January 12th at 4:30pm?"

Harper's heart sank. It was the evening before the LSAT. "That's the only option?"

The receptionist's fingers flew across her keys. "In the evenings, yes," she confirmed. "I see that's your preferred timing. If you wanted something earlier in the day, I have a Wednesday or a Thursday. Dr. Bluffton advises you give yourself the rest of the day to recover, however, so I wouldn't recommend trying to squeeze it in over lunch."

Harper looked up at the photos of smiling families on the wall. "Friday will be fine," she said, resigned. If that's what it was going to take, so be it. It would be the first of many things she would have to learn to juggle if everything worked out. Not *if*, Harper thought, practicing holding the idea in her mind, *when*.

The receptionist held an appointment confirmation card over the counter. "There you go," she offered. "Merry Christmas."

"Merry Christmas," Harper returned, tucking the card into the pocket of her coat. She glanced at her watch, still time to make an evening appearance at the office for another hour of work or test prep. She had recently felt herself in an unspoken power struggle with Tate, constantly aware if the light in his office was still on when she left. He had a decided advantage given his lack of a family or a partner waiting at home. She had noticed him watching her from his office as she waited at the elevators when leaving for her appointment that afternoon. She hoped he would still be there when she returned. Let him wonder where she had been. Let him think she was off doing important, scholarship-winning work.

She stepped onto the elevator and switched her brain from future-mom to future-ass-kicking-lawyer mode.

Chapter 11

There were two events leading up to the holidays that Harper looked forward to every year: the Horowitz, Walsh, and Pickett Christmas party and their celebration with Maggie and Seth. It may have been naïve, but a part of Harper desperately wished that somehow these reliable holiday rituals would remain disentangled from the decisions clouding the new year. Hindsight, however, would prove twenty-twenty.

The firm's holiday party fell annually on the last Friday before Christmas, a Friday night that Harper found herself in her office, late, looking for a very specific piece of case law for one of the junior partners. The office was nearly empty, everyone having left early to prepare at home or changing into their formalwear at the office before calling a car and heading to the Ritz for cocktail hour. Harper had expected to run home, change, and pick up Bryan before heading to the hotel, but everything had taken just a bit longer than expected, and then Andrea Thompson had stopped in with a very particular request.

In her time at the firm, Harper had watched with some envy as Andrea ascended through the ranks of associates to an eventual junior partnership. She was whip smart, unafraid to take on anyone in the courtroom, and fast becoming the star litigator on Robert Horowitz's handpicked team of corporate trial lawyers. She had also graduated from Northwestern, and Harper could never quite ignore the fact that the trajectory of Andrea's career was the very path to which she had also aspired.

For her part, Andrea had never treated Harper as anything but a peer, often seeking her services on tough cases because she claimed to trust Harper's work above the associates she had assigned to work for her. Which is how she ended up in Harper's doorway that evening–blonde hair swept into a tight chignon at the base of her neck, burgundy evening gown studded in silver beads shimmering in the fluorescent, hallway lights–asking for an obscure legal precedent she *thought* she remembered hearing about from an appellate level case in Florida. Her team had searched all afternoon and came up empty. Could Harper help?

Harper might have been inclined to say no or that it would have to wait until Monday, but when Andrea mentioned Candace had specifically recommended having Harper look into it, she knew she would stay as long as it took.

This had been happening more and more, Harper realized as she pulled another tome from the shelves in the thirtieth-floor library. For the past month, the office had been divided into two separate camps: those who admired and supported Candace and, by extension, Harper, and those who were loyal to Lyle Pickett and, therefore, Tate. Harper had always known that the politics of the firm and its partners simmered just below the surface of daily business. To see it play out so openly, and with her and Tate at the center of the chaos, was more than a little unsettling. Most days, she worked with her office door closed to avoid extra conversation.

Nevertheless, the workload continued to increase. Though Candace had not explicitly stated that Harper was required to take on more than her normal assignments, nor were most of the people requesting her services likely to be part of the scholarship committee, Harper couldn't help but feel like it was in her best interest to meet each request with a smile, expediency, and her best work. With the partners in particular, it was hard *not* to feel like every filed brief, reviewed document, and retrieved piece of research was a mini-evaluation of her value to the firm and her potential as a lawyer.

On the day she called the fertility clinic, she had promised Bryan that she would find a way to maintain balance, a promise he promptly reminded her of the first two nights she didn't arrive home until after 8:00pm. She apologized profusely, and Bryan smiled, kissed her forehead, and put their dinner plates in the microwave to reheat. He was unfailingly patient, which only enabled Harper to make the same mistake again. Not that she didn't feel guilty about it. In fact, it was in those moments she most questioned why she had so eagerly decided to try again for a baby. She was already overwhelmed just trying to be a good wife.

She glanced at her watch. It was already 6:30, and she had asked Bryan to be home and ready by 5:00. She dropped her head in her hands. The last text she sent had been at 5:15, and she optimistically, and incorrectly, asserted that she was wrapping up and would be home soon.

As if on cue, her cell phone rang.

"I'm sorry! I'm sorry," she answered on the second ring. "I didn't realize how late it was." She collected the books in one arm while pinching the phone in the crook of her neck. "I just need to run back to my office and grab my bag and then..."

"Babe, breathe," Bryan responded. His tone was even and kind, and Harper instantly relaxed despite her frenzied scurrying around the library to shelve her books. "Where are you now?"

"Still in the library," Harper admitted. "Just for another minute."

"Then I'm coming up," Bryan replied.

Harper froze, a book poised in her hand midway to the shelf.

"Coming up where?"

"To your office," said Bryan. "I'm in the lobby."

Harper sighed. "You're here?"

"Yep," Bryan confirmed. Harper heard the elevator chime through the phone. "Don't worry. I brought the dress and shoes and the silver clutch that you couldn't find this morning."

Harper slid the book into its place. "Thank you. You didn't have to."

"If I hadn't, I'd still be sitting at home alone, drinking my second whiskey and soda," he interrupted with an exasperated chuckle.

"I'm sorry," Harper offered again, rushing toward her own elevator.

"It's fine," Bryan assured her. "It's your party. I'm just the arm candy. So, if you'd rather I sit in my tuxedo all night and watch you work, I'm here to please."

Harper's elevator doors opened at the same time that she heard Bryan's chime through the phone, and they stepped out, side by side, in the small lobby of the twenty-eighth floor. After seven years together and five years of marriage, the sight of her husband in black tie still stirred butterflies.

"Hey," she said, ending the phone call and smiling through a heavy sigh.

"Hi," Bryan replied. He carried a black garment bag draped over one arm and held out his other to pull her into his side. He kissed her gently on the forehead. "Long day?"

"Obviously." Harper leaned into him.

"Want to talk about it?"

"Not now," replied Harper, pulling away slightly.

"Want to go drink on the company dollar instead?" He held out the dress.

She took his hand and led him toward her office. "Absolutely."

Twenty minutes later, the black town car that Bryan had hired special for the occasion rolled to a stop, and Harper stepped out onto the street in front of the Ritz feeling anything but glamorous. Her emerald green velvet dress had been hanging in the closet for weeks and had fit like a glove when Harper tried it on at the store. Tonight, she felt it fit more like a sausage casing. She had struggled with the zipper in the stall of the restroom, trying to convince herself that it refused to slide because she couldn't reach it to pull at the right angle and attempting to ignore the way the fabric clung just a little less comfortably around her waist and hips. Finally, she gave up and texted Bryan for backup.

He didn't struggle as she had, but Harper could not deny that the saleswoman had not needed to use one hand to pull the fabric together at the waist to help the zipper move forward. Standing behind her in the mirror, Bryan kissed her shoulder and told her she looked beautiful, and while she believed him, she couldn't help but be distracted wondering if it was the stress of the LSATs or the artificial hormones coursing through her system that was responsible for the extra few pounds she now carried around. Bryan didn't say a word; he just offered his hand and escorted her down to the car.

The party was already in full swing as they entered the ballroom. Guests clustered around high-top tables, dotted with tea lights and swathed in silver and white tablecloths; their eveningwear sparkled in the dim light of four enormous, crystal chandeliers suspended down the middle of the room. In the corner, a jazz combo improvised solos around the standard holiday classics. They were flanked on either side by two large evergreen trees, flocked with artificial snow and twinkling with white lights.

The bar had been open since five, with heavy appetizers and a number of carving stations positioned around the perimeter, and from the buzz of the crowd, Harper could tell that a lot more liquor had been consumed than prime rib. She nodded to a few friendly associates and fellow paralegals as they made a preliminary lap of the room, trying to shake the feeling that even here, some people still held to the lines drawn by office politics. It did nothing to squelch the feeling when Candace Walsh, elegant as ever in a sapphire gown dripping with crystals, waved her over to a high-top table on the far end of the room to introduce her to a small group of senior partners who Harper knew of by name only.

"Harper is one of our best paralegals," Candace provided as a way of introduction. Harper dutifully shook hands around the table. "She has shown tremendous promise as a budding legal mind."

"Oh, that's right," said the partner to her right, fixing Candace with a knowing grin. He was tall and broad shouldered, with patches of gray at both temples and frameless glasses that flashed in the reflected light of the chandelier as he shifted his gaze to Harper. "You're Candace's protégé for the academic endowment." His tone held an edge of superiority that immediately made Harper's skin crawl. "It's not every day the great Candace Walsh plucks someone from obscurity." The man took a swig from the tumbler in his hand. "You're a very lucky young lady."

Harper felt Bryan tense beside her.

"Luck has nothing to do with it," Candace said breezily. "Harper's an excellent candidate, and she works hard for us." She threw Harper a wink, and the knot in Harper's stomach loosened slightly.

"I'm sure she is," said the man, sipping again from the glass in his hand. "But I've heard Lyle say the same thing about his guy." He took another drink. "It's a cute game you're both playing."

"This guy is an ass," Bryan murmured low, leaning into her side. "Let's get out of here."

Harper nudged him with an elbow.

"You two can dress them up however you want," the man went on, his eyes sliding up and down Harper's body. She shifted uncomfortably under his gaze. "Excellent paralegals don't make excellent lawyers by default."

Harper's hackles rose.

"Oh, seriously, Dale." Candace rolled her eyes. "Could you be any more condescending?"

"Just out of curiosity," Harper chimed in before she could stop herself. "When was the last time you worked on a case without a paralegal?"

Dale's eyes flashed, and he set his glass on the table. "I have an associate to handle that type of work for me," he retorted with an insincere smile.

Harper's pulse quickened, but she forced her tone to remain even. "But your associate certainly consults with a paralegal on occasion?" she asked.

"Of course," Dale conceded. "I didn't mean to suggest you didn't have your place."

Harper's annoyance quickly rose to anger. "It's not that," she pressed on with as much calm as she could muster. "It's just, seeing as your work relies on the work of an associate *and* a paralegal, it would seem far more likely that an excellent paralegal could do your job than you could do mine."

Candace snorted into her champagne flute, and Dale picked up his glass from the table and downed the rest of his drink. "Well, she's plucky Candace. I'll give you that."

Harper turned to Bryan. "Ready for a drink?"

"More than," Bryan confirmed.

"Excuse us." Harper smiled around the table. "Nice to meet you all." Her gaze locked with Candace, who gave her a small nod, amusement dancing behind her eyes.

"Goodnight, Harper. It was good to see you again, Bryan," she offered in dismissal.

Bryan guided her gently from the table and toward the bar on the opposite side of the room. "I hate that guy," he said when they were safely out of earshot. "What a prick."

"Yep," Harper agreed with a small sigh.

"He had no right to talk to you that way," Bryan went on, clearly agitated. "And Candace could have done more to stand up for you."

"Candace was fine," replied Harper, feeling suddenly defensive. "She's already vouched for me. It's not her job to fight all my battles."

"You shouldn't have those kinds of battles," Bryan insisted. "That guy was an elitist, chauvinistic asshole."

"He was equally dismissive of Tate," Harper countered. "That hardly counts as chauvinism."

Bryan stopped a few paces from the bar and turned to her. "I doubt he gives Tate the same once over he gave you."

Harper did not have a reply. Bryan was right, and she detested the ogling. That it would happen in front of a named partner, a female partner at that, was testament to the pervasive nature of the toxic masculinity that existed among some of the firm's older, male demographic. It was not, however, the chief concern that bothered her as she walked away from the conversation. Rather, it was the insinuation that Harper was *less* than, and would always be, not because she was a beautiful woman, but because she was a paralegal. She knew that for every person who had chosen a side, there were likely five more who could not have cared less about her, Tate, or the scholarship. She had not, however, imagined a faction that believed she didn't even deserve to be considered. Now, she couldn't help but wonder whether they would always consider her beneath them, regardless of her level of success.

Bryan laid a hand on the small of her back. "Is it just me, or does this party suck a little this year?"

Harper glanced around the room, trying to remember what she normally loved about it. The fancy décor and the formalwear and the good food and the relaxed camaraderie were all still there. She saw a table of paralegals from the cubicles laughing and knew that if they joined them, she would quickly get lost in office gossip while Bryan talked sports or business with the boyfriends and husbands. After a few drinks, the dancing would start, and they could lose themselves in the glitz and the glamor like they had so many years prior. But she suddenly felt like she didn't belong there, and she didn't belong across the room where the junior associates unwound from their eighty-hour work weeks, and she clearly didn't belong with Candace and the partners. If they left now, they could pick up food on the way home, and Harper could be in her pajamas on the couch with her LSAT book and a Christmas movie in the background within the hour.

She turned and looked up at Bryan, feeling the velvet of the dress pull at her hips. She self-consciously smoothed a hand over the ruching. At the same moment, Tate Bishop stepped through the main doors on the opposite end of the ballroom looking debonair in a white tuxedo jacket with black satin lapels. Harper made up her mind instantly.

"It totally sucks," she agreed. "Let's go home."

•   •   •

The friends celebrated Christmas two days later on Sunday afternoon in Bryan and Harper's living room. The Bears game hummed quietly in the background while Bryan and Seth strung lights on the artificial tree propped up in the corner. Harper decorated the trays of sugar cookies that Maggie had lined up on the kitchen counter. They were the same, easy traditions they had followed for years. But despite all the history Harper and Maggie shared, and the almost familial bond between the four friends, there was no denying the energy in the room was off.

Harper piped white icing onto snowman shaped cookies and tried to pretend that nothing was different. It was an unnatural tension that rarely existed in their friendship, but one which neither woman seemed certain how to overcome. Lately, their conversations between stretches and shavasanas at Sunday yoga class had been superficial, focused more on the goings on at the restaurant and the firm than their own homes and marriages. Though Harper texted throughout the week, Maggie's schedule continued to make her responses sporadic, and the growing pressure at the firm made it difficult for Harper to cut out for even a quick breakfast or lunch date.

The irony of the situation was not lost on Harper. Somehow, she had found herself exactly where Maggie hoped to be: childless and on the verge of a huge advancement in her career. Meanwhile, Maggie and Seth now unexpectedly found themselves where she and Bryan imagined being months ago. It all felt wrong, and yet somehow, being together in the days before Christmas still felt right, even if she wasn't sure how to dive into conversation.

"How are you feeling?" Harper settled on the most benign question she could think of asking. She dropped mini chocolate chips into the shape of a smile across the snowman's face.

"Tired," Maggie admitted, leaning against the countertop. "Dinner service sucks. I just spent $150 on orthotics because my back aches the next morning, and I'm not even out of the first trimester."

"Sit then," Harper encouraged, standing up to drag her own stool into the kitchen.

Maggie waved a hand. "I'm fine." She glanced at the oven. "The last tray is about finished, and then I'll sit down to help decorate."

An uneasy silence settled between them again, broken by a sorrowful moan as a Lions' running back broke free from the line and dashed toward the end zone.

"Get him! Damn it!" Seth wailed at the television, pounding a fist on the back of the couch.

Bryan wound the string of lights around the tree. "The Bears still suck, my friend," he chuckled.

Harper noticed with both relief and envy that, despite the atmosphere in the kitchen, there did not appear to be any unspoken tension between the two men. If anything, Seth and Bryan had been talking more since the news of the baby. She turned her attention back to the cookies, wondering how best to move the conversation forward. The timer chimed, buying her a few precious seconds of consideration as Maggie turned and checked the oven.

"How's work?" Maggie asked before Harper could provide a better question. She turned back to the counter with a tray full of warm cookies.

"Great," replied Harper, a little too enthusiastically.

Maggie raised an eyebrow.

"Fine." Harper amended with a shrug. "Mostly it feels like all I've earned so far are awkward office dynamics and more work for myself."

"Any regrets?" Maggie asked, not looking up. She slid the remaining cookies onto the cooling racks.

Harper hesitated. After everything she handled at work during the week, she then gave up much of her weekend studying. She had put in four hours the night before timing herself in an online practice exam, the first full test she had taken, practice or otherwise, since undergrad. She managed a 166, which somehow seemed equal parts encouraging and disheartening. There were four practice tests left in the book's online companion program, and she planned to take one a week until test day. Already, she had spent another ninety minutes that afternoon before Maggie and Seth arrived, reviewing 'Deductions and Inferences' and 'Mixed Setups,' her two lowest scoring skills. It was time-consuming and exhausting, but she didn't regret it.

"I don't think so," said Harper. "Right now, it's a lot of work with little guarantee. There's still a real chance I lose the whole thing to Tate."

Maggie scoffed. "And to think, not long ago you almost let him talk you into moving to New York with him."

"New York was never on the table," Bryan called with a forced laugh from the living room.

"AW! C'MON!" Seth hollered as a linebacker rushed a gap in the line and stripped the ball from the quarterback's hand, scooping it up and running in the opposite direction.

Bryan turned back to the TV. "Tough break man."

Maggie picked up a piping bag of yellow icing and began to trace the stars. "Not to be a naysayer, but have you considered what you'll do if Tate wins?"

Harper's mouth went dry. "I'll still have my job," she replied, wondering where Maggie was going with this.

"Is that enough?" asked Maggie.

Harper's pulse jumped as she felt the words, yet unshared, ready to pour out. No, it wouldn't be enough, but if they were raising families together, she was convinced it would fill whatever void existed when she gave up the idea of law school again.

"That's the question I keep asking myself," Maggie went on before Harper could respond. "If I let go of Indie Lime now, having built it but not seen it through, will I regret it? Is it enough to have launched it? Is it fair to think a baby will fill the space the restaurant leaves behind?"

Harper set the piping bag on the counter and looked at Maggie.

"They're not remotely the same thing. So why choose?" she asked. "Don't give up on the restaurant. You may need to rethink it, probably train up a sous chef or bring in an interim executive, but if anyone can figure it out, you can. This is your dream."

It surprised Harper how easily and automatically the encouragement came, as if she wasn't wrestling with the same questions and challenges. The words seemed hollow in hindsight.

Maggie raised her eyebrows skeptically, and Harper saw the glimmer of tears ready to fall. "That's not really how it works." Her voice wobbled, and she swallowed hard. "It's my name on the menu. If I was Gordon Ramsey or Bobby Flay, my name might be enough. But it's not."

"Yet," Harper tried to encourage.

Maggie shook her head. "Beyond that, the hours are terrible, and I'm on my feet all night, and I have no maternity leave to speak of. We can't close because I can't afford the space without the restaurant operating. And there's no way my investors will continue to fund a business model without stability at the most important position." She cradled her head in her hands. "There's a reason only 5% of top chefs are women."

"If you've got a contract with them, then…" Harper started.

Maggie interrupted with a hard, bitter laugh. "You should know better than anyone the time and energy rich people will spend finding ways out of what should be binding legal documents."

"What would make you feel better?" Harper asked, hoping beyond reason the answer might be something along the lines of 'if we were doing this together.'

"Honestly," Maggie said quietly, not making eye contact. "If this had never happened at all."

An icy fist clutched at Harper's heart. "Maggie," she breathed.

Maggie looked up, her expression ragged. "You know we didn't want this."

Harper stole a quick glance at Seth, who sat wringing his hands over the last two minutes of the football game. "Seth seemed thrilled the night he came to tell Bryan," she offered, regretting the words immediately. Maggie looked as if she had been slapped, and Harper suddenly realized she had barely talked to Seth that night. He might have come to Bryan in equal dismay, and if he hadn't, that knowledge did nothing to help Maggie now. "I'm sorry. That wasn't fair. I don't know what Seth and Bryan talked about."

"Seth and I are on the same page," asserted Maggie, an edge to her tone. "And if we decide not to keep it…"

"What!" blurted Harper at the exact moment Seth cursed loudly at the television.

"I'm sorry," Maggie said. "I know you and Bryan were trying, so I'm sure this seems like an unconscionable decision to even be considering…"

"I've started a fertility workup at the clinic," Harper interjected quickly. "I've already done the bloodwork and started the hormones. I have imaging scheduled in January."

Maggie stared at her. "That's great," she said weakly. "I'm happy for you."

"No," Harper moaned. "You don't understand. I called the clinic the morning after I found out you were expecting. I thought we would do this together, Maggie. I know you said you didn't want this in the past, but I thought if we did it together that…"

"That what?" Maggie said in disbelief. "That being pregnant together would somehow overrule all the things I wanted for myself?" She looked away and blew out a heavy breath. "You know Harper, when Seth and I decided to be child free, some people called us selfish. But I was never so selfish to believe that someone should give up all their goals and plans to follow mine instead."

"That's not…" Harper started.

"Tell me something," Maggie went on, her voice rising. "Did you ever have your own reasons for wanting a family, or was my pregnancy a good enough reason to jump in and avoid having to do any soul searching yourself? Because you weren't so sure the day we talked at the restaurant, but you're pretty certain all of a sudden."

The game was over, and Bryan turned off the TV. The room went eerily quiet.

"And if you don't get the scholarship, and we don't have a baby, will your family be enough?" Maggie continued. "Will a baby be enough for *you*? *Just* you? Can you answer that question for yourself? Because until you can, I don't think you get to judge me for at least considering whether it's worth trying to hold on to a version of *my* future that I have been very clear about wanting for a very long time."

"Mags," Seth moved to the kitchen. "You don't have to defend anything."

Harper felt Bryan at her shoulder, but she couldn't look away from Maggie. The tension between them was suddenly gone, replaced by something Harper feared far worse. Resentment. Not that Harper had the freedom Maggie craved, or even that Maggie knew what she wanted and Harper didn't. Rather, Harper's vision of her future was deeply twined with a version of Maggie's that she had never asked for. One she didn't want. Harper wished she could deny Maggie's words, but they both knew that she couldn't. It made them cut that much deeper.

"You're right," Harper whispered, voice hoarse. "You're right, Maggie. I'm sorry."

Silence hung between them.

"I think it might be time to call it an evening," Seth said finally.

Harper felt Bryan shift behind her. "Yeah, ok. Let me grab your coats." He and Seth stepped into the entryway, giving the two women a guise of privacy.

"I'm sorry," Harper tried again, pleading. "You know we'll support whatever decision you make."

Maggie looked at her skeptically. "I hope you mean that," she said, her voice laced with pain. Seth draped her jacket over her shoulders, and she slid her arms into the sleeves.

"Ready?" he asked.

Maggie nodded, looking sadly away from Harper. "Merry Christmas, Bryan." She kissed him on the cheek.

Bryan squeezed her in a one-armed hug. "Merry Christmas," he replied. He patted Seth on the back, murmuring something that Harper couldn't understand as he closed the door quietly behind their friends. He turned around slowly to face Harper. "What just happened?" he asked, voice unnervingly calm.

"Did you know they were thinking about terminating the pregnancy?" Harper asked, distraught.

Bryan sighed. "The night Seth came to tell me they were pregnant, he thought Maggie would at least want to talk about it."

"You were laughing and having a beer over it!" Harper exclaimed.

"I was trying to help my best friend through a moment of crisis. Give him some perspective, some normalcy, like you should have done for Maggie."

Harper ran a hand through her hair in agitation. "I tried," she lamented. "She didn't *want* to talk about it."

"Maybe because she knew your reaction would be completely out of line," Bryan suggested.

"What's that supposed to mean?" Harper crossed her arms defensively over her chest. Bryan mimicked the pose, and she realized how childish she must look.

"Seriously? You told her to keep the baby for *you*, that the whole thing would be fine, not because of anything she wants, but because you are desperately racing to get pregnant at the same time. Not for *us*. For *her*." A pained expression twisted his features. "Don't you get how messed up that is, Harper?" His voice rose. "Not just for Maggie. How do you think *I* felt hearing that?"

"Well, what did you think when I rushed to call the clinic the next morning?" Harper asked, more accusation than question. She realized her admission, and her blood ran cold.

Bryan's mouth moved, but silence stretched between them.

"It's one thing to be conflicted," he said finally. "I can understand that. I just thought, maybe, you made your decision based on us, feeling the pull of something we could share, the way I did, not fearing that you would miss out on a pregnancy with your best friend who doesn't even want to be pregnant. Forgive me for giving you the benefit of the doubt." He crossed to the bedroom door, looked back at her sadly, and sighed before closing it between them.

The apartment fell silent and, for the first time in their entire marriage, stayed that way for the next twenty-four hours.

Chapter 12

After Helen's death, Harper developed a love-hate relationship with going home to family for Christmas. On one hand, she craved the time with her dad and sister, her two new nephews, and the other friends and family that would pop in over the holidays. On the other, her mother's absence was most keenly felt in the week between Christmas and the new year. Her dad tried, but never quite captured the magic in the same way. The decorations were slightly askance; the cookies were slightly overdone; the wrapping paper bunched in the folds, and all of it pointed back to Helen's empty chair.

In the aftermath of the disastrous holiday parties, Harper briefly considered whether it might be easiest not to go home at all. Bryan's parents had opted to cruise for Christmas, and as he was an only child with limited extended family to consider, at the time it had been a relatively simple decision to spend four days back in Minnesota with Harper's family. But the decision was far from simple now.

With her sister's twins in the fold for their first Christmas, Harper knew she and Bryan would face an increasing number of invasive questions about their own plans to start a family. She could already hear well-meaning aunts and uncles wondering aloud whether next year might bring another little stocking hanging over the mantle. Of course, they had no way of knowing that Harper had suffered through the gender reveal and baby showers wondering if, maybe next month, it might be her turn for good news. Nor could they have guessed that she finished her fertility meds just weeks before the twins were born. That Lyla's pregnancy had aligned with Harper's struggles was an unfortunate coincidence Harper bore with as much grace as possible, but she wasn't looking forward to mustering the same poise again.

Moreover, she worried that particular line of questioning might threaten the fragile peace she had found with Bryan. Harper had broken the silence first, leaving work early the night after the holiday party disaster and racing home to spend an hour making his favorite beef stroganoff from an Emeril Lagasse recipe she once used to impress him when they were dating. He walked in with rosy cheeks, frustratingly brushing snow from his coat. But despite the tension that permeated the apartment, Harper saw his eyes twinkle as he wiped the fog from his glasses and took in the bubbling baking dish freshly pulled from the oven.

"Welcome home," Harper whispered, her voice already thick with emotion.

Bryan took a deep, slow breath. "Smells good," he replied.

They stared at each other a long moment before Bryan stepped into the kitchen and opened his arms. Harper closed the gap between them, bracing herself against him.

"I messed up," she confessed into the damp wool of his coat.

"Mm hm," he murmured. His voice rumbled in his chest, humming against her ear.

Harper looked up at him. "I'm sorry," she said, tears pricking the corners of her eyes. "I ruined everything."

He leaned down and kissed her gently.

"We'll figure it out," he assured her. "Let's eat."

Harper wasn't entirely certain how to "figure out" what was quickly beginning to feel like an existential crisis, but she started by renewing her promise to Bryan to leave the office on time. She had kept the promise every night since, even when it required her to ignore an overflowing inbox or the light still shining in Tate's office. She sent a dozen messages of apology to Maggie, all of which went unanswered. Eventually, she changed tack and sent flowers to Indie Lime. In reply, Seth reached out an olive branch, assuring her that the effort had not gone unnoticed.

By the time the holiday arrived, Harper had solved very little, but also had very little to gain by creating more drama and canceling on her family. Lingering hesitations aside, she and Bryan left for Minnesota on Christmas Eve.

Now, sitting in her dad's kitchen on Christmas morning, Harper sipped coffee and watched snow flurries drift past the window. The LSAT book was open in front of her, but she hadn't worked through a full practice passage in the hour she had given herself before she expected Bryan out of bed. She thought instead about her mom, remembering what it was like as a kid, waking up to the gifts perfectly wrapped under the tree, bacon already cooking on the stove, a plate of cookies for Santa partially eaten, a perfect crescent-shaped bite missing from one of the sugar cookie stars. There were so many ways her mom made the holidays special for Harper and her sister. She wondered if she was cut out to do it herself someday.

Seeing her sister around everyone with the twins the night before had given her a snapshot of what that future could look like. Her father doted, and her aunts and uncles dispensed their best advice and worst jokes about parenting. The babies gurgled and cooed in their matching Christmas outfits, and everybody agreed that having young kids around brought extra magic to the holidays again. Over and over, Lyla and Brady were congratulated, while Harper and Bryan were, as expected, prodded about their intentions and when they might gift her father with a third. They managed tight smiles and perfected a noncommittal, laissez-faire response.

Part of Harper could not imagine *not* watching her kids run around with their cousins someday. It was more than just growing her own family and giving her father a grandchild. It was continuing the family he had first started with her mom, making sure a piece of Helen's legacy lived on to the next generation through Harper. Not having a chance to see her grandchildren was one of the few things Helen had expressed truly regretting in the final days of her life. That she would have grandchildren was a foregone conclusion Harper had never had a reason to challenge. Sitting in the kitchen, looking out over the toys still sprawled across the living room and the extra little stockings hanging above the fireplace, expectation and obligation sat heavy on her heart.

She glanced at the book on the table, pushed it aside, opened her laptop, and ran a quick search.

When is the best time to have a baby in law school?

Harper skimmed a few of the links at the top of the list, an assortment of blog posts, comment threads, and community forums. They revealed a wide range of opinions and experiences. Year one was an overwhelming adjustment; year two, according to many comments, was the hardest; by year three the load lightened considerably, but there was also the bar exam to worry about and searching for jobs. No one seemed to agree on which of these factors created the best (or worst) set of circumstances.

She opened a second tab and searched: *How hard is it to have a baby and be a lawyer?*

It felt juvenile even as she typed it, but as she read the stories of being passed over for partnership or pushed off complex cases after returning from maternity leave, she confirmed a nagging suspicion that starting a family while actively pursuing the scholarship may make her look like a bad long- term investment. When she thought about her colleagues at Horowitz, Walsh, and Pickett, she could name the female attorneys she had seen pregnant at the office on one hand.

Of course, there were exceptions. Glowing "tell-all's" about life in a big, New York City firm while raising two kids on Park Avenue with a husband who left a lucrative career in finance to support his wife as a stay-at-home dad. Q&As with women who had chosen a different legal environment, started their own firm, dictated their own hours, or worked as an in-house counsel or for a non-profit. There was even an extensive piece in *The Atlantic* extolling the virtues of firms that were adapting their business models to be more family friendly, in the process allowing more female lawyers who may have previously left the field to continue to practice in a corporate environment.

But more so than any one article that she read, it was a comment left by a fellow reader that struck Harper the most.

Of course, a woman CAN be a lawyer and a mother at the same time. DUH! But ladies, remember, just because we CAN do it all, doesn't mean we HAVE to do it all. Pursue the career. Pursue the family. Pursue both. But whatever you pursue, do it because it's right for you, not because a stranger on the internet told you it was possible and now you feel beholden to someone else's standards or expectations.

Harper pulled the notepad she was supposed to be using to draw logic diagrams out from under the test prep book. She drew two simple t-charts.

BABY. She labeled the first one in her tidy, looping cursive. *LAW SCHOOL.* She labeled the other. She began a list of pros and cons under the first heading.

Pros: share a child and a family with Bryan; continue Mom's memory; impact the next generation; have a family for the future–grandkids; watch and help someone learn, grow, change.

Cons: expensive; need for child care; stressful; lifestyle changes; current fertility questions; schedules and time.

She looked over the first list and noticed, with some pride and relief, that all the reasons were her own. Maggie's surprise announcement and Bryan's preferences aside, she could articulate her own reasons both for and against the prospect of motherhood when she gave herself a real chance to think about it.

She moved to the other list.

Pros: fulfills dream; love the work; career security at firm; professional and personal challenge; keep promise to Mom; keep job while taking classes; more potential money and opportunity long term

Cons: crazy schedule; stressful; scheduling work and school; less time with Bryan = lifestyle changes; baby?

With an uncomfortable twinge of apprehension, Harper realized that many of the cons from the first list showed up similarly on the second. Whatever the path forward, there was no denying it would be a busy, stressful, all-consuming season of change.

Footsteps on the stairs behind her pulled her attention back to the kitchen, and she stuffed the legal pad into the pages of the test book.

She slammed her laptop closed just as her sister stepped into the kitchen, a baby tucked in each arm.

"Good morning," she whispered. She glanced between Harper's computer and the book. "Sorry, I didn't realize you were working."

"It's fine," Harper assured her. "Need a hand?" She reached toward one of her nephews.

Lyla passed him gently to Harper. "That'd be great. They're always hungry at the same time," she chuckled with an eye roll. "It's Simon's turn with me, so I'll warm up a bottle for Zeke if you want to help feed him."

Harper looked down into the big, blue eyes staring up at her and smiled. "Yeah, of course."

Considering one arm was completely incapacitated with 15 pounds of infant, Lyla moved swiftly around the kitchen with impressive efficiency. She hummed to herself and the baby, and within minutes, she handed Harper a perfectly temped bottle and a white, quilted burp cloth.

"You're on," she smiled, nodding toward the two recliners in the living room.

Harper moved from the table and crossed to the chair opposite her sister. The weight of the baby was an uncomfortable, foreign object, and she shifted around until she found a stable position that allowed her to prop her arm on the armrest to better cradle Zeke's head in the crook of her elbow. Though she knew she was old enough and, technically, more than capable to care for a baby, there was still a part of her that felt like a six-year-old child who should be told to sit on a couch surrounded by pillows and reminded to use both hands. The casual nature with which Lyla handled not one but two babies seemed a completely alien concept to Harper. She offered Zeke the bottle, and he took it enthusiastically, his little hand reaching up to rest on one side of the plastic cylinder while his mouth puckered around the rubber nipple and sucked eagerly.

"You're a natural," said Lyla, sleepy eyes on Harper. She leaned back, a blanket draped casually over one shoulder under which Simon squirmed and nursed.

Harper's heart skipped a beat. "Thanks," she whispered, watching Zeke's impossibly blue eyes droop as he made progress on the bottle. "You seem…"

"Sleep deprived?" Lyla laughed quietly.

"I was going to say well-adjusted, all things considered," Harper said, shifting the baby in her arms.

"Number one rule of parenting," Lyla adjusted the blanket to peer down at Simon's progress. "Fake it until you make it."

"What's the number two rule?" asked Harper.

Lyla shook her head. "I don't know," she said. "Probably keep them alive."

Harper chuckled lightly, not wanting to disturb the baby resting in her arms. "Well, seems like you're a smashing success on both accounts."

Lyla turned Simon to the other side. "We're figuring it out." She flinched and closed her eyes, hand working under the blanket to dislodge, what Harper imagined were, little jaws clenched around sensitive skin. After a moment, she relaxed back into the chair again and blew out a breath. "Brady got almost no time off of work, which was hard, obviously."

Harper felt a pang of guilt. "I should have come."

"You did," Lyla replied.

"For a weekend," bemoaned Harper. "It wasn't enough, and I'm sorry."

Lyla shrugged. "You have work. I get it. Brady's mom stayed with us for the two weeks after he went back. That was a God-send. I cried for three days after she left because I was so tired, and it was so overwhelming. But it wasn't really the help I missed." She paused, clearing emotion from her throat.

"Let me guess," Harper said quietly. "You missed Mom." She had felt the same way a dozen times, when it had been Lyla, not Helen, who had zipped her into her wedding dress, or Maggie, not Helen, who took her calls about work or good news. Thinking of Maggie caused her heart to pang.

Lyla looked away, brushing at the corners of her eyes. "It was like losing her all over again, not being able to call with a question or send a picture or just get the reassurance that everything would be ok."

"I love the pictures," Harper promised. "And everything *will* be ok." Zeke whimpered and squirmed in her arms, and she tipped the bottle further to start the flow of milk again.

"I know," Lyla said with a sigh. "But I think about her all the time now that I'm a mom." She looked at Harper. "It's like I was living with the memories, and they were getting me by, but they're not enough anymore. It's a new hurt that she's not part of this, that I can't share this with her."

Or me, thought Harper, uncertain what comfort she could offer. A sudden temptation to open up about the fertility clinic surprised her, but she quickly brushed it aside. Since her mom's passing, she felt a keen sense of responsibility to protect her dad and sister against further heartache. There was nothing they could do about the negative pregnancy tests or the fertility issues. There was nothing they could do to help the process. They could only worry about it. So, in the absence of being able to provide them any answers or comfort or future hope, the best thing to do, in her mind, was to shield them from the knowledge at all.

"She would be proud of you, Lyla." Harper whispered. "I'm sure of it."

Lyla smiled sadly. "She'd be proud of you too, getting ready to go to law school."

"If Mom were here, I already would have gone to law school," Harper reminded her.

"Right." Lyla bit her bottom lip. "Sorry."

Harper shrugged. "Now, Mom would probably tell me it was time to follow your example and start settling down instead."

Lyla's brow furrowed. "Oh, I don't think so," she insisted. "Mom made you promise."

Harper's chest tightened, and she struggled to keep her tone light. "Sure, but that was years ago. I think by now she would have different expectations."

Lyla shook her head. "Mom knew how important it was to you. I don't think she always understood it. You wanted very different things for your life than she wanted for hers, but she tried to support that the best she could. She didn't want you to change your dreams for anything, even her diagnosis. Even her death."

Harper could not speak around the lump in her throat.

"I understood why you didn't go then," Lyla continued. "But for what it's worth, I admire what you're doing now. I think it's brave. I can't imagine going back to school, starting a new career."

"Doesn't *mom* count as a new career?" asked Harper.

"Sure," Lyla agreed. "But that's not what I mean. Going to law school after a decade takes balls, Harper."

Harper laughed. "So does raising twins."

Lyla rolled her eyes. "Stop deflecting the compliment for a second and just think about what you're actually doing. Plenty of women our age are leaving careers to start a family or stay at home with their kids. How many are starting law school? Imagine if I suddenly announced I was going to be a doctor."

"You could," Harper offered.

"Now? Never," Lyla insisted. "Even if I wanted to, I can't imagine giving up the time with them. Not to mention the expense." She slid Simon from under the blanket and transferred him onto her shoulder to burp. "Once your morning routine includes saying goodbye to these smiling faces, you see the appeal of being there for all their little moments." She looked at Harper. "It's hard to do both. Work and home." The admission came out quietly, a private confession that Harper couldn't help but take as a personal warning.

She nearly asked then. Is it worth it? Did you know it would be? But before she could form the right question, Zeke spit out the nipple of the empty bottle and burst into an ear-piercing scream. Almost instantly, Brady appeared at the bottom of the stairs, moving toward Harper with outstretched arms and already clucking quiet reassurances to the crying baby. He lifted Zeke from the crook of her elbow up onto his chest.

"Thanks," he said with a tired smile, taking the burp cloth Harper held out to him.

She watched him walk around the kitchen with bouncy, rhythmic steps, soothing the baby in a sing-song voice. She looked over at Lyla, head tipped back, eyes closed, Simon dozing on her shoulder. She felt the emptiness of her own arms and missed the warmth of the baby tucked against her ribs and the enormous eyes, momentarily enraptured with her and only her. She understood why people wanted it, and left jobs for it, and paid thousands of dollars for treatments and surgeries and hormones all in the name of acquiring it. Lists aside, she felt it, viscerally.

Yet, as she stood, offered the chair to Brady, and collected her computer and book from the kitchen table, she also couldn't push aside the nagging questions of her own motivations and desires. She slipped into her dad's office and closed the door, dampening the wailing baby, acutely aware that she wouldn't be able to do so with a child of her own. The realization settled into a tight ball in her stomach as she laid her work across the desk. Then she put in her earbuds, opened her test book, and began working on the next logic problem.

Chapter 13

Harper didn't set New Year's Resolutions, but if she had, a simple 'figure your shit out,' would have sufficed. The week after the holidays the firm bustled with new year business and old cases that managed to drag themselves onto the brand-new calendar. The stream of associates and partners looking for Harper's help never lessened, but with fewer than two weeks until the LSAT, most people seemed aware that Harper was burning the candle at both ends and offered at least passing words of encouragement and advice from their own experiences. As a thank you for her help before the holiday party, Andrea Thompson had even dug up her set of handwritten flashcards to which she credited the 170 both she and her college roommate had managed.

Harper accepted each pearl of wisdom graciously, though privately wished that someone would realize that the most helpful course of action would be to stop piling on the work and let her get through the test. Three nights in a row she returned home on time only to hurry through dinner and a rushed conversation with Bryan before diving into a few hours of studying before bed. In the morning, she'd start the cycle over. It was the closest she could get to balance, and she realized it was just a small taste of what law school life would feel like. She didn't know how she would do it with a baby in the mix. Nevertheless, the HSG remained circled on the calendar the day before the exam.

Overwhelm aside, there were two silver linings Harper found in the run-up to both tests. The first was that, regardless of the outcome, once it was over it was over. January 13th was the last testing date that fit within the window for submitting her applications, so there would be no scheduling a retake to better her score. Whatever happened after that Saturday morning, Harper was sure it would be the last time she prepared for the test. While there was a lot that remained uncertain about her future, the finality of walking out of the room knowing that what was done was done, for good, forever, was undeniably refreshing. Bryan even suggested having the fireplace recommissioned to burn the prep book when she was finished.

The second was that it was becoming increasingly clear that Tate was suffering under the same pressures as Harper. Despite his impeccably tailored suits and polished oxfords, Tate had appeared uncharacteristically disheveled since the holidays. One morning he came wearing mismatched socks. Another, he walked around in a new suit coat still sporting a tag tacked to the flap of his jacket. Harper heard he spent three hours one afternoon trying to track down his cell phone, which he'd left behind in an Uber at lunch. He had taken the Uber home in the first place because he arrived at the office that morning only to realize he had forgotten his watch, belt, and cufflinks. They were small and seemingly insignificant mistakes. But to a man as image conscious and put together as Tate, they were tantamount to showing up naked.

But more than all his superficial wardrobe gaffes, word in the cubicles was Tate was struggling where it really mattered: his applications. Allegedly, Lyle Pickett had been seen with a list of law programs within a hundred-mile radius of the office that would accept an LSAT score under 160. Harper had completed three more of the available online practice tests, scoring as high as a 169 on her latest attempt.

"You're way ahead, I think," Andrea told Harper encouragingly when she stopped by to pick up a brief. "And you've got Candace on your side if Lyle tries anything weird to give Tate an edge at the last minute."

"Great," said Harper with a forced smile, wondering what it would take for her to reach Andrea's level of confidence.

But the knowledge that Tate may be floundering did not guarantee Harper's own success. So, she worked. She studied. She made extra copies. She wrote extra briefs. And she checked in with Candace each afternoon to see if there was anything more she could do to sell her dedication to the firm.

Which is why she was surprised to find Candace already waiting for her with a thick file folder when she arrived Thursday morning. In their brief encounter the afternoon before, Candace had nearly laughed Harper's unceasing enthusiasm out of her office.

"Relax," she insisted. "Spend some time with your husband. *Don't* study for a change. You don't do me any good if you're burned out before you even start your first year."

Harper left at five and caught up on two episodes of *The Amazing Race* over takeout Chinese and a bottle of wine with Bryan. She had not considered the exam until Bryan's breathing deepened beside her, and she slipped gently out of bed to take her last practice test. It had been a good night, one that made Harper wonder, as just about everything made Harper wonder these days, about upsetting the balance of the life they already had.

Two hours later, when she finished the test and saw that she scored a 170 for the first time, she remembered how insistent the pull of a dream could be.

"Good morning, Candace," said Harper, attempting to capture the casual familiarity she hoped was developing between them. "I'm sorry. I seem to have kept you waiting." She glanced at her watch. It wasn't even eight o'clock yet. Her curiosity piqued. "I must have missed that we had an early appointment."

Candace waved a hand, glancing out the narrow office window crusted with patches of blowing snow. "We didn't," she assured. "Did you take my advice and have a quiet night at home?"

"I did," Harper confirmed, sliding out of her coat. "I waited to take my last practice test until after Bryan was asleep, at least."

Candace stifled a laugh. "You remind me of me. Relentless."

The compliment bloomed in Harper's chest, a warm glow that she worked to keep from rising to her cheeks. "Thank you," she managed.

"I didn't say that was a good thing," Candace chided affectionately. "Or do you not believe in burn out?"

"I scored a 170," Harper offered, settling in behind her desk. She had tried to remain indifferent to the number since it had lit up her tablet screen at 1:00am, but now, with Candace, the woman who vouched for and would invest in her, she wanted her to know that it was worth it.

Candace's eyes flicked wide. "Well done," she said, unable to suppress her smile. She looked at Harper and the empty hallway outside the door. "Between you and me," she whispered, "Lyle's guy…"

"Tate," Harper interrupted.

Candace nodded. "Yeah. Lyle's struggling to get him over 160."

Harper couldn't stop the corners of her mouth from twitching, but it didn't feel as good as she expected. She thought back to the condescending partner at the Christmas party. She didn't want to know in what kinds of office conversations her own name had been mentioned and what kinds of reactions it might have elicited.

"Don't get cocky," Candace warned. "He can get into plenty of schools with a 160, and surely you know by now that, right or wrong, in this field you're often going to have to be twice as good to get the same look as a man with half your talent."

"Right," Harper agreed quietly.

"But," Candace's eyes sparkled. "A 170 would force anyone to take a hell of a look. No doubt."

This time, Harper couldn't stop the flush in her cheeks. "Thanks," she grinned. "So, what can I do for you this morning?"

Candace laid the file on the front edge of Harper's desk. "Something personal."

Harper pulled the folder toward her and flipped through the first few pages. Financial documents, declaration of assets, various insurance policies. "What's this?" she asked, skimming over a car title.

Candace sighed. "A favor," she admitted. "I wouldn't ask, but I've already had you elbows deep in the other related financial documents."

"The Urban City deal?" Harper asked, confused why the deed to a condo was now part of the transaction.

"Not exactly," said Candace. "Mark's divorce."

"I don't understand."

Candace folded her hands in her lap and looked out the window.

"Mark is still highly motivated to sell, and we should be able to move ahead with things. But he announced to the family over the holidays that he and his wife were separating."

"Merry Christmas," Harper muttered sarcastically.

"Of course," Candace went on, "his wife is smart enough to know that dragging things out allows her leverage. She can easily interfere with the sale and make things inconvenient."

"She's an owner?" asked Harper, paging through more of the documents.

Candace nodded. "I need information. I need you to find something in there that could be used as a carrot to keep the acquisition on track and settle the divorce with as little mess as possible. You're not unlike Ainsley yourself, a driven, ambitious, millennial woman. What would you want? What would motivate you to move things along?"

Harper blew out a breath. She didn't know.

"I suppose you can't go through the files yourself," she said, question lingering in her tone.

"That's right. For the same reason I didn't go through the business financials," Candace confirmed. "If he didn't want me going through his company assets, he sure as hell doesn't want me going through his marriage."

"What am I looking for?" Harper asked.

"Leverage," said Candace with a shrug. "Something she would be unwilling to give up, or unwilling to give Mark. Something that she is as invested in as Mark is invested in the company. Something she might fight for, or not want to fight over if it was offered as the key to a quick and clean settlement."

"You don't think there's any chance they'll figure it out and stay together?"

Candace sighed. "He says no."

"And no prenup?" Harper guessed.

"They were college sweethearts, and Mark insisted he knew what he was doing." Candace shook her head slowly. "I've always liked Ainsley, but Mark's timing could not be worse given the acquisition, and I'm sure she knows it. I'd like to find a quick and mutually beneficial way to make this go away."

Harper flipped back to the top page of the file. "I'll see what I can find."

Candace pushed herself from the chair. "Thank you, Harper. I know how valuable your time is these days." She nodded toward a stack of files in the basket on Harper's desk as she moved to the door. She had one foot in the hallway before she turned around and raised an eyebrow. "A 170, really?"

"Really," Harper confirmed with a smile.

Candace shook her head, chuckling. "Lyle's going to lose his mind." Then she stepped from the office, turned the corner, and was gone.

Harper spent the morning with the documents in the file, finding little in the way of leverage. There was a property in Chapel Hill and a small condo in Chicago, but Harper doubted very much that was what a jilted wife whose husband was about to come into millions of dollars was looking for. There was a well-established retirement fund and money in the bank accounts, but a modest amount really, considering the payout that was coming. Best she could tell, Mark and Ainsley lived comfortably, but not what Harper would call extravagantly. The big money was coming from the sale, and she couldn't imagine his wife walking away without a piece of it.

There were only two pages in the file that didn't make immediate sense. The first was a trust set up three years prior. Money had been added in small, but regular, increments for six months, then abruptly stopped. A year later, four additional payments had been added of the same amount in the same monthly increments, then stopped. Nothing had been added since, though what was put in the account remained there.

The other was a statement from a joint checking account that had been opened about six months prior to the trust. Though it was not the account that the money for the trust appeared to move in and out of, the significant sums of money that moved in and out of this account seemed, somehow, intrinsically linked to the other. If money was moving into the trust, the checking account balance remained stable. If money was not moving into the trust, the checking account balance fluctuated wildly. Stranger still, all the payments seemed to go to one vendor, an address that Harper found familiar but could not place.

She stopped just after 1:00pm and made her way to the breakroom to heat her leftover Chinese. There was still a pile of other work on her desk to get through, and she would only work a half day tomorrow to make her appointment at the clinic. Her goal had been to finish her assignments before leaving, making sure everyone had what they needed before the weekend so that she could be clear minded for both the appointment and the exam. She wondered how much longer to spend on Candace's wild goose chase before getting the afternoon back on track.

The microwave timer pinged, and Harper retrieved her steaming plate. Spinning around quickly to rush back to her office, she collided with navy wool and starched cotton. Harper wobbled on her heels and took a clumsy step backward. Tate folded his arms across his chest.

"Andrews," he said warily.

Harper suddenly realized how good she and Tate had become at avoiding each other. It had been weeks since they had been in a room alone together.

"What are you doing here?" she asked, awkwardly trying to navigate the tension that had been forced between them.

"Grabbing my lunch," he said, pointing at the refrigerator behind her.

Harper glanced over her shoulder before stepping to the side, allowing him to pass by her. "Sorry," she said, embarrassment threatening to erupt on her cheeks. She tried to think of something more to say that wouldn't come off as stilted or patronizing. While she didn't want to lose to Tate, she couldn't bring herself to be intentionally cold either. She turned quickly and headed to the door.

"Andrews," Tate called after her. Harper froze. "A 170?" he asked with a whistle. "Gerry Collins overheard Candace as she left your office this morning. Good show."

She turned around slowly, surprised to find something akin to genuine admiration in his expression.

"It was just a practice test," she said, feeling a sudden consideration for Tate's feelings. "No big deal."

Tate put his container in the microwave and leaned up against the counter facing her. "It's a big deal," he said, his tone warm. "If anyone would know right now, I would."

Harper saw the exhaustion etched across his face, the same shadows around his eyes that she expertly hid under concealer every morning.

"For what it's worth," he went on, "I regret what this has done for life at the office." He stuffed his hands in his pockets. "I've always appreciated having you as an ally."

It struck Harper that he hadn't used the word friend.

"I would have done it differently if I could have," Tate said, turning toward the microwave as it chimed. "If I could have changed the timing of things. Been part of a different selection cycle. I wasn't trying to take something from you."

"It's not..." Harper interrupted. She stopped. Timing. Cycles. The financial documents in the folder on her desk snapped into focus, the potential connection becoming suddenly and uncomfortably clear. If she was right, then the 'sure thing' that Candace was looking for was, ironically, the most uncertain part of Mark's life. "Oh," she breathed.

"Oh, what?" Tate asked, one eyebrow raised.

Harper shook her head, bringing herself back to the present. "Nothing," she said hurriedly, dropping the Chinese container in the nearest garbage can. "Thanks, Tate." She rushed from the breakroom before he could ask further questions.

Back in her office, she laid the two financial statements side by side along with her desk calendar, marking out when money went in and out of each account. She counted weeks, dividing the time into cycles as she had watched Dr. Bluffton do. Her heart pounded. It was little more than a hunch, albeit a strong one. She looked again at the address and payment information on the checking account statement, suddenly realizing where she had seen it before. She swiped her phone screen, loaded her own banking application, and swiped through her recent transactions. Her heart fell as she found it, and she reached for the phone on her desk with a trembling hand.

"Is she available?" Harper asked Greta. "I'm coming up."

Five minutes later, Harper looped up and down the hallway outside the office while Candace finished a phone call.

"That bad, huh?" Greta asked, watching Harper's progress with obvious curiosity.

"I don't know," Harper admitted. "Maybe." If she was right, and the checking account seemed to confirm she was, this was going to stretch Candace's ability to respect whatever boundaries she was trying to hold with Mark.

"Harper!" Candace called a moment later, her voice muffled by the glass door closed between them.

Harper stopped her lap of the hallway, glancing nervously at Greta, who jumped up from her desk. She held open the door and gestured Harper through. "Good luck," she whispered as Harper crossed the threshold.

"You have something?" Candace asked, waving Harper into the office. She held out a hand expectantly as she moved behind her desk, and Harper rushed forward with documents.

"I think so," Harper admitted, unable to keep the hesitancy from her voice.

Candace's hand fell a few inches. "I asked for a sure thing," she said, gently chiding.

Harper looked at the documents. "I know," she admitted. "It's just, I don't think you were expecting this."

Candace waggled her fingers, beckoning Harper forward. "Show me."

Harper handed her the first paper. "They have a trust fund. They've been adding money to it intermittently. Money moves in for a few months, and then a few months pass with nothing." She watched Candace's expression, looking for a hint of recognition.

"Ok," Candace said slowly. "But there's nothing here to make things interesting."

"No," Harper agreed. "What's more interesting is *why* they would open a trust, and why they would only add to it intermittently." Her heart rate increased as she handed Candace the other document. "There's a separate checking account that money moves out of in the months they weren't contributing to the trust."

Candace slid her gold-rimmed reading glasses up the bridge of her nose. "These charges are to the same vendor," she said, glancing up and down the page. "What is 'Family Health Holdings'? Do we know where the money is going?"

Harper swallowed hard. "We do," she admitted. "Lakeview Fertility Clinic. It's a private clinic here in the city." Candace looked up, meeting Harper's eyes, and Harper forced herself to finish her hypothesis. "I think Mark and Ainsley were trying to have a baby. Based on the amount of money moving out of the account, my guess is that they were at the clinic for IVF."

"That doesn't explain the trust," Candace said, laying both papers on her desk and bracing herself on her fingertips.

"I'm speculating," Harper admitted. "But money only moves from one account or the other. If they started a cycle that they thought was successful, they may have put money into the trust for the baby."

Candace sucked in a sharp breath and sagged into her desk chair. "They stopped putting money in the trust when they lost the pregnancies."

Harper shrugged, her nerves buzzing. "I'm speculating," she reiterated.

"But you're sure the charges from the checking account are going to the fertility clinic?" Candace asked, pulling the page toward her.

"100%" Harper confirmed.

Candace let the page fall to her desk. "Ok," she said after a moment. "So, where's my leverage in all of this?"

It was the part that made Harper most uncomfortable. She wasn't actually sure what kind of leverage this was, how Candace could use it, or if it even *should* be used. But Candace had asked her what would motivate a driven, ambitious, millennial woman, and as a driven, ambitious, millennial woman who also happened to be a patient at the same fertility clinic, she could guess what she would be most concerned about if she was in Ainsley Archer's shoes.

"If they have embryos left," she started, carefully, "could there be custody to consider?"

"Embryos?" Candace asked in disbelief.

"I'm…" Harper started.

"Speculating," Candace interrupted. "I know." Her hands trembled slightly as she removed her reading glasses and rubbed her eyes.

It unnerved Harper to see her rattled. She felt slightly queasy wondering what the next steps might be and whether Candace would ask her to dig in deeper. "What happens now?" she asked.

"Now, you go back to your office and give someone else a headache this afternoon," said Candace. There was an unexpected sharpness to her tone, and Harper tried not to take it personally. It was, she reminded herself, as much a personal as a professional revelation for Candace. She turned to the door, walking the length of the room before she heard Candace sigh behind her.

"Harper?" It was measured, gentle even.

Harper turned around automatically. "Yes, Candace."

"When you have a moment, see if you can get me a copy of the Lakeview Fertility Clinic patient contract. We need to find out if they specify a chain of custody or plan for embryos remaining after treatment."

Harper nodded. "Absolutely," she affirmed.

"And Harper?" This time, Candace smiled.

"Yeah?"

"Good luck on Saturday."

Chapter 14

When she checked into Lakeview Fertility Clinic the next afternoon, the first thing Harper thought about was not its new and unlikely connection to Mark Archer. Rather, it was Kara Grobbert, who had a brand-new picture of her growing family on the wall of success stories. She cradled a small, yellow wrapped bundle in her arms surrounded by a thin man with a black shock of hair and two toddling boys wearing matching plaid shirts. Kara beamed with the same smile she had flashed at Harper that day in the waiting room, and Harper stared up at the picture with undeniable ambivalence. Not that she wasn't happy for the Grobberts or indifferent to their success. Indifference would have been easier than the complicated mix of emotions Harper wrestled with instead. Kara got her picture on the wall with three healthy babies. Harper got an invasive imaging procedure on her way to what may or may not prove to be a healthy and viable first attempt that she may or may not have to juggle with law school.

The receptionist looked up and smiled. "You're all set. We'll call you back in just a few minutes." Harper did not reply, but nodded once in recognition and took a seat in the waiting room.

She had been in a bad place about the appointment all morning, and not just because she finally took fifteen minutes over breakfast to Google what to expect and the potential outcomes. As soon as she had, she was grateful she had been too distracted to look sooner. Preparing for the LSAT would have been that much harder while also worrying about the logistics of moving around on the x-ray table with a catheter and uterus full of imaging dye.

"This sounds like the pelvic exam from Hell," she admitted to Bryan, anxiety rising as he refilled her coffee mug.

He kissed the top of her head reassuringly. "Do you want me to come?" he asked. "I can reschedule a couple of office hours and meet you at the clinic."

Harper had seen plenty of women at the clinic waiting with their partners, but she had never been compelled to have Bryan there. It wasn't so much that she was trying to keep him away, but that she felt she could handle it without putting him through the stress and worry and hassle.

She shook her head. "I'll be fine," she insisted.

"You're sure?" he asked, squeezing her shoulders.

She was.

Until she wasn't.

Now, sitting in the waiting room, stomach tight with nerves, Harper wished she had someone. She glanced around, wondering if any of the other women scattered across the matching chairs were on her same path today. Not that she would ever have the gumption to slide over and strike up a conversation as Kara Grobbert had, but it suddenly struck Harper as odd that this wasn't talked about more, even among women going through the same thing in the same office waiting room. She was sure she could find a Facebook page or a local city support group. But why didn't she have women in her life with whom she could share this? Her mom was gone. Her sister was busy with two babies of her own, and Harper wasn't willing to be an imposition. Women at the firm who had children seemed to talk about them rarely.

Three weeks ago, she could have asked Maggie to be here.

The realization hit Harper in the heart, and she drew a sharp breath as she wondered about her friend. Was it possible that somewhere in the city, she too was sitting in a waiting room, alone? Did she worry about what others waiting might wonder about her? Or, more likely, was Seth there to hold her hand? Regardless of the decision, she couldn't imagine Seth not standing by her.

She wondered if any part of Maggie thought about her. Though Harper had imagined sharing pregnancies and babies, she never thought about having to forge ahead on the more difficult paths. Infertility. Unwanted pregnancy. They couldn't have expected this. Yet, here they were. Or rather, here she was. On her own, while Maggie struggled elsewhere. For the first time in their entire friendship, they were heading in opposite directions, completely alone.

Harper vaguely remembered her high school health class. There had been a lot more hands-on, experiential learning since then. But one thing she knew they had failed to teach her was what to do at this moment. She learned STDs and anatomy, the mechanics of reproduction and ways to prevent pregnancy before the proper time. But she never learned what to do when it all went wrong, and the wrong people were pregnant, and the right people couldn't seem to get there, and the rest of the people didn't know how to talk about it. It now seemed that would have been far more useful knowledge. Maybe talking about it then might have made it feel less foreign to navigate now.

"Harper Andrews?" A petite, dark-haired woman in the clinic's signature seafoam green scrubs stood in the doorway next to the reception desk, holding a file and scanning the room. Harper raised a hand as she collected her bag and stood. She smiled as Harper approached. "How are you today?"

"As good as I can be, I guess," Harper replied, obediently following through the door and down the hallway to the right.

"I'm Sam," the woman offered as they walked. "I'll be assisting Dr. Bluffton as the radiography tech."

"Great," Harper murmured, trying not to come across as too unfriendly. The woman was, after all, about to be very up close and personal.

"Is it still snowing?" asked Sam.

Harper wondered how many patients found this kind of banal small talk soothing before procedures. "A little," she replied, playing along. "The roads are mostly clear."

Sam stopped at a wide door on the left. "That's good." She gestured into the room. "We'll be in here."

Harper's pulse fluttered. "Great," she muttered again.

The exam room was large and dimly lit, with screens and monitors along one wall, and a large table surrounded by imaging equipment in the center. There was paperwork on a high-top desk next to the door that Sam referenced as they entered before handing Harper a gown and instructing her to undress from the waist down. Harper glanced awkwardly around the room, searching for a hint of privacy. The irony was not lost on her that she was about to have her most intimate parts not only exposed, but essentially photographed, yet here she was looking for personal space to take her pants off.

"There's a restroom in the corner," Sam offered, pointing toward an unmarked door on the far side of the room.

"Thanks," Harper replied automatically.

The bathroom was white and ceramic tile and smelled of hospital-grade cleaner. She undressed quickly and left her clothes folded neatly on a metal shelf next to the sink. Squinting into the fluorescent light reflected in the bathroom mirror, nervous energy roiled her stomach and drained the color from her face. She rubbed her eyes in the bright light, telling herself it would be over soon and worth it someday. Maybe. It was almost a relief to step back into the soft, dim lighting of the exam room. Almost. Her eyes fixed on the tray of silver instruments Sam was arranging beside the x-ray table, and her heart ticked faster.

The door to the exam room opened, and another woman in scrubs entered. Her blonde hair was twisted into a knot on the back of her head, and a surgical mask dangled from one ear.

"Hi, Harper," she declared, extending her hand as she stepped into the room. "I'm Dr. Masters. I'm the radiologist helping Dr. Bluffton today."

Harper offered her hand in return. "Nice to meet you."

"Dr. Bluffton will be ready in just a minute. In the meantime, do you have any questions about the procedure?"

Thanks to her last-minute Googling, Harper was comfortably informed. On the recommendation of multiple women online, she took three ibuprofens before she left work. There wasn't much else that was suggested could help, nor was she convinced more information would be reassuring.

"Are there any potential risks?" she asked.

Dr. Masters shook her head reassuringly. "It's a relatively common and safe procedure. Once in a rare while there will be an infection or allergic reaction, but the risk is low."

"Ok," Harper replied, her pulse continuing to climb.

Sam brought a clipboard from the desk near the door. "If you don't have any other questions, here's the consent form for today's procedure."

The form was a double-sided page in 10-point font, and Harper was quite certain most patients trusted the doctor enough to sign it without even skimming. Her legal mind, however, would not allow it, and she took a few steps towards the backlit screens to have better light to read the document. She was on the second to last bullet point when she heard the door open, and Dr. Bluffton entered the room. She smiled at Harper under the light of the monitors.

"Don't criticize the legalese. It's a standard form."

Harper looked up. "I'm sure," she said. "Force of habit."

"Take your time," Dr. Bluffton nodded, crossing the room and inspecting the tray of instruments.

Harper swallowed hard as she slid the pen from the top of the clipboard and signed her name on the bottom of the page. "All set." She handed the clipboard to Sam, who set it on the desk before joining Dr. Masters and Dr. Bluffton near the x-ray table.

"Ok, Harper," said Dr. Masters in a voice that Harper deemed much more enthusiastic than the current situation warranted. "Let me walk you through this."

Dr. Masters helped Harper onto the table and into position for Dr. Bluffton, who maneuvered the cold, metal instruments into position between Harper's legs so that the catheter could be inserted. Harper closed her eyes and breathed deeply in through her nose and out through her mouth.

"I'm just going to clean things up with a little iodine," Dr. Bluffton narrated from the end of the table. "Now comes the catheter. Slight pinch."

Harper considered the sensation neither slight nor a pinch. She felt like she had been shishkebabbed.

"You're doing great," Dr. Bluffton assured her, returning the silver speculum to the instrument tray. "Just relax for a second before we inject the dye. Dr. Masters, go ahead and slide her back on the table where you want her."

Sam and Dr. Masters moved behind Harper, supporting her head and shoulders as she pushed herself backward.

"Right there is good," Dr. Masters decided. She reached over the top of Harper and adjusted the x-ray equipment. "Once we inject the dye, you may need to move a little to help us get the best angles. Sam will help."

"Ok," Harper nodded. Her heart hammered, and she could feel herself sweating under the hospital gown. So far, everything had been as described. She was not comfortable, per se, but she also wasn't suffering. The worst, according to the online testimonies, was yet to come.

Dr. Bluffton reached for a large plastic syringe, holding it up so it was just within Harper's line of vision. "There's no needle here," she assured her. "This attaches to the catheter to inject the dye. You may feel some discomfort." She moved to the end of the table. "Here we go. Take a deep breath."

Harper did as she was told, holding the breath a split second before the pain grabbed her. It seized her all at once with such intensity that her stomach rolled. She sucked in a sharp gasp and tried not to curl instinctively into a ball on the table.

Dr. Masters moved quickly, guiding the equipment into position and taking the first images. "You're doing great," she encouraged, adjusting Harper's hips on the table for the next round of films.

Harper could not reply. A white-hot poker was stabbing into her abdomen, prodding again and again and again. She saw Dr. Bluffton move to the monitor where the x-rays had appeared on the screen. "Can we get a better look at that left side?" she asked calmly.

"Sure thing," Dr. Masters concurred. "Harper, we're going to need you to slide up a little further and have you roll toward me." She moved the x-ray equipment up and to the side to give Harper space to maneuver, but Harper could not seem to make herself respond to the directions she was given. She felt awkward and disoriented, sliding one way, but stopping when the flexible tubing still snaked inside her caught on the edge of the table. She rolled a few inches, then stopped. "That's ok," Dr. Masters assured her. "Sam, can you come up here by her shoulders, please? Harper, if you just sit up a little, Sam will help move you back."

Tears pricked in the corners of Harper's eyes as she took a deep breath and pushed herself up on her elbows. Her lower abdomen screamed in protest. Sam hooked her arms under Harper's and guided her back gently.

"That's good there," Dr. Masters instructed. She moved the machine back into position. "Harper, keep your hands up there by Sam so they're clear of the image. I'm going to help you roll your hips toward me, ok? One, two, three."

Harper did her best to move herself the way she was directed, feeling Dr. Masters' hands on her back and her butt guiding her to just the right angle. A quiet moan of discomfort escaped her lips as Dr. Masters stepped back to check the picture with Dr. Bluffton, forcing Harper to hold the position herself. For a moment, she thought about how immensely unfair it was that she had been led to a dark room to be probed and prodded while all Bryan endured was the potential embarrassment of being handed a cup and a stack of magazines. Then the pain radiated through her again, and Harper focused only on Bryan and that, if nothing else, she was doing it for him. *He should have been here,* she thought. *I should have told him to come.*

A single tear slid onto her cheek, and Sam reached over and brushed it away. She squeezed Harper's hand. "Almost done," she whispered. "The worst is over."

Harper nodded in acknowledgement, grateful for the gesture. She did not let go of Sam's hand, nor did Sam make a move to pull away when both doctors stepped back to the table.

"You did great," Dr. Bluffton said warmly. "We got everything we needed. We're going to get you cleaned up, and then we'll talk about what comes next."

"Ok," Harper whispered. Her throat was tight, and the unspilled tears threatened to fall. But the pain had lessened to a dull, yet insistent, ache.

Dr. Bluffton removed the remaining tube and covered the instrument tray with a paper cloth while Dr. Masters wiped down the x-ray machine and moved things back from the exam table.

"You can sit up when you're ready," Dr. Bluffton instructed, patting Harper's knee. "Take your time." She tossed her gloves in a bin by the door and glanced at her watch. "Sam will bring you over to my office after you're changed."

"It was nice to meet you, Harper." Dr. Masters offered, following Dr. Bluffton to the door. "Take good care." They stepped into the hallway, leaving the room dim and quiet.

Harper took a few deep breaths and released Sam's hand. "Thanks," she said, gingerly pushing herself up to a sitting position. She rested a hand on her lower abdomen. "That was..." She hesitated, taking another deep breath.

"Intense," Sam finished for her. "I know. I'm sorry."

Harper shook her head. "You don't need to apologize. I signed the form."

Sam kept one hand on Harper's back as she slid toward the end of the table. "Yes, but somehow that doesn't quite capture the experience of it, does it?"

"No," Harper admitted with a wince as her feet hit the floor and she pushed herself to standing.

"You might feel a little woozy," Sam warned. "And there are sanitary pads in a basket in the restroom. You may consider one for the next twenty-four hours."

Twenty-four hours. Harper drew a shaky breath. She couldn't imagine thinking straight for the LSAT at the moment.

"Thanks," Harper said, shuffling toward the bathroom door.

"If you need anything, just call," Sam offered. "Take your time."

Standing in front of the bathroom mirror, Harper wondered how much the fluorescent lighting was responsible for her sickly pallor. She splashed cool water on her face and around the back of her neck, slipped off the gown, and retrieved her clothing from the shelf. The thick pad she affixed to her underwear was obtrusive under her tailored trousers, and she wobbled as she stepped into her heels. Her body felt fragile and tender, like she would break apart if jostled too hard on the street. She leaned on the sink, forcing herself to breathe deeply.

"Harper," Sam's kind, concerned voice floated under the door. "Are you ok?"

"I'm fine," Harper called, her voice shaking. "Just another minute." She stared up at her reflection again. Her mascara was smudged in the corners where the tears had pooled, and her hair was mussed from being slid around the table. She raked her fingers through it and dabbed at the black marks on her face with a damp paper towel. The pain had ebbed further to a faint throb that she pushed her attention from, thinking instead of whatever news Dr. Blufton was about to deliver. Her hands shook as she tossed the paper towel into the wastebasket and reached for the doorknob, heartbeat stuttering with the familiar twinge of nerves. She closed her eyes, took a final, steadying breath, and stepped back into the exam room.

•   •   •

It was neither entirely positive nor was it all bad news. Dr. Bluffton struck a tone of cautious optimism. The left fallopian tube was blocked, a fact to which Harper could attribute most of the crippling pain during the exam. The right tube, however, was fully functional, and Dr. Bluffton showed Harper where on the image the amorphous tendrils of dye indicated the desired result. That only one tube was open, she explained, was likely a major contributing factor to their difficulty in conceiving. It also had an undeniable impact on their plans moving forward.

"It's not that medication can't work," Dr. Bluffton offered. "You've already taken the prescription we gave you for this cycle, so you might as well see the calendar through the next few weeks. The HSG procedure has even been known to boost your odds a bit," she encouraged. "In the long run, however," she added, tempering her enthusiasm, "we might be more successful moving ahead with the IUI or IVF process. We can eliminate some of the random chance and make sure we're taking the best advantage of the healthy follicles you have."

Harper nodded along, numb, barely digesting the words, wondering vaguely how she would explain it to Bryan, but more pressingly when she could leave the office, get out of her work clothes and into an oversized t-shirt and her favorite sweatpants. She understood there was hope, but also that things weren't quite right, and that there would be more steps, time, and money. She understood that the cycles of appointments, medications, intercourse, and ultrasounds could easily consume more time and energy than they already had. And she understood that tomorrow she was taking the next big step toward law school, which continued to feel completely at odds with the conversation she was currently having.

As conflicted as ever, Harper accepted Dr. Bluffton's laminated folder of pamphlets on various treatment options and two printouts of frequently asked questions, along with the reassurance that, however Harper and Bryan decided to proceed, she was optimistic. Only as

Harper moved to the door did she remember she could now kill two birds with one stone.

"As long as all the options are on the table, could I take a contract for treatment along with me as well?" she asked casually. "Just to review."

A look of confusion flashed across Dr. Bluffton's face. Then she smiled.

"Force of habit, right?" she asked, opening her file cabinet and retrieving a thick packet.

"Right," Harper agreed, grateful that it wasn't entirely untruthful.

On the ride home, Harper stared at the folder on the seat next to her and wished for the third time that afternoon that she let Bryan come if for no other reason than she wouldn't have to go home and explain it to him on her own. He could have heard it from the doctor. He could have asked his questions to the doctor. They could have left the office together, and in doing so, left some of the burden and heartache behind with the doctor as well.

She rolled to a stop at the curb in front of the apartment, stepped carefully across the icy sidewalk, and was halfway up the stairs when their door flew open and Bryan appeared on the landing.

"I saw you pull up," he explained, hurrying down the steps to take her bag.

An unexpected lump lodged in Harper's throat as he pulled her into a hug from the step above her. She swayed in her place, and he pulled her tighter to him. His heart thundered level with her ear. For a long moment, it was the only sound.

"Are you ok?" he asked gently.

Better to get it out all at once, Harper decided.

"No," she admitted. "There's a blockage. Just on one side. Dr. Bluffton thinks we should consider other options."

Bryan pulled back and looked down at her. "Harper, stop. It doesn't matter. I mean, it does, but…" He set the bag down and took both her hands. "Are *you* ok?"

Harper's bottom lip trembled, and she fought to keep her composure. Bryan's eyebrows furrowed, and he pulled her to him again.

"You should have let me come," he murmured.

"I should have let you come," Harper agreed, her voice cracking. She nestled into his arms, feeling all the safety and security and assurance that had been missing from the past few hours. The stability and comfort of his arms was home. "I'm fine now," she reassured him, relaxing into the embrace. Her tone was even, and as she looked up into his sea glass eyes, she almost believed it was true.

Chapter 15

Eighteen hours later, staring at the start screen for the last section of the LSAT exam, Harper felt anything but fine. It had been a grueling morning, and she was less confident about the outcome than she had been during any of the practice exams. Little things kept throwing her off: a passage phrased with slightly more nuance than in her preparation book; the rumble and shudder of the air vent in the small library cubicle at Lancaster University she reserved for testing; the thought of having to answer to the entire office on Monday how she thought she had done. She was grateful that the test was no longer administered in large auditoriums or high school gymnasiums where she might have watched the back of Tate Bishop's head bent over his own test and wondered how she was doing comparatively.

The intermission timer ticked in the corner of the screen, and Harper finished her granola bar and stood from the table, stretching her arms wide overhead, careful not to pull or strain her abdomen. The pain was gone, but the knowledge of what was wrong and the intensity of the appointment had not left her. She felt fragile, physically and emotionally, and after her morning of intellectual gymnastics, the mental exhaustion threatened to push her over the edge.

The clock flashed red as the final minute counted down, and she tossed her wrapper into the can by the door and rolled her shoulders a few times before settling back into her chair and pulling a yellow legal pad toward her. While the sections of the test were presented in a random order, the focus of those sections was no secret. Thus, Harper knew that no matter how run-down she felt, she would have to find a way to rally for the next thirty-five minutes. Most test takers considered her remaining section, analytical reasoning, to be the hardest of the exam. It almost didn't seem fair, Harper thought as the clock disappeared and a gray "START" icon flashed to the center of the screen, that some test takers got these questions first when they were fresh and eager, adrenaline leading the way. She felt that boost working through the complex reading passages earlier that morning, but would have been just as comfortable slogging through them at the end of the test, half delirious. It would have been no different from a long day at the office.

Analytical reasoning, however, required its own kind of focus and attention. The section comprised of four logic "games," each requiring the test taker to reason through a scenario based on a set of conditions and answer corresponding questions. The setups were notoriously complex, often complicated by competing concepts, and best represented by the kinds of diagrams that Harper had been practicing all month. Though it was the most difficult section of the test, it was also the most learnable, with each game built from the same components: ordering, grouping, subsets, mismatches, and conditionals. Recognize the parts, recognize the setup. Recognize the setup, recognize the solution.

Harper clicked into the test and read the first question.

An advertising firm has six pitch meetings scheduled over three days–Monday, Tuesday, and Wednesday–with one meeting in conference room A and one meeting in conference room B each day. Each meeting will be led by a different executive–Chad, Devin, Elizabeth, Frank, Grace, or Hannah. The assignment of executives to pitch meetings must meet the following conditions:

Chad must hold his meeting on an earlier day of the week than Grace

Devin and Hannah must hold their pitch meetings on the same day.

Frank must hold his meeting in conference room B

Elizabeth and Frank cannot hold their pitch meetings on the same day.

Question 1: Which one of the following could be an accurate assignment of executives to conference rooms for the three days?

Harper scratched the first diagram on the legal pad, listing off the six executives down the left of the page, with spaces for conference rooms A and B and the days of the week to the right. She began filling in combinations of possibilities based on the parameters, working until there were three complete scheduling scenarios fully diagrammed. She double checked the given information, assuring she had not overlooked a condition. Confident that everything was accounted for, she scrolled down to her list of options, double checking her notes before settling on her answer.

Question two required her to add a new condition to the setup, and she adjusted the diagram accordingly. Question three changed which days Devin and Hannah could meet. Question four changed which meeting rooms Chad and Devin could use. Question five threw the entire diagram out the window and asked if one specific condition was known, how many others could be assumed. She looked over the five selected answers a final time before clicking the arrow to advance to the next page. Ten minutes had already elapsed. One down, three more to go.

Twenty-five minutes later, as the seconds of the session ticked away, Harper sat with her head in her hands, utterly overwhelmed with relief, fatigue, and nerves. It was over and completely out of her control. She had already updated her scholarship information with Candace so that her materials included her current personal details, work history, and references, and she would finalize her applications to the University of Chicago and Northwestern in the days ahead. In three weeks, the scores would be released, and she would have a better sense of what chance she actually had. In the meantime, there was nothing to do but wait.

She packed her laptop and scratch papers into her backpack and slipped on her coat. She had parked in Bryan's spot next to the science building on the south side of campus, and she hunkered into her scarf and flipped up the hood of her black puffer coat as she stepped into the snow and wind cutting across the quad from off the lake. The sidewalks, already patchworked with black ice, had drifted over, and she tread lightly, trying to picture what it would be like to be back on a campus, walking to classes and visiting the library more than once on a rare Saturday morning. It would be a far cry from undergrad, hustling back to the firm in between lectures and exams, returning home to her apartment and husband every night. Yet, she had always been comfortable in academia. There was something about walking in the hulking shadows of the academic buildings, cold and stoic in the swirling snow, that woke up her imagination to the real possibility that she was about to start life as a student again. The allure was nearly tangible.

The drive home crawled along snow-crusted city streets, giving Harper ample opportunity to overthink and reassess her test answers. She parsed through each part, worrying about the questions on which she hesitated and trying to recall every wrinkle of each logic game. She wondered how Tate was feeling, if he found himself more confident after his years at the firm than he had after undergrad years prior. A cynical part of her wondered if he and Lyle Pickett had already spoken to his father about what it would take to get him into a top tier program. It wasn't fair, but she knew a passable test score plus a sizable donation could be just as good, if not better, than high academic marks alone.

She thought briefly of texting him to ask how it went, but wasn't sure if her sudden curiosity would come across as genuine or prying. Their conversation in the kitchen had been civil, but not exactly friendly. At the memory of the awkwardness, she decided against it.

The Lakeview exit materialized through the swirl of snow, and Harper's thoughts flashed to Maggie and how, under different circumstances, she might take the ramp into the heart of downtown for an early celebration at Indie Lime. It was hours before dinner service, but Harper knew Maggie would be there, prepping, cleaning, putting in the hours, doing whatever it took. There had been one text since Christmas, a response to Harper's general well wishes for the new year. Just two words. *You too.* Given the radio silence stretched between them, any reply felt like an improvement, but nowhere close to enough to drop in unannounced. Harper wondered if the staff knew about the baby, and in the next uncomfortable moment, she wondered if there was still a baby for the staff to know about.

She slipped and spun her way back home to the apartment. Besides the contract she took from Lakeview Fertility Clinic the previous afternoon, she had brought nothing home related to work, and she was half convinced Bryan would already have the test prep book destroyed. Not that she needed it. She looked up. The windows of the apartment glowed invitingly in the swirling snow, and she dashed from the car and up the stairs, eager to be back in the cozy comfort of home with no obligations for the rest of the afternoon. She opened the front door and was met by the scent of evergreen candles and the chatter of ESPN. Bryan looked up from the couch as she shook the snow from her coat and stepped inside.

"How'd it go?" he asked immediately, muting the TV and rising to meet her at the door.

Harper unwound her scarf and kicked off her boots. "Ok," she answered vaguely.

"That's all I get?" Bryan huffed with a laugh.

"It was a lot," she offered. "I'm wiped." She leaned into him, kissing him lightly before burrowing her face into his chest.

"But how do you think you did?" he pressed again. There was, Harper noticed, a sweet, earnest eagerness in the question. Genuine excitement amid their other uncertainties. She pulled back to look up at him.

"I think it went pretty well," she said noncommittally. "I don't want to get my hopes up."

Bryan beamed and pulled her to him again. "Well, I do. Congratulations."

"It's a little early for that," Harper said, stepping out of the hug. "We've still got to wait for scores, and then admissions decisions, and then the scholarship." She offered Bryan her hand and led him to the couch where they sat down, side by side. Harper curled up in her favorite corner with Bryan's arm securely around her.

"I'm proud of you, no matter what happens," said Bryan. His thumb absentmindedly traced circles on Harper's shoulder. He gazed at her for a long minute. "I've been sitting here all morning thinking that I haven't said that enough," he admitted. "I know I've been focused on what this will mean for our family, but that doesn't change the fact that you're just incredible for taking on the challenge."

Contentment spread through Harper like warm sunshine, and she nuzzled into the crook of his arm. "I'm sorry that I haven't always balanced things will."

Bryan ran a hand over her hair. "I told you we would figure things out, and we will." He held her tight, her head on his shoulder, and they watched the talking heads on ESPN gesticulate and eye roll in muted silence. After a long moment, Bryan shifted, leaning Harper backward toward the arm of the couch. His mouth came down on hers tenderly at first, then more urgently as his hand snaked along her hips, across her torso, then into her hair.

Harper broke the kiss with a coy chuckle. "What are you doing?"

"What does it look like I'm doing?" Bryan asked, leaning in again.

"I know what it *looks* like." Harper laid a hand on his chest. "But I'm exhausted, and starving, and slightly overwhelmed, so I'm going to need a minute, a sandwich, and a nap."

"We can nap." Bryan crooked an eyebrow.

"I'm serious," Harper laughed.

"So am I," Bryan insisted. He sighed in mock frustration. "Fine," he teased in an overblown whine. "Make your sandwich. Take your nap. Fewer excuses when I come back for a second pass before dinner."

Harper laughed, pushing him further back as she stretched out on the couch. "This is quite the celebration you're trying to instigate. Feeling pretty lucky, are we?"

"I don't need luck tonight," he replied in the low, smooth murmur that had been known to make Harper blush. All she could do now was laugh.

"What are you talking about?" she snorted.

Bryan dropped the flirtatious act, his head tipping in confusion. "It's Day 11," he said, as if it was the only piece of information Harper should require for understanding. When she did not respond, he nodded toward the kitchen. "Doctor's orders."

Harper turned, her heart sinking as she caught his meaning. On the refrigerator, where she dutifully posted it after returning from the clinic weeks ago, was Dr. Bluffton's calendar. She hadn't thought about it when she came home from the appointment yesterday, and Bryan would never have insinuated, given the circumstances. But even from the couch, she could make out the little smiley faces drawn on days ten through eighteen.

"I knew you had other things on your mind, so I just figured I would get the ball rolling, help you decompress." Bryan shrugged, an embarrassed look replacing the brazen confidence of a moment earlier. "But you're right, it's been a long morning." He glanced out the window. The snow piled against the sill, and his gaze slid out of focus for a moment as he watched it drift. "No rush," he added a moment later, eyes finding Harper's again. "I don't think we'll be headed out anytime soon." He pulled the blanket off the back of the couch and tucked it around her.

She smiled up at him. "Thank you."

Bryan leaned over and kissed her forehead. "Relax," he whispered. "I'll make some lunch." He unmuted the TV as he headed for the kitchen, turning the volume to a low murmur as the talking heads on ESPN came back to life.

As she dozed, Harper tried to let go of the needling guilt of pushing Bryan away. She knew he would never pressure her to follow through, but she also felt an unavoidable sense of obligation to the plan as it had been laid out before them.

She thought back to her blustery walk across campus, the feelings she had about taking on the role of student again, the anxious excitement of waiting for her results, planning for the future. It was a different yearning than she felt toward being a mother. It was her own. There wasn't any expectation to it. She was motivated by desire, not duty. Twenty-four hours ago, she laid on the exam table wondering if three minutes of immense discomfort were worth the eventual outcome. She had spent every spare moment for a month and a half preparing for an exam that she labored tirelessly over all morning and, through it all, never asked herself the same question. Babies and law school were not the same thing, which is perhaps why she had never quite been able to picture them together. But the real question, she wondered as she slipped toward unconsciousness, was not if she *could* picture them together. The question was whether she really wanted to.

Chapter 16

Three things kept Harper distracted while she waited for her scores to be released. The first was the incessant stream of work at the office, which had only increased now that everyone knew the test was finished. Though Andrea Thompson promised it hadn't been her doing, a whole new contingent of junior partners seemed suddenly interested in procuring Harper's services on their cases. When she finally asked who they had all been working with previously, she was surprised how many openly admitted to working with, and subsequently leaving, Tate. She was not flattered. Competition or not, she knew Tate's work was good. She wanted to beat him, but she didn't need to tear him down. She stopped agreeing to review cases he had already started.

Despite delivering the contract from Lakeview Fertility Clinic to Candace's office personally on the Monday after the LSAT, she had not been asked to look into the matter further. Still, as much out of personal curiosity as professional, Harper had reviewed a copy of the agreement and found that it contained non-binding language suggesting conceiving partners have a plan for any remaining embryos. It did little to hold either party to a future course of action, however.

One sentence in particular, near the end of the document, made Harper believe the clinic was not in the business of wading into divorce proceedings. *Terms of the consents agreed herein may be altered through mutual consent of all undersigned parties.* She couldn't know what kind of ethos Mark and Ainsley may have had about their decision going in. Maybe they had long ago agreed on what would happen to any remaining embryos when they were finished having children. What she knew, however, is that while they might be finished with each other, they had never been finished growing their family. They barely even started. That meant that whatever they might have planned to do was, at least now, up in the air along with everything else they would divide from their life together. Given her own situation, and despite her stable relationship, she found the vague, gray areas of this particular form of custody law unsettling.

To go along with the contract, she also found precedent in Illinois law regarding partners with differing ideas on what to do at the end of their treatment. She included the ruling in the folder with the contract should it prove to be useful, but Candace had merely glanced at it before thanking her for her expediency and wondering aloud how Harper had managed to get to the clinic over the weekend. She gave no indication as to whether she had confirmed any part of the embryo hypothesis, and curiosity aside, Harper wasn't willing to push it with Candace. She needed to stay in her good graces because the second thing competing for her time was the finalization of her law school applications. A glowing recommendation from Candace Walsh was as good as gold.

Given her history with the university and its proximity to the firm, Northwestern was an obvious first choice. The University of Chicago, however, was the most prestigious program in the city, and Harper knew that acceptance there would be difficult for the committee to ignore. She also wanted to be realistic, however. It was late in the process, and she was far from the traditional candidate. The scholarship meant nothing if she didn't have a school to attend. Considering Bryan's standing on the faculty, Lancaster seemed the most obvious safety school, though the fact that he never suggested it made Harper wonder if he might be bothered by his wife showing up on campus as a newly minted law student.

She broached the subject one night after giving up working on her personal statement. She had been considering, yet again, whether the story of her mother's diagnosis made for a compelling focal point.

Every time she tried to write it, the words refused to come out the right way. She closed her laptop in frustration.

Bryan stood behind her chair, rubbing the tension from her shoulders. "Stuck again?"

"Yes," Harper moaned, letting her head fall forward as Bryan pressed a thumb into a knot at the base of her neck. He eased up as she flinched under his touch.

"Give it time. You'll find it," he assured her.

Harper sighed. "Time is the one thing I don't have. It's already the end of January. All the spots could already be spoken for." Her voice rose, laced with nervousness. "Just because they let people submit their materials this late doesn't mean they're holding space to accept late applicants."

"Hey," Bryan soothed gently, leaning down and kissing the top of her head. "They'll have a spot for you. Or they'll make a spot for you. They just don't even know they want you yet."

Despite her uncertainty, Harper breathed easier at his simple, easy confidence. "Just in case," she said, pivoting in the chair to better face him. "I've been thinking it makes sense to have a backup plan."

"Oh?" Bryan asked with polite intrigue. He stepped around the small table and pulled out the other chair. "I kind of thought we already had one."

Harper's brow furrowed. "We do?"

Bryan shrugged, looking shy. "I meant with the clinic."

"A baby should not be a backup plan," Harper interrupted quickly. Her heartbeat skittered. It was the thing she was supposed to say, she knew. You weren't supposed to back your way into parenthood. But it wasn't like she hadn't considered it herself.

"I know that," said Bryan, quickly. "I didn't mean to imply…"

"Well, then, what do you mean?"

Bryan looked away and blew out a breath. When he turned back, Harper could read the obvious conflict in his expression. "I meant," he started slowly, "that I've been wondering if there's any scenario in which we take law school back off the table?"

Harper sucked in a breath. "Do you want there to be?" she asked, already dreading the answer.

Bryan shook his head. "Not if it's what you want," he assured her. "But I don't just mean getting into school. Because we know you can get in. If not Northwestern or the University of Chicago, I'm sure Lancaster would take you in a heartbeat."

The tiniest wave of relief rippled through Harper that the thought had at least crossed Bryan's mind before she could suggest it.

"I'm talking about the scholarship," Bryan continued. "If you got into school but didn't get the scholarship, is this something you're prepared to give up again? Is there any turning around from this? Because if there's not, we should talk about what that means for everything else."

Everything else.

There it was.

The conversation she knew they would have about the feelings she still couldn't wrap her head around.

She knew she was supposed to know. She expected to feel a certain way by now. She couldn't imagine giving up either future, but still couldn't imagine both at the same time. It felt too harsh to admit that she felt a calling toward being a lawyer in a way she never felt a calling toward being a mother. That she felt pressured toward being a mother in a way she never felt pressured toward going to law school. She didn't want to acknowledge that the whole reason she was clinging to other people's plans and expectations was to avoid being held accountable for her own decision–because what if she made the wrong one and forever regretted her choice? Weeks of pressure and tension bubbled up from her very core, threatening to burst out in a guttural scream. "I guess I hadn't really thought about it," she deflected, the lie coming out so weakly that Bryan's reactionary scoff nearly came out as a laugh.

"Well, that would be the first thing in our entire marriage that you hadn't really thought about," he said, tone more unbelieving than unkind. "You analyze for a living. You were consumed with the test. Now it's the applications. Is there any part of you that can actually imagine *not* accepting one of the offers that we both know is going to come?"

"We don't know that," Harper started.

Bryan smiled, but it didn't reach his eyes. "Of course we do," he sighed. "That's what you wanted to talk about, wasn't it? A backup plan? A safety school in case Chicago or Northwestern doesn't pan out; a safety school that assures you'll have somewhere to go?"

"I have to be accepted into a program to even be considered for the scholarship," Harper insisted. "I have no chance at all if I'm not in school."

"But once you're accepted to a school, is your mind made up? You know we could afford the Lancaster tuition without a scholarship."

Harper took a breath to answer, but held it, not responding. In her heart she knew that, yes, if an acceptance letter and a scholarship offer both materialized in the weeks ahead, there would be very little that would keep her from pursuing it. In her mind she had linked not winning the scholarship with not going to school, but she realized now that Bryan was right, and there would still be that choice.

Heads. Tails. Heads. Tails.

"I don't want saying yes to me to mean saying no to you," she whispered, voice cracking. "I don't know how to do both, Bryan. But I don't want to choose either, and that's where I'm afraid we're headed–toward a choice I don't know how to make."

Bryan's expression softened. "How can I help?" he asked.

"I don't know," Harper admitted. "But I'm not ready to make final decisions yet. Can't we see what the schools say, and what the firm says, and what Dr. Bluffton says after this cycle finishes before we make the call?"

A storm of conflict swirled in Bryan's eyes, and he hesitated before responding. "So, you don't want to talk about taking a baby out of the picture?" He swallowed hard, and Harper watched his Adam's apple ripple the dark stubble along his throat. Her own mouth was suddenly so dry she was afraid she wouldn't get the words out, assuming she found them at all.

"No," she said finally, realizing as she did that, despite all her misgivings, it didn't feel untruthful. "It's just weird to be in the middle of everything right now, not knowing how it's all going to play out."

Bryan looked away, lost in thought. "Ok," he said finally. "So, how do you feel about that?" He nodded toward the kitchen.

"What?" she asked, turning to follow his gaze.

Bryan sighed. "It's Day 17."

As she realized the implication, Harper's stomach sank, an automatic and increasingly familiar reaction that was quickly becoming her visceral association with their most intimate moments. It broke her heart. Still, she could not give him hope in one breath and stave off his advances in the next. Besides, they were already committed to this cycle. She allowed herself to be helped to her feet, and Bryan pulled her toward him. Her head fell onto his shoulder as his arms wrapped around her, and they held each other, hearts beating in steady unison, seeking to put the tension and applications and doubts behind them so they could do what needed to be done.

Bryan leaned down and kissed Harper's forehead. "I love you," he whispered.

"I love you too," she murmured. Her lips brushed the skin just above his shirt collar, and she felt goosebumps break out under her touch. She looked up and kissed him, feeling his hands slide along her hips. Resigned, she let him lead her to the bedroom.

Thus, her third and most insistent distraction became a renewed obsession with whether she would find herself pregnant at the end of the month. She woke up the next morning intensely aware that continuing to brush her misgivings aside was not so much avoiding having to make a final decision as setting herself up to surrender to the outcome of a decision already made for her. As she stepped from the shower and stared at her muted reflection in the foggy glass of the bathroom mirror, she wrestled with the reality that it might not matter how she felt about it anymore. The eventual outcome may already be in motion.

Butterflies erupted in her stomach as they had in the early months of trying. The possibility. The anxiety. Month after month of waiting and imagining what it would be like to see two thin, life-changing lines appear. The eventual letdown when, month after month, the test either came back negative or there was no reason to test at all. In the beginning, she and Bryan had waited in the bathroom together, impatiently counting down the seconds before checking the tiny window. Eventually, Harper found it easier to take the test alone, unable to muster the false hope and optimism required to hold a conversation about their hypothetical future family for the three minutes it took for a plastic stick to determine her fate. She would share the result later without fanfare while they brushed their teeth or while commercials played during Sunday Night Football. Ultimately, she stopped bringing up the tests all together, the continued letdown unspoken yet understood between them.

Her apprehensions were now different than they had once been, somehow weightier and more tangible, but she also couldn't ignore the kernel of desire that grew in her chest when she thought about the possibility of taking yet another pregnancy test. She rested a hand over her lower abdomen, wondering.

"What are we doing?" she muttered under a heavy sigh.

Thus, for three weeks, Harper worked; she wrote; she waited. Though Candace continued to refuse her help on anything related to Urban City Apparel or the divorce, Greta called with assurances that all the requested and required references for her law school applications had been completed. Harper filed her personal statement, took her prenatal vitamins, and checked off the boxes on the calendar. She was constantly aware that while the whole office waited for the LSAT scores, it was not one but two potential test results with a stranglehold on her future. Which is why it seemed only appropriate to Harper that when she woke up the morning the scores would be released, she subsequently realized she was late.

Part 3

Everything that Matters

Chapter 17

Thin, gray light filtered through the living room curtains as Harper paced, waiting for the coffee to finish. She knew vaguely that it may not be her best option given the potential circumstances, but she was jittery enough already without skipping her morning dose of caffeine. She poured a full cup before sitting down at the kitchen counter and considering her options.

There was a box of pregnancy tests in the bottom drawer of the bathroom vanity. She could have the answer in three minutes if she wanted it. It certainly wouldn't be the first time she started her morning locked in the bathroom before Bryan woke up. But she remained rooted to her spot at the counter.

The clock on the stove glowed 6:00am. Scores were released at 8:00am through an online management system. She imagined opening the email in her office, the glass wall a fish bowl letting others gauge her reaction to whatever number flashed on the screen. The thought churned her stomach. So too did the idea of sitting at home and trying to work up the courage to open the bottom drawer in the bathroom. She heard Bryan stirring and wondered if he had done the math and put together the timeline. They had spent more time watching the calendar this month than ever before. But when he shuffled, bleary-eyed, into the kitchen a moment later, his thoughts seemed only on the LSAT score.

"You ok?" he asked. He wrapped his arms around Harper from behind.

"Mm hmm," she hummed, leaning back into him. Her heart fluttered as his hands settled lightly over her stomach. "I was just trying to decide what to do with myself until 8:00."

"Stay home. Go in late." Bryan suggested, giving her a final squeeze before making a move toward the coffeepot. "Relax. You've earned it."

Harper shook her head. "I can't just sit here and wait. I need a distraction. I thought I might go for a drive."

"In rush hour traffic?"

Harper shrugged. "Makes it harder to refresh my inbox incessantly for the next two hours."

"I guess," Bryan admitted, closing his eyes as he took a sip of coffee. "You want company? You can drop me off on campus, make a big loop back to the office."

Harper's eyebrows rose behind her coffee cup, and her heart skipped. While an extra hour with Bryan might calm her nerves about the test scores, she was quite certain it would have the opposite effect when it came to thinking about a baby. She wondered if he would want to be surprised by it. Little shoes in a gift box on the coffee table, or a onesie hidden among the laundry, or a pregnancy test left strategically out in the open. She hadn't made those kinds of plans. At least not yet.

"I'll be fine," she assured him. "Besides, you don't actually need to go in for hours. I'm just going to clear my head a bit. I'll let you know as soon as I hear anything."

Bryan rubbed a hand over his face. "You're sure that you're ok?"

"Just nerves," Harper insisted quickly. She moved around the corner and kissed him lightly on the cheek. "Promise." It was the truth, she told herself, even if he didn't understand all the factors fueling the day's anxiety. "I'll call you when I know."

Thirty minutes later, she headed north out of downtown along the lakeshore. On her right, a jagged landscape of icy peaks jutted out from the shoreline, glittering in the reflection of city lights. Far out in the darkness, the first traces of watery morning light glowed along the horizon line in faded pinks and golds. She'd left without a specific destination in mind, yet by the time she reached Lake Shore Drive, it seemed all too obvious where she would end up. She drove in silence, whizzing by the familiar exits that would take her back into the heart of the city, wondering briefly if Tate was already in his office, fretting over his inbox. For the first time she considered, really considered, the possibility that he could beat her, that his score was high enough, or hers low enough, that he would shock the entire office and come out on top via his own merits. Beyond losing the scholarship, Harper realized, she would have to contend with the entire dynamic of the twenty-eighth floor shifting. Everyone expected her to perform. Her stomach twisted.

She reached the city limits. Chicago gave way to Evanston, and Harper changed lanes, following, but not really needing to follow, the arrows toward the Northwestern campus. A steady stream of students in black North Face parkas lugging backpacks and messenger bags materialized from the surrounding apartments and duplexes as she drew closer. A few brave cyclists donning reflective armbands and headlamps navigated fat tire bikes through the gray sludge piled along the gutters. She found a parking spot a few blocks from the famed Weber Arch and allowed herself to be swept into the flow of sleepy students shuffling their way toward early morning classes.

She felt slightly foolish for having come. The law school wasn't even on the main campus in Evanston. But it hadn't been law school that drew her to her alma mater. It was nostalgia, and, if she was honest, her mother. She flipped her hood up to guard against the stiff breeze whipping off the lake.

Winding through campus, small clusters of students broke off, rushing to lecture halls and science labs. Harper remembered her days doing the same. It felt like eons ago. A different age. She read the optimism and certainty and self-assurance on the faces around her; a part of her wanted to warn them it wouldn't all go as they imagined. That it was wishful thinking to believe that the dreams they were carefully curating and cultivating were guaranteed by a diploma. She was certain she never imagined coming back after more than a decade to avoid having to take a pregnancy test on the same day she waited for her second set of LSAT results. Would she have wanted a warning about how it all turned out? Would she have made different choices had she known?

By the time she reached the edge of campus and the path that wound past the shoreline studded with colorful boulders, her cheeks were wind whipped and her nose was numb. The sky was awash in pink and orange, throwing golden light like glitter across the ice-slicked rocks. They glowed and sparkled like hot, molten glass, dazzling in the first rays of the morning sun. Harper was mesmerized. She wandered to a bench and sat facing the lake, watching the sun come up, and thinking about her mom along the same path, on the same bench, waiting for Harper's decision, her enthusiasm unflappable even in the face of terminal illness.

"Now what?" Harper asked herself aloud, the wind whipping away her words. Tears pricked at the corner of her eyes and she ran a mittened hand over her cheek. She tried to soul search her way to an answer about the pregnancy. She had heard that some women "just knew" in the days before they took a positive test, their innate, maternal, gut instinct confirming the truth before doctors or science even had reason to suspect. But if this sixth sense was supposed to feel like anything other than a cold, hard pit in the bottom of one's stomach, Harper didn't have it.

She looked out at the lake where stormy gray whitecaps churned three hundred yards off shore where the ice had not formed. The space in between was a barren, pock-marked, wind-swept moonscape of ice that red signs staked every fifty meters along the path warned was "volatile." The ice along shore routinely heaved and buckled, and even when the ice was good, conditions could change rapidly. As she sat there looking over it, Harper heard the great sheets groaning and grinding against each other. The lake wrestled with itself. Caught in between two seasons. Fighting against its very nature, its own essence. Harper had seen the signs a hundred times as a student, but staring at the boundary line where the waves crashed up and over the thin shelf of ice, she understood its meaning, felt it even, for the first time.

Her cell phone chimed, and her heartbeat stumbled. She pulled off a mitten and dug in her coat pocket, hand falling on the cool plastic case just as a second notification vibrated beneath her fingers. Harper glanced at the digital clock displayed on the lock screen above her two waiting text messages.

7:58.

Below that–

Andrea Thompson: Seriously? You're really going to leave us all hanging this morning? Candace is looking for you!

Then–

Candace: Let me know when you have them.

Harper clutched her phone in both hands, dropped her elbows onto her knees, and hung her head, feeling suddenly sick to her stomach. She was right not to wait at the office where everyone could watch, waiting for any indication: a raised eyebrow, a slumped shoulder, a hint of a smile. As it was, she would have an audience from the moment she stepped off the elevator. At least this way, regardless of the result, she would have a chance to practice her composure first.

Her phone flashed to 8:00, but no notification arrived. She stared at the phone screen, simultaneously willing the email to appear and dreading its arrival. She jumped as it pulsed in her hands.

Bryan: ??? The suspense is killing me!

Harper's hands shook as she typed. *Me too!* The flashing ellipses appeared immediately below her reply.

Bryan: Nothing?

Harper: Not yet!

She kicked at the snow beneath the bench as the minutes ticked by. 8:05. 8:10. She logged into her online account to make sure she hadn't missed it. Nothing. She refreshed her inbox again, then checked the spam folder. Still, the scores did not arrive. 8:15. 8:20. The delay was not unprecedented. Despite all the scores releasing at the same time, the online forums were full of stories from people who waited, sometimes even hours, for their report to show up. There was nothing to do but wait it out. But with each passing minute, the sense of dread in Harper grew. It was irrational, but she couldn't help but feel like good news traveled fast and should have arrived by now. The more time that passed, the more convinced she was that she had inexplicably flopped. By 8:35, she decided that, scores or no scores, she was freezing and could only put off the office for so long. She pushed herself from the bench with a resigned sigh and walked back into the heart of campus.

She was just through the Weber Arch when her phone pinged again, and Harper startled so badly that she nearly fumbled it into the snow. She closed her eyes, took a deep breath, and looked down at the screen.

Andrea Thompson: Where are you??? Tate=164!

Harper stared at the message equal parts relieved that the number wasn't higher and sick to her stomach at the possibility she underperformed at the same level that Tate had exceeded expectations.

On my way, she typed with trembling hands, tucking her phone back into her pocket before stuffing her frozen fingers back into her mittens. The phone pinged again, but Harper ignored Andrea's reply, unwilling to expose her fingers to the cold now that warmth and feeling were spreading back through them. Only when she was back in the car, the heater blowing on her face and toes and her GPS showing thirty-five minutes to the office, did she pull the phone from her pocket to send her ETA.

The message was not from Andrea.

One new email waited in her inbox.

Harper's stomach lurched, and she threw open the driver's side door. A blast of cold air filled the car as she dry-heaved into the slush along the curb. She took a few gulps of cold air, trying to calm her racing heart, before pulling herself back into the driver's seat and willing her thumb to press the tiny banner on the home screen. The email opened, a blue hyperlink button in the center of the screen prompting Harper to retrieve her results from the online database. She swiped out of her inbox and opened her message thread with Bryan.

Harper: They're here!

It took less than a minute, but it felt like a frustratingly long time before his reply arrived.

Bryan: And???????????

Harper: Haven't looked yet.

Her phone rang instantly. "Hello," she answered weakly.

"Harper," Bryan's voice floated through the car's speakers, gentle and laced with concern. "What's the matter? What are you waiting for?"

Harper took a shaky breath. "Tate got a 164."

"So what?" Bryan scoffed automatically. "You beat it."

"What if I didn't?"

"I 100% believe you did," insisted Bryan.

Harper pinched the bridge of her nose, both comforted and frustrated by her husband's blind assurance. "Why?" she prodded. "How?"

Bryan's voice was warm and even on the line. "Because there's nothing and no one I believe in more in this world than you, Harper. Trust me, open the email."

She suddenly wished she was back at home on the couch, with a blanket in her lap and Bryan's arm over her shoulders. It was foolish that she had all but run away, and she felt guilty that they weren't sharing this moment together in person. It was, after all, not only her life that was about to change.

"Bryan." Her voice cracked. "I'm late."

"It doesn't matter," he insisted. "You already knew that they might not show up right at 8:00…"

"No," Harper interrupted. "Not the scores. Me. *I'm* late." A weighty and expectant silence stretched between them, interrupted only by the heartbeat thundering in Harper's ears.

"One thing at a time," Bryan said finally. His voice was even and reassuring.

Harper swallowed hard. Now that she'd brought it up, it seemed too significant to just brush aside, but there was nothing to gain by pressing the issue either. She swiped back to her inbox and stared at the blue link.

"Ok," she said, more confidently than she felt. "I'm ready. Three…two…" Her thumb brushed the screen, launching a new window which remained empty for a heart-stopping moment before loading her score and percentile rank in bold, black numerals.

175.

99th percentile.

Just five points away from a perfect score.

Her breath caught before a cry burst from her, part laughter, part sob. She rested her head on the steering wheel and cried tears of joy and relief and, if she was honest, tears of lingering apprehension. A whole minute passed before she remembered Bryan was still on the line.

"Babe? Are you still there?" She sniffled hard and thought she heard Bryan do the same.

"Was I right, or was I right?"

Harper wished she could jump into his arms. "You were right."

"Harper," he said, and this time, the emotional hitch in his voice was clear. "You're going to be a lawyer."

Harper laughed, pure joy and disbelief. "I'm going to be a lawyer," she repeated, relishing how the words sounded. She leaned back in her seat and closed her eyes, letting her heart rate relax and the thrill of success wash over her.

Only later, after she ended the phone call and merged back onto Lake Shore Drive heading toward the office, did she wonder if, despite the nerves and anxiety that came with the unknowing, she would feel just as euphoric to learn she would be a mother.

Chapter 18

"You're not pregnant," Dr. Bluffton announced with, what sounded to Harper like, a well-rehearsed balance of sympathy and pragmatism. She clicked out of the test results displayed on the computer screen. "I'm sorry," she added quietly. She folded her hands on her desk, watching Harper through her thick-framed, blue reading glasses.

Harper wondered how many women had sat in this exact chair and broken down at the same news. She could see that Dr. Bluffton was analyzing, waiting to console or calm as required by Harper's reaction. Thus, she felt more than a little guilty that her feelings in that moment were detached acceptance and a hint of relief.

It was for this very reason that Harper had considered not coming to the clinic for confirmation. There were plenty of places around the city where relief was the common, even expected, reaction to a negative test. She could have dropped in at any of them without a question or a second look. But somewhere in between accepting the congratulations of every paralegal and associate on the twenty-eighth floor that morning and leaving Candace Walsh's office that afternoon, she decided that the most mature and measured thing to do was to face the outcome like an adult, in her own doctor's office. She had already played her brooding and avoidant card for the day.

Admittedly, the meeting with Candace had given her confidence, if not about impending motherhood, then at least about her overall competence. She left the office with Candace's assurance that she would personally see to it that the scholarship committee compare the applications with all due haste, given that admission to a program was now a mere formality. Harper briefly wondered aloud if Lyle wouldn't be making the same case for Tate, considering he had unexpectedly over-performed.

Candace waved dismissively. "Don't worry about Lyle Pickett or Tate Bishop," she insisted. "You're far and away the favorite to win. We'd have to put down a mutiny among the paralegals and half the junior partners if you didn't."

Despite her effort at professional humility, Harper beamed, which Candace encouraged further by requesting she attend the upcoming meeting regarding the Archer's divorce settlement. "As an extra set of eyes and ears," Candace offered. "We may need to get creative, and you were the one who figured out that Lakeview Fertility Clinic might be worth something."

Harper swallowed hard at the mention of the clinic, but she floated from the office feeling more assured than she had in weeks.

Now, sitting in Dr. Bluffton's office, Harper recognized that feeling as a different kind of relief. The relief at seeing her LSAT score, accepting Candace's congratulations, and being named the clear favorite over Tate had radiated through her; warmed her heart. It was a relief that glowed from within, flushing her cheeks with pride and shining in her eyes. Relief that she had achieved something. Relief that she made it. Relief that she was, in fact, doing the very thing she had set out to do.

Hours later, and here she was relieved again, not because things had finally worked out, but because they hadn't. The drugs had failed. The plan hadn't worked. The desired outcome was still, at least, a cycle away. There was no warmth or pride, just a cold detachment, an acknowledgement that this was easier. Better. The feeling was short-lived, quickly giving way to shame, then dread, then heartbreak as she thought of taking the news home to Bryan, letting him know that, yet again, it hadn't happened. Relieved or not, it was impossible not to feel like she failed him. She sighed and looked down at her hands, emotions churning in her stomach.

"Your disappointment is understandable," Dr. Bluffton said gently. "I'm sure it feels like you'll be starting over from square one."

"Uh huh," Harper murmured, careful not to reveal too much of her inner turmoil.

Dr. Bluffton leaned back in her chair and removed her glasses. "If you want the truth, it would have been remarkable if this first cycle had proven successful. I think we have a much better chance if we use medically assisted conception. IVF gives us the most control and the highest success rates, but even an IUI would allow us to tip the scales in your favor a bit."

"IUI?" Harper asked, vaguely remembering the acronym from the informational packet she'd been given after her last appointment.

"Intrauterine insemination," Dr. Bluffton clarified. "People sometimes sophomorically refer to it as the turkey baster method. It's generally a less expensive and less invasive option that many couples choose before resorting to IVF. Of course, nothing has to be decided today." She rolled her chair out from behind her desk and toward a framed diagram on the wall.

"The earliest we'd start thinking about an IUI is the start of your next cycle," she continued, pointing to the start of the illustrated timeline in the frame. "We've already established that is late. So, either we wait for nature to take its course, or we jump start things for you and then count from that point on." She moved her finger along the line. "There are a few ultrasounds to make sure things are progressing as they should be. A few pills to encourage ovulation. And then, provided everything looks right, you and Bryan come in on day 15, and we inseminate."

She turned and faced Harper. "You're an obvious candidate, and you're essentially able to start as soon as you're ready, so it's a very viable next step." She rolled the chair back behind the desk. "IVF is obviously a bit more involved," she said. "I'd want to start with some additional testing to look at hormone levels, and then we'd need to time things out to plan an egg retrieval. If it's something you're thinking about, retrieving eggs now, while you're younger, is better than, say, pushing it out two or three years."

Something in her tone caught Harper's attention, and she looked up from her hands and met the doctor's eyes. "I only mention it," Dr. Bluffton continued with professional nonchalance, "because I know you've been studying for your LSAT, and if you're thinking about waiting until after law school, your window will have shrunk by a few years. I make a point to never pressure a patient over their biological clock, but I will always counsel that it is a real factor. Of course, we can freeze eggs and embryos as well, which buys you some time." She leaned back in the chair. "You wouldn't be the first woman to schedule her procedures around finals or board exams."

She smiled collegially, and Harper wondered if perhaps the doctor was speaking from her own experience. She glanced around the office, but there was no evidence of children or a family photo. Dr. Bluffton cleared her throat, turning Harper's attention back to the conversation.

"Thank you," Harper said, pushing her chair back from the desk. "This is a lot to think about."

"If you decide to move forward," Dr. Bluffton continued, "we can get tests or prescriptions set up quickly. Just let us know how and when you want to proceed." She stepped around the desk and extended a hand. "Don't lose heart," she encouraged, clasping both of her hands around Harper's.

"Ok," Harper agreed, unwilling to commit to a more definitive response. Her head was swimming with timelines and the insinuation of opportunity slipping away. She had come to the clinic for clarity, a simple yes or no; she was leaving with an answer that was still paved with uncertainty. "I appreciate your fitting me in this evening."

Dr. Bluffton smiled and gestured toward the door. "Of course. Feel free to call with any questions; it can be a lot to process."

That, Harper thought, stepping into the hallway and following the signs back toward the lobby, was a laughable understatement.

•   •   •

Twenty minutes later, the first thing Harper noticed coming up the stairs to the apartment was the smell. The rich scent of aromatic spices and chili peppers hovered in the hallway, making Harper's mouth water before she even made it through the front door.

"What smells amazing?" she asked as she stepped into the apartment and slid out of her coat. The table was set, and candles were lit around the room, twining hints of evergreen and eucalyptus through the savory aromas of meat and herbs. "Did you cook?"

Bryan looked up from the couch. "Welcome home," he replied with a smile, jumping up and crossing the room to meet her in the entryway with an enthusiastic kiss. "No, I didn't cook," he said, pulling back with a laugh. "But yes, that smell is dinner." He leaned in to kiss her again. "I thought you would want something special to celebrate." He released her from his embrace, stepped to the refrigerator, pulled out two bottles, and set them on the counter side by side. One was champagne. The other, sparkling grape juice.

"I wasn't sure which one." His eyes searched Harper's for an inkling of clarity. He shrugged. "You said you were late."

Harper's heart lurched, and she moved to Bryan, wrapping her arms around his waist and tucking her head into his chest. "We're not pregnant," she murmured into the softness of his sweatshirt pressed against her cheek. "I stopped at the clinic on the way home to have them run the test."

Bryan stiffened, his arms tightening the embrace ever so slightly. Then the moment passed, and he sighed, and Harper felt him relax into her again.

"Ok," he said, kissing the top of her head.

"Ok?" she asked, glancing up at him.

He shrugged, and Harper watched the tension in his shoulders as they rose and fell. "One thing at a time."

Harper nuzzled against him once more. "One thing at a time," she agreed, resisting the temptation to mention the rest of her conversation with Dr. Bluffton. "Can we start with whatever the 'one thing' is that's responsible for that smell?"

"Absolutely," Bryan smiled. He turned and opened the oven where three silver pans wrapped in aluminum foil were being kept warm. "I didn't know what exactly the occasion called for. You're the first wife I've had who scored a 175 on her LSAT." He said it teasingly, but the grin on his face was all adoration and pride, and Harper blushed under his gaze. "Lucky for us, I know where to find the best food in Chicago." He donned a pair of oven mitts. "One gourmet celebration dinner, courtesy of Indie Lime."

Harper froze as Bryan removed the foil, revealing a steaming heap of crawfish, a rich, braised beef stew, and pasteles wrapped and steamed in plantain leaves. "Maggie did this for us?" she asked quietly, feeling the distance stretching like a gulf between her and her best friend. "Did you see her?"

"I didn't have the chance," Bryan admitted. "She was back in the kitchen." A shadow flickered over his expression, and Harper knew instantly he was keeping something from her.

"What?" she insisted.

Bryan took off his glasses and rubbed the bridge of his nose. "I don't know. Maybe it's nothing."

"Tell me."

Bryan sighed. "It's just, when I talked to Seth and asked if he thought Maggie would do me an enormous favor by making the meal, he told me it was no big deal; I should just call it in as takeout."

"Takeout?" Harper said, instantly confused. "Indie Lime is a gourmet restaurant. Maggie's not serving takeout."

"Except she is," Bryan went on. "When I got there tonight, the dining room was all but empty. The vibe was completely off, and there's a new website with a carryout menu and a link to DoorDash."

Harper folded her arms and leaned against the counter, pondering the possibility that the restaurant had gone mainstream casual in just two months. She immediately regretted that, even in the face of their disagreement, she had not done more to support the early days of the business. It might not have been their every night kind of fare, but it was her job to cheerlead, and she had let Maggie down. Again.

"They could have been booked with later reservations," she suggested, trying to convince herself as much as Bryan.

"Maybe," said Bryan. "But it didn't feel that way. The host seemed like he was grateful to see even a takeout order walk through the door."

Harper's curiosity prickled uncomfortably. "Did you ask Seth about it?"

Bryan shook his head. "Not yet. He didn't seem plussed when he mentioned it, so maybe it's nothing. It just wasn't what I was expecting."

"Yeah," Harper agreed, distracted. "Maybe."

They filled plates and moved to the candlelit table. Bryan raised his champagne flute.

"To my incredible wife, who is going to be an incredible lawyer. Cheers to you, Babe."

Harper smiled, touching her glass to Bryan's. "Thank you." She sipped the champagne, bubbles tickling her nose and bursting brightly on her tongue, and pushed from her mind any lingering guilt over the bottle of sparkling grape juice still sweating on the counter.

They dug into the meal, savoring the magic that was Maggie's cooking. Despite the obvious change in business model, the food was, undeniably, still five-star quality. Maggie, Harper knew, wouldn't be able to do it any other way. Which is why, for as good as it was, and as comfortable as it was to sit in her own kitchen instead of trekking across town for a dinner reservation, Harper couldn't brush off the feeling that it wasn't right. Indie Lime was exotic rum and vibrant energy and the rattle and clatter behind a bar lit in a dozen shades of green. It was not aluminum pans topped in foil waiting in plastic carryout bags. She had listened to Maggie talk about owning her own restaurant since they were kids, and she could say with all certainty that DoorDash wasn't the dream.

She stabbed another piece of braised beef, so tender that it immediately fell apart on the fork, and took small comfort in the fact that whatever was going on behind the scenes, Maggie was still cooking with her whole heart. The food was divine.

"You're thinking pretty hard over there," said Bryan, and Harper realized she had paused mid-thought, her fork suspended halfway between her mouth and the plate, her eyes unfocused as they stared into the flickering candle flame. Her gaze slid to his, candlelight dancing as flecks of gold glitter in his green eyes.

"Sorry," Harper chuckled, taking another sip of champagne. "How was work?"

Bryan shrugged. "Fine. The usual. Uneventful. We don't need to talk about my day. I want to hear about yours. Tell me what happened when you got to the office this morning."

Harper pushed aside her nagging worry over Maggie and breathed a contented sigh. "It was really amazing," she admitted, unable to keep the smile from her lips. She launched into a play-by-play of her return to the firm: her text to Andrea Thompson on the way in, assuring her that the legend of the flashcards remained intact; sending Greta her score and waiting for Candace's reaction; the afternoon meeting and Candace's implied assurances. "This could really happen," she said, breathless with both disbelief and excitement.

"It *is* happening. So, how does it feel?" Bryan leaned back in his chair and sipped his champagne.

Harper considered. It was impossible to not feel both the weight of expectation and the thrill of what came next. It felt like it had at twenty-two, daunting and exciting, overwhelming and exhilarating. The day had been a rollercoaster, but the adrenaline that coursed through her when she thought about the opportunity before her was intoxicating.

"It feels great," she admitted, finishing the final bite of stewed beef. "I've been waiting for it a long time."

Bryan smiled. "I'm glad." He pushed himself up from the table, collected both plates, and paused to lean in for a kiss. "I'm really, really proud of you," he said quietly.

Harper's throat tightened. "Thank you," she whispered, suddenly emotional. "I love you." A tear slipped down her cheek.

"Hey." Bryan said, setting the plates back on the table and dropping to a knee. "What's wrong?"

"Nothing," Harper sniffed, wiping quickly at her eyes. "It's just been a lot today."

Bryan reached for her hand. "So, these are *happy* tears?"

Harper laughed through a sniffle. "Kind of."

"Kind of?" Bryan looked between Harper and the bottle of grape juice, now warm, on the counter.

"Yeah," Harper confirmed, feeling the tears start fresh again. It felt like days ago that she had driven to Northwestern, watched the sunrise over the lake. She had all the results and perspective now that she hadn't had then. Some things had worked out, and at the same time, others hadn't. There were questions still waiting to be answered. "Dr. Bluffton wants us to talk about IUI or IVF," she said, voice unsteady.

Bryan's brow furrowed, and his lips pulled into a tight line. Harper saw the sadness in his eyes. "I doubt she said it had to be tonight," he finally offered.

Harper took a steadying breath. "You're right," she admitted.

Bryan brought her hand to his mouth and kissed her knuckles.

"Then it can wait," he said. "We've waited months already. Tonight won't be the difference maker."

Harper nodded, brushing away the tear streaks.

"Ok," Bryan gave her a small smile. "I'm going to clean up the kitchen. Why don't you go get yourself cozy, unless you had intentions of going out and getting crazy to celebrate?"

Harper managed to chuckle. "No, cozy is good."

"Good," Bryan stood up, taking both Harper's hands in his own and helping her to her feet. He kissed her lightly before reaching for the plates and returning to the kitchen. Harper's cell phone chimed from the front pocket of her bag, and she retrieved it before retreating to the bedroom. She sat on the edge of the bed before glancing down to read.

Tate: Congratulations...

Harper stared for a full minute, wondering at the meaning of the ellipses, waiting for a follow-up text that never arrived. In some ways, it felt fitting. Everything about their friendship had been left completely hanging. She had assumed Tate would learn of her score through the same inter-office grapevine that she had learned his. However, she was slightly ashamed that he'd been a big enough person to reach out while she continued to dwell on how much remained changed between them.

Thanks, she replied. *You too.*

She hesitated another moment, waiting for the read receipt below the message. A check mark appeared, but Tate did not reply.

Harper closed out the thread, nearly tossing her phone to the side absentmindedly, but Maggie's name at the bottom of the screen caught her eye. She clicked into the text thread, a mostly unanswered string of Harper's attempts to reach out. She thought about Maggie, Indie Lime, and the fact they had drifted so far apart she didn't even know what was happening with the restaurant anymore. Her heart suddenly ached for her best friend. Maggie, more than anyone, would have been the person who could have steadied Harper through the day. The LSAT. The clinic. She didn't need to have babies together. She wanted to do life together again.

She opened the thread and tapped out the message.

Harper: I'm still sorry. You can still be angry. But thank you for dinner, and if you need anything, I'm always here.

She set the phone on her dresser, changed into her favorite yoga pants and faded Northwestern sweatshirt, pulled her hair into a ponytail, and washed her face. Mascara pooled in raccoon patches under her eyes, and she sighed in exasperation. As she opened the bottom drawer and reached for a cotton ball, her gaze fell onto the open box of pregnancy tests, and her hand faltered. Just looking at them made her tired. The day of her biggest triumph marked by yet another failure. No, not a failure, she thought. It wasn't her fault, nor could she have tried harder. Still, her sudden success and her ongoing frustration could not have been more at odds with each other.

She sighed and kicked the drawer closed, settling for a Kleenex to remove the offending makeup smudges.

Back in the living room minutes later, she was relieved to find the bottle of sparkling grape juice had disappeared. Bryan was waiting for her on the couch, champagne flutes refilled, and she settled in next to him, pushing the pregnancy test as far from her mind as she could. Only later, when she returned to the kitchen to set the coffeemaker before bed, did she realize Bryan had, mercifully, thrown away the calendar on the refrigerator door as well.

Chapter 19

January turned to February, and though winter dragged on in a monotonous series of perpetual slush puddles and heavy, gray skies, Harper couldn't help but feel like everything else in her life was careening toward an inevitable and dramatic inflection point. With her scores reported and her applications submitted, there was very little to do but wait for a decision on her admission; and though Candace had assured her that the scholarship was essentially a foregone conclusion, the committee had announced a final decision would not be made until acceptance letters were in hand. Thus, all Harper could do was wait and watch the snow drifting and swirling out her office window as she powered through endless mountains of work.

And while she waited, she worried. Worried that it would somehow still fall apart. Worried that, once in school, she wouldn't be able to hack it with her younger, more academically gifted classmates. Worried that, at some point, having to face the question of babies and family would push her and Bryan apart.

It was that last worry that made Harper hesitate when Bryan suggested he come with her to the follow-up appointment at the clinic. Managing her appointments alone felt like the one shred of personal control she had left in a process that often seemed like it was happening *to* her. So much of trying and hoping and testing and waiting felt more akin to fate than medical science, and to this point, leaving things to fate had worked. Kind of.

When Bryan reminded her of the HSG appointment, Harper bristled defensively. But before she could switch into argumentative lawyer mode, Bryan dropped down on the end of the bed, head in his hands, palms pressed to his eyes, holding back tears.

The response was so unexpected that Harper stopped, mid-objection, hand frozen in an ambiguous gesture she was about to use to emphasize her point.

"Babe?" she asked gently, cautiously. She perched on the edge of the bed next to him.

Bryan looked sideways at her, his eyes shining. "I would never minimize what you have to deal with as the woman in our situation," he said quietly. "But this is not something that's only happening to you. This is *our* family. It's my future too."

Harper felt a response bubble inside her, but she swallowed it down, laying a hand on Bryan's back as he continued.

"You don't know what it feels like to be the one not there. Knowing you suffered alone when I could have been there for comfort. Knowing you received bad news alone when I could have been there to hold your hand. If you think you've made it easier on me by shielding me from it, you haven't. It kills me to sit back passively, waiting for bad things to happen to you."

Harper's throat tightened. A full minute passed before she could speak. "I'm so sorry," she said, finally. "I didn't mean to cut you out."

"I know," Bryan said, allowing Harper to pull him into her shoulder.

Harper thought about how many times Bryan had held her–after negative tests, after months they'd not needed a test at all, after appointments and procedures had broken her down. He had always been stoic in her moment of need, which was clearly not without its own emotional toll.

"You don't always have to be the bearer of bad news," he continued. "And I never want you to feel like you're doing this alone."

"That's not how I feel," assured Harper quickly.

Bryan sat up and took both of Harper's hands in his own. "You're one of the smartest people I know, Harper. This isn't about me being there to ask the right questions or walk you through it. But I can't help but feel like we're getting to the end of this, and I've somehow been both in the middle of it and barely a part of it."

Harper's stomach dropped. "We've already said that law school doesn't have to mean letting go of a family," she offered.

"It doesn't have to, but it might," Bryan interjected. "And it's not just law school. We're down to just a couple of options, options I'm not even sure we want to pursue. But at the very least, I want to be a part of the conversation."

Harper leaned into his shoulder. "We'll go together."

Which is how she arrived at this moment, watching her husband, who had heard so much about her doctor, shake the hand of her doctor, who had heard so much about her husband.

"Bryan!" Dr. Bluffton exclaimed, coming into the room and immediately extending her hand in greeting. "I'm Amy Bluffton. It's wonderful to meet you. And it's always good to see you, Harper," she added, gesturing toward a trio of chairs in the corner of her office.

It was hard not to notice how different it felt with Bryan there. He reached for her hand, instantly steadying her nerves as they took chairs side by side.

Dr. Bluffton looked between them. "I'm sure you've got questions," she started, "and, as Harper knows, my goal is always to be as upfront and straightforward as possible. So, should we jump right in?"

Harper gave Bryan's hand a reassuring squeeze.

"Ok," Bryan said, hand flexing around Harper's in return. "Harper said you'd like us to consider either IUI and IVF, so can you start with walking us through both processes?"

Dr. Bluffton nodded as she launched into a detailed explanation of the steps and timelines of both procedures. Harper paid partial attention, having already been walked through the same speech at her last appointment. She had a hard time believing Bryan actually needed as much of an explanation as he was getting. He had read the pamphlets before the appointment, and she would be shocked if he hadn't also done a cursory Google search on his own. But Harper supposed he wanted to appear an engaged and thoughtful partner, the same way that Dr. Bluffton clearly wanted to be seen as a knowledgeable and thorough physician.

"And we've already ruled out surgery on the blocked fallopian tube, right?" Bryan asked, surprising Harper. It was never an option they had discussed at length, nor one that Harper had given much consideration.

"That's right," Dr. Bluffton confirmed. "It's an invasive procedure with limited upside."

"Everything feels invasive," Bryan admitted.

Harper had to agree.

"It's reasonable to feel that way," Dr. Bluffton assured them. "It's obviously a more aggressive approach. But, also one over which you have a great deal of control. We can time your cycles, pick your preferred windows for conception. Work around law school a bit if needed?" she added, gaze shifting to Harper.

Harper gave a nervous laugh. "That'd be a definite plus."

Dr. Bluffton smiled. "Congratulations." She reached for her legal pad on the table between them and scratched a few notes. "I'm assuming that having a baby in the first few months of law school would be less than ideal?"

Harper looked at Bryan, and they both confirmed with a nod.

Dr. Bluffton made another note on her pad. "So, we're a little early in talking about cycles now. It would, however, be completely reasonable to think about an egg retrieval later this spring to prepare for implantation in early fall. That'd be the IVF route. Given that IUI doesn't require retrieval first, we could start monitoring hormones and drugs, say, late summer. In either case, we'd be aiming to line up 40 weeks with your first summer break window."

Harper looked over at Bryan. A deep vee furrowed between his green eyes. "What are the odds?"

"IVF? First attempt, around twenty-five percent," said Dr. Bluffton. "There are a number of factors we can't always anticipate. If we do multiple cycles, the total rate of success typically goes up. By a third cycle, for example, the success rate is over fifty percent."

The numbers did not immediately inspire optimism in Harper, and the idea that the more she failed the better her odds became did little to induce her confidence. From the way the vee deepened on Bryan's forehead, she could guess at his own trepidations.

"IUI?" he asked.

"Ten to fifteen percent," Dr. Bluffton replied, clicking her pen against the pad. "About the same chance as natural conception in couples with average fertility." Bryan nodded slowly. "It's a lot to think about," Dr. Bluffton admitted, "but you have a little time to decide." She shifted her attention to Harper again. "In the meantime, we'll keep you on birth control to regulate your cycle and hormones. That way, we'll be able to jump in whenever you decide you're ready to go."

It was, Harper realized, the doctor's foregone conclusion that they would decide at some point they were ready.

"Thank you," Bryan said, his tone clearly indicating he had heard enough. "This has been really informative."

"Like I've told Harper," Dr Bluffton said, setting her legal pad on the side table as she pushed herself from the chair. "If you have any other questions, please don't hesitate to reach out. I know it can be a lot to navigate, but the important thing to remember is that you still have options and a path forward."

Bryan looked at Harper with a forced smile. "That's good to hear," he said, gently placing a hand on the small of her back. "We'll be sure to reach out."

Dr. Bluffton guided them to the office door and held it open. "Good to see you both. Take good care," she added as they stepped into the hallway. The door closed behind them, and they looked at each other a moment before Bryan pulled Harper into a hug.

"Are you ok?" Bryan asked, resting his chin on Harper's head. "You didn't say much."

Harper sighed. "I didn't know what to say," she admitted. "We both know what the procedures are. I just don't know what to ask or what I'd need to hear to help me know what we should do."

Bryan kissed the top of her head. "Me either," he admitted. "I don't want to put you through either one."

Harper looked up at him, surprised. "What?"

He shrugged with a sigh. "I mean, I get the science; I respect the science. If there was a guarantee, I'd feel better about subjecting you to more drugs and injections and procedures. I just…" he hesitated. "I just can't imagine asking you to put yourself through it, especially in school. But if it's something you feel strongly about, then we'll talk about it." His eyes met hers, but Harper couldn't hold his gaze. She was far from enthusiastic about the idea, but refusing treatment reduced their odds dramatically and, perhaps, permanently.

"I don't know," she murmured. "We've already gone this far."

"We don't have to decide now," Bryan said, keeping an arm around her shoulders as they made their way back toward the lobby. He threw a cursory glance at the wall of success stories as they stepped back through the door, passed the front desk, and headed toward the elevator bank.

The lobby was glass, and the windows were plastered with thick, heavy snowflakes that had started falling during the appointment. They drifted and swirled in the golden cones of the streetlights, sparkling in the blue glow of the February twilight.

"I'll go get the car," Bryan offered, pulling on his stocking cap. "Be right back." He dashed out the door, leaving Harper in the lobby with her thoughts.

The appointment had been neither surprising nor exactly as she would have expected, in part because she had not known what to expect. Despite having danced around the complications of law school and a baby and worrying the two might be incompatible, she had never come close, not really, to saying she was ready to give up the idea of one for the other, especially when there were options still on the table. She'd always kicked the can down the road. But with Bryan's one admission, that he was undecided and, perhaps, ready to say enough, she realized that road was rapidly approaching a dead end. The thought quickened her pulse, and a flush rose to her cheeks.

She glanced around the lobby, finding a set of restroom doors in the corner. Inside, she splashed cool water on her face, gripped the edges of the sink, and stared into the mirror. She had wished for a baby and dreamed of law school, and now one was in reach while the other was slipping away. Was Bryan really willing to stop trying? Was she? Was it over? Did she hope it was?

Hope was a funny thing. It ebbed and flowed. Drove some people to fits of passion and others to their knees in prayer. Hope was fickle and fleeting–and it was all she had. Hope that whatever came to pass was enough and that she would find her peace with whatever else was let go along the way.

She dried her hands and was about to return to the lobby when she heard a sniffling from the handicap stall behind her. Harper froze, turning to the bank of stall doors, leaning down far enough to spy a pair of brown leather boots. She listened for a moment, the only sounds a vent humming in the ceiling and the quiet, uneven inhalations of someone trying to regain her composure. Harper backed quietly toward the exit, but before she could reach it, the doors on the handicap stall swung open, and a woman–tall, blonde, in a beautiful, burgundy peacoat and cashmere scarf–stepped toward the counter. Harper caught her eye in the mirror, immediately envying that despite her tears, the woman's makeup somehow still looked impeccable.

"Hi," the woman said weakly.

"Hi," Harper replied hesitantly. She had no desire to become a Kara Grobbert type, oversharing with a woman she'd never met, but she didn't feel compelled to walk away either.

"Sorry," the woman said, dabbing demurely at the corners of her eyes.

"No, no," Harper assured her quickly. "It's fine. Are you ok?" She immediately regretted how stupid the question sounded. The woman was crying in a public restroom. She was obviously not ok.

"Ugh," the woman sighed heavily. "No," she admitted. "Bad news."

"I'm sorry," Harper replied automatically.

The corner of the woman's mouth twitched. "You're just the innocent bystander in the bathroom. Definitely not your fault," she said. "Not anyone's fault, really. Unless you want to blame my husband." She added it under her breath almost inaudibly, and Harper's curiosity prickled. The woman turned to Harper, leaning a hip against the counter. "Have you ever just assumed your life was going to go one way, only to have it completely flipped on its head?"

"Yes," Harper responded honestly, wondering why she felt obliged to continue the conversation at all. "I just applied to law school at thirty-four years old."

The woman gave a small smile at Harper's candor. "That's amazing."

Harper shrugged. "It's complicated. My husband and I are in the middle of fertility treatments." It surprised her how easily the confession slipped out.

The other woman nodded slowly. "Lakeview? Dr. Bluffton?" she asked.

"Yeah."

"Me too. Or, at least, I was." The woman brushed her fingers through her hair.

Harper suddenly understood the tears in context. "Your husband's fault?" she asked, remembering the vague accusation.

"More or less. We're divorcing," she said bluntly. "Infertility is hell on a marriage. Miscarriages are worse. He can't do it anymore."

"I'm so sorry," Harper replied, uncertain what else there was to say.

The woman turned toward the mirror and raked her fingers through her blonde waves. "The thing is, it's not that I blame him. We've been through a lot. We're not partners anymore. We're barely friends. It's just, this is all there will be for me. He can go off, meet someone else. For me, I'm out of options." Her eyes welled with tears again, and she leaned over the sink, letting them fall into the marble bowl. "I'm not sure why I'm telling you any of this," she laughed weakly. "This place does things to people, I guess."

An uncomfortable realization came over Harper, her suspicion raising the hair on the back of her neck. The blood rushed behind her ears, and she knew she should choose her next words very carefully. The truth tumbled out before she could think better of it.

"You could sue for custody." Her stomach lurched at having said the words aloud, and the other woman looked up, surprised.

"There's no way he would ever let me keep the embryos we created together. We'd be in court for years."

"Yes," Harper agreed. "But there *is* legal precedent."

The woman's brow furrowed. "So, this is your soon-to-be-a-lawyer expert opinion?"

Harper wondered how to backpedal the conversation into safer territory. "Probably not," she tried. "Money's easier."

The woman laughed, hard and sharp. "How much money would it take to make you feel better about never having children?"

Harper's thoughts drifted uncomfortably to the scholarship.

The woman washed her hands. "Lawyers have equations they use. I'm sure you'll learn all about that in school." There was a tinge of bitterness in her tone that set Harper's nerves on edge.

"You should only give up the future you designed for something that is utterly life-changing," Harper replied, growing more certain by the moment that she should have left the conversation when she had the chance.

"Fair enough. A lot of zeros then."

Harper's cell phone chimed in her pocket, and she pulled it out and glanced at the screen.

Bryan: Where'd you go?

"My husband," Harper said, nodding to her phone before returning it to her pocket. "I hope everything works out for you…?" she hung on the last vowel, a question, an invitation to confirm what she was already certain of.

"Ainsley," the woman said, taking the cue and extending her hand.

Harper tried to keep her hand from trembling as she reached to accept the gesture. "Harper."

"Good luck in law school, Harper," Ainsley offered. She motioned them both toward the door. "And with Dr. Bluffton."

"Thanks," Harper said, feeling the heat rising up her neck. She held the door for Ainsley, who gave a quick glance and wave over her shoulder and headed toward the doors on the far side of the lobby.

Harper watched her go, heart racing, wondering how much Ainsley Archer would ask for when she found out that she had accidentally conspired with her mother-in-law's paralegal protégé.

Chapter 20

Harper didn't know how long it would take her bathroom run-in with Ainsley Archer to make it back to Candace, but she was certain that it would. So certain, in fact, that for a week after it happened, she seriously considered going to Candace and proactively admitting the mistake. Ethically, Harper was pretty sure she hadn't crossed a line. It wasn't as if she'd approached Ainsley on her own, nor had she pried for information. Ainsley had shared it all in a moment of perceived, anonymous confidence, and Harper had responded as a neutral third party. But she knew the optics were odd at best and suspicious at worse. And Harper worried that the meeting, no matter how coincidental, could have real implications on the settlement when someone realized that it wasn't just a random woman in the bathroom, but a paralegal at the firm representing her soon-to-be ex-husband, who suggested Ainsley hold out for much more than she was offered, or worse, sue.

That Candace had invited her to the settlement meeting only increased the likelihood that the connection was made. Had Harper been able to hole up in her office and work on her overload of cases, she was confident she could ride out the meeting in relative anonymity, far from suspicion or recognition. But that Candace had extended the invitation specifically as a show of confidence made declining it now feel impossible.

Which is why, when the time came, she handed off the patent law case research she was working on to a pair of brand-new paralegals in the cubicles, dropped a stack of filed motions on Andrea Thompson's desk, and headed for the elevators to meet Candace in the private conference room on the thirty-second floor. She had decided on a weak semblance of a plan. Play dumb. If Ainsley arrived and showed any sign of recognition, Harper would pretend to be slow on the uptake, genuinely surprised at the coincidence, and see how Ainsley presented it to the rest of the room. Ainsley had no reason to know or suspect that Harper knew or suspected any connection.

She approached me, Harper reminded herself as she jammed the elevator button. Let Ainsley explain the coincidence.

The doors slid open, and Tate Bishop pushed himself from the back wall of the elevator. He stopped at the sight of Harper waiting just beyond the doors.

"All right, Andrews? You look like you're about to vomit."

Damn, Harper thought, cursing her fair complexion for giving away the slightest hint of emotion.

"I'm fine," she answered in an overly cheerful tone that immediately betrayed her insincerity.

Tate chuckled. "For someone aspiring to be a lawyer, you need to learn to lie better."

Harper felt the flush flame in her cheeks.

"I don't suppose it has anything to do with your admissions decisions?" Tate asked, clearly fishing. He stepped out of the elevator, holding out his hand to prevent the door sliding closed behind him.

Harper rolled her eyes as she stepped past him. "It's been like three weeks, Tate. Why would I be expecting to hear anything already?"

Tate shrugged. "I don't know. Rolling admissions. I guess I figured if I was getting letters, you must be too. On the off chance you're waiting to hear from Loyola or the University of Illinois, my decisions arrived last night."

"Congratulations," said Harper, genuinely happy for him. "Those are good programs."

Tate stuffed his hands in his pockets. "Sure," he said. "But I didn't get in. I've just been up to tell Pickett. Needless to say, given the competition," he nodded at Harper, "he feels like he hitched his wagon to the wrong horse."

Harper felt two inches tall in her three-inch heels. "I'm sorry."

Tate shrugged again. "There will be others, maybe. Either way, it's yours to lose now. Don't screw it up." He moved his hand from the doorway. "Good luck with your meeting."

The doors closed, leaving Harper staring at her pale expression in the polished chrome; her pulse quickened as the elevator climbed. She knew they were at the end of the admission cycle and that decisions could, theoretically, come anytime, but she hadn't been ready for them now. Not when she was in the midst of figuring out how to stay in Candace's good graces while avoiding a potential future run-in with Ainsley Archer. She thought about Tate–swaggering, confident, brash–having to go face Pickett with the news of his rejection. It churned her stomach to imagine having to face Candace the same way.

She took a deep breath as the elevator pinged on the thirty-second floor, and she stepped out and turned toward Candace's office. The door to the conference room was closed, and the windows were frosted up six feet from the ground, but Harper already heard the murmuring of voices inside. Her stomach lurched at the prospect of walking through the door and revealing her real identity to Ainsley and her panel of lawyers. She would never be able to keep the recognition off her face. Tate had read her too easily. She wondered what Candace would do if she never showed up, if standing her up was worse than the scene she may be about to create. Candace had put all her faith in Harper. Was this how Harper was really about to repay her?

Harper's hand shook slightly as she reached for the door handle.

"There you are," Candace announced, coming through her office door. "Greta's been calling you for the last five minutes. Everyone's here, ready to start." Her eyes narrowed as she approached Harper. "What's wrong?"

It was the moment of truth. Harper's mouth went dry.

Heads. Tails. Heads. Tails.

She forced herself to swallow. "I need to talk to you," she managed, an urgent whisper.

"Fine, when the meeting is over…"

"Now," Harper insisted.

Candace raised an eyebrow, giving Harper a critical look before turning and gesturing back toward her office. Harper followed on her heels. The door had barely swung closed before Candace faced Harper, arms crossed. "What is it?" she demanded.

Harper's heart thundered in her ears. "I can't go into that meeting," she admitted. "You don't want me there."

Candace tipped her head in confusion. "Fine," she said shortly. "If you don't want to be there, I'm not going to force you. But seeing as you waited until the last possible moment to bail out, care to tell me why?"

"I met Ainsley Archer at the clinic," Harper confessed. "In the bathroom. I didn't know who she was, at least at first, and she didn't know me. But we talked. She mentioned the divorce."

"You did what!?" Candace caught herself mid-outburst and lowered her voice. "This lapse in judgment aside, I know you're not incompetent, so I'm guessing you put two and two together?" she speculated.

Harper nodded.

"But you didn't remove yourself from the conversation either?"

Harper shook her head, and Candace turned back toward her desk, taking a few paces into the office. "Why the hell were you back at the clinic, anyway?" she asked, spinning back toward Harper in confusion. "We already have what we need from their records."

Harper's mouth opened, but she could not answer.

Candace closed her eyes and composed her expression. "Here's what you're going to do. Go back to your office, close your door, and don't so much as step into the breakroom for a cup of coffee until Greta calls you to let you know they've left the building. You didn't know, so you didn't do anything wrong, but we don't need to introduce any variables at this point."

Harper's stomach tightened. "I told her there was precedent," she added quietly, "for custody. I told her she'd have a case if she wanted to press the issue."

Candace's eyes widened. "Damn it, Harper," she hissed. "Before or after you realized who she was?" She quickly held up a hand. "Never mind, don't answer that. It's better if I don't know." She squeezed her eyes closed and pinched the bridge of her nose. "Anything else I should know?"

Harper stared at her shoes, eyes tracing the lined pattern of the carpet. "No," she said.

"Good," Candace said curtly. "As long as you're staying out of the way this morning, you might as well start going through that court case argument by argument. Figure out an angle. I will not let you blow this up because you got loose lipped in the girls' bathroom."

The dig stung, but Harper nodded.

Greta wrapped her knuckles against the glass, and Harper jumped. She looked down the hallway, then back at Candace, tapping her watch.

"Go. Find me a fix," Candace said, striding to the door and holding it open for Harper. "Now."

Harper rushed from the office. As she stepped back onto the elevator a moment later, she realized that she'd been holding her breath the whole way. She blew it out dramatically as the doors slid closed, and the elevator descended, putting as much distance as possible between Harper and the Archers.

•   •   •

Minutes dragged to hours as Harper holed up in her office and waited for the all clear from Greta. At first, she did as Candace asked, pouring herself into the case law surrounding Illinois custody precedent, but forty pages into careful annotations about infertility, family planning, the value of a family, and the perceived importance of having children, she had to take a break. She could not remember a more personally taxing assignment. She pulled a granola bar from her bottom drawer, all the lunch she was currently cleared to enjoy, and pushed the legal tome aside, resting her elbows on the desk and staring into her blank computer screen.

She expected to feel foolish for not telling Candace sooner, but it wasn't embarrassment that bothered her now. It was a shame. Her choice to wait had been inherently selfish, made of self-preservation rather than what made sense for the case and the client. Candace could be tough, but had never been unfair, and Harper realized that her decision was wrapped up in personal emotion, the same feelings of failure and loss she felt every time she stepped into the clinic–like she screwed up and was going to come up short again. She was programmed to expect adversity. She lived with her feelings in self-preservation mode. It wasn't who she wanted to be.

She tossed the wrapper in the can under her desk and clicked her computer screen to life. Four windows of court records filled the screen, and she opened a new tab and logged onto her law school application database. Her fingernails drummed on her mouse while she waited for the page to load. Thus far, she had fought against the impulse to check the status of her applications. When the letters arrived, they arrived. But after Tate's revelation at the elevator, her curiosity nagged her. Status links appeared on her portal page, but apprehension stilled her hand. This was the last hurdle. The *real* last hurdle. Not Candace's opinion or the firm's scholarship, though they certainly meant something.

She hovered her mouse over the links, feeling her stress build as she hesitated. It was not so unlike waiting for two blue lines to appear on the bathroom counter. Her entire future, dreams, seconds away.

The phone on the corner of the desk rang, breaking the tension of the moment.

"Hello," she answered on the second ring.

"The Archers have left the building," Greta drawled dramatically. "You're in the clear."

Harper relaxed into her desk chair. "Thank you, Greta. Should I come up?"

"Decidedly not," said Greta. "She's in a mood."

"My fault," Harper admitted.

Greta huffed a tight laugh. "Don't give yourself so much credit."

"I…" Harper started, but there was a sharp click, and the line went dead.

Harper set the receiver back in its cradle, gave the links on her screen a final glance, then closed the tab and returned to the pages of court records.

The next time she looked up from her screen, daylight had faded from the narrow window in her office, and the lights of the city sparkled in the indigo dusk. She pushed *print* on her report, standing and stretching as the pages spooled from the printer behind her. She had not found a fix, or a loophole, or a sure-fire strategy, but she was certain that it was a comprehensive overview of every wrinkle and argument made over every nuance of fertility and impending parenthood. It left her completely spent. She picked the papers off the printer, still warm in her hand, and sighed. Somewhere in the pages and pages she read and the hours of testimony she reviewed, she came to a gut-wrenching realization.

This wasn't her.

This woman, the plaintiff, was so certain, so desperate, so persistent, so sure that it was her destiny to be a mother that she fought the would-be-father in court for years, all for the mere *chance* at a pregnancy and a child she knew she would carry, deliver, and raise alone. She was not only willing to do whatever it took medically, but legally, and arguably morally, as well.

That wasn't Harper. She could draw a line. Would draw a line. Had, if she was honest, already drawn a line she was afraid to admit.

She tucked the report in a cream, Horowitz, Walsh, and Pickett folder and left it neatly in the center of her desk. She would deliver it in the morning, accept whatever chastisement Candace doled out, and resolve to do better. This was the thing for which she was willing to do anything. This dream. This future.

Her cell phone rang as she zig-zagged through the cubicles toward the elevator. Bryan.

"I'm just about to get in the elevator," she answered. "I'll call you back in a minute."

"Ok," Bryan said, the syllables so heavy that Harper instantly knew something was wrong.

"What?" she asked, heart leaping to her throat, hand hovering just shy of the down arrow. "What happened?"

"Don't panic, but Seth called. Maggie needs you."

Fear pooled in Harper's stomach. "Bryan, tell me! What's wrong?"

"She's ok. I mean she's not hurt. But she's in trouble."

Harper's hand slammed repeatedly into the silver elevator button. "Where is she?" she demanded, chest tight.

"The restaurant," Bryan said. His voice was even but sad in a way that was already breaking Harper's heart. "They're shutting her down."

"Tell Seth I'm on my way." She pushed through the elevator doors before they fully opened. "I'll be there as soon as I can."

Chapter 21

The dining room at Indie Lime was dark when Harper arrived, the only light coming from the impressive, green glass fixture over the bar. Her hand hesitated briefly on the front door as she skidded to a stop and peered through the window at the lone figure hunched over on a bar stool, her back to the street. Harper's heart seized. She was both desperate to see her friend and already gutted that their reconciliation was happening on these terms. She looked up at the glowing neon over the window. It was peak dinner hour. Just a few months ago, she was here under such different circumstances. Was it really only a few months? It felt like a different lifetime.

The restaurant was eerily quiet as Harper stepped into the space, the squeaking of her rubber soles on the floor interrupting the heavy, contemplative silence. Maggie did not turn around, and Harper, feeling suddenly intrusive, stepped out of her boots and padded across the room, her wool socks a whisper on the polished hardwood.

"Maggie?" she said quietly, approaching the bar.

Maggie looked up, her eyes red rimmed. Her expression was unreadable as she lifted a sweating tumbler and took a sip of a nondescript, clear liquid. The ice cubes clinked against the crystal, and Harper tried not to jump to any conclusions. She set the glass back into the water circle it had left on the bar.

"Seth called you?" she asked, her voice hoarse.

"He called Bryan," Harper clarified.

Maggie nodded once, eyes falling back to the tumbler. She turned the glass slowly in her hands. "So, I guess you know then."

There was so much Harper didn't know, though the meaning of Maggie's words was clear. She pulled out a second barstool, pausing as if waiting for permission. When Maggie didn't object, Harper took a seat. "The investors are idiots," she offered.

Maggie laughed once. It came out hard and bitter. "If that's true," she lamented, "then they were idiots when they wrote me the check."

"That's not what I meant," Harper amended quickly.

"I know."

An expectant and uneasy stillness settled between them, as if each was waiting for the other to make the next conversational move.

"Did they say why?" Harper finally asked.

Maggie shrugged. "The numbers since the opening have dropped off, and they don't like the projections. Never mind that it takes most restaurants two years before they turn a profit, and it's part of the risk they took on." She sighed. "They disagreed. They think it's too unreliable, unsustainable. I didn't prove the concept. The restaurant landscape is constantly changing. Keeping staff is impossible. The initial buzz died too quickly. The menu wasn't as strong as it needed to be. We were only dragged along because of the holidays. It's all bullshit. They help mitigate those kinds of factors all the time." Maggie paused, sipping from her glass.

Harper wasn't sure how to respond. She had known since the night Bryan brought home the takeout containers that things at Indie Lime were obviously different, but she never imagined it was coming undone. She hadn't known because Maggie couldn't tell her. And Maggie couldn't tell her, because Harper had blown her response to the last life-altering piece of news Maggie had delivered. She was desperate not to make the same mistake again. She remained quiet, glancing around the room, remembering the magic of opening night. The buzz. The energy. The atmosphere. It was impossible to imagine it any other way. A wave of guilt rippled through Harper. She had missed it. She had missed all of it.

Maggie looked up sadly. "You know, there were always two strikes against me. I'm a woman, and I'm black. Do you know how many black women have Michelin stars?"

"One," Harper responded quickly. The restaurant was in Chicago, and Seth had taken Maggie for their anniversary just before it was officially recognized. She talked about it for weeks after. Every plate; every bite.

"Right," said Maggie quietly.

"That doesn't make you a liability," Harper insisted. "It makes you a trailblazer."

Maggie shook her head, a sad smile pulling at one corner of her mouth. "It might have, once. But not anymore. Strikes one and two are forgivable. Strike three, and I'm out."

"Strike three?" asked Harper.

"The baby," Maggie whispered.

Harper barely dared breathe. She would not have dared ask. She tried not to stare at the tumbler, to wonder at its contents, to glance–despite knowing it was far too early to make out any trace of a bump–at Maggie's chef's coat. The joy and relief that burst in her chest at the revelation were replaced a moment later with rising anger over Maggie's insinuation.

"You told them?" she asked, the most neutral response she could manage.

"Not directly," replied Maggie. "I quietly began exploring options that would allow me to take a leave of absence. A visiting chef takeover. Training up a sous chef. Truthfully, I hadn't even decided what I wanted yet."

"They can't push you out because you're pregnant!" Harper burst. "That's illegal."

"It's not," Maggie leaned an elbow on the bar, propping her head in one hand. "Because I signed this." She slid a stack of papers across the counter to Harper. "It's our operating agreement."

Harper took the document, eyes flying over the page, landing on a flagged and highlighted section near the bottom. The wording was obscure, intentionally vague, and no doubt included to subtly, yet legally, address a situation such as this. Harper closed her eyes and let out a deep sigh as she realized what her friend had agreed to. "Did you know your equity as a partner was contingent on active employment?"

Maggie rubbed a hand across her face. "Technically? Yes. Though I didn't think it would matter. It's a two-year agreement, after which the terms are renegotiable."

"If I would have known this was in the contract…" Harper started.

"Then what?" Maggie scoffed. "You would have told me not to sign it? I had a lawyer, Harper. A real one. Not my best friend playing pretend."

The words landed like a slap.

"He told me the risk was low," Maggie continued, the defensiveness rising in her tone. "It wasn't like we were planning the pregnancy, and who starts a restaurant they don't intend to see through the first two years?"

"Even so," pressed Harper, doing her best to brush past the personal slight, "this doesn't mean they can push you out right now. You should still have at least six months to plan, prepare, and continue to prove the concept."

Maggie propped her other elbow on the bar, cradling her head in both hands. "Why?" she asked, resentfully. "So that they can take it all away in six months instead."

"If it was successful in six months, they'd be fools not to take you back after a leave."

"If it was successful in six months, they'd figure out the best person to hand it off to and keep the ball rolling without me. It happens all the time." Maggie's voice had risen to a tear-filled lament, and she pressed the palms of her hands into her eyes. "I've been fighting for it for years, and I thought I had it. I don't want to fight for another six months."

Harper sat quietly, listening to her friend's sobs echo through the space. She knew Maggie was right. It was the same executive pressure she worried about if she found herself pregnant at the firm. Minutes passed, and the crying died away, and Maggie's breathing evened. She wiped her eyes with the sleeve of her sweater before turning to Harper.

"Go ahead and ask," she said, voice weak.

"Ask what?" replied Harper, genuinely confused.

Maggie managed a small smile. "About the baby," she said. "I'm sure you've wanted to ask since the moment you walked in the door and found me at the bar of all places."

Harper stole a peek at the empty glass.

"Club soda," Maggie explained, "with a twist." She plucked the lemon wedge from the edge of the glass and bit into it. Harper's own mouth puckered as Maggie sucked on the lemon. Maggie chuckled weakly. "The cravings are ridiculous."

"When did you decide?" Harper asked, nervously tripping over the words. She'd been invited to this conversation, but it still felt like fragile ground.

"A few weeks ago," Maggie admitted.

"What changed your mind?" The question escaped Harper before she could decide whether it was too much too soon.

Maggie let the silence hang between them a long time before she replied. Her fingertips drummed rapidly on the bar. "You know," she started, "I don't think I ever fully understood how hard your struggle was once Candace offered you a chance at that scholarship. I had never considered it both ways. It had only ever been the restaurant for me." She hesitated, gazing wistfully around the room. "When I met Seth," she continued, "he agreed to take children off the table, and then we just went on with our lives. It was easy." She looked at Harper earnestly. "Until it wasn't," she admitted. "Being presented with both options, and knowing that I might have one but not the other, and wondering if it was time to change priorities, and knowing everyone had an opinion about what they thought the right answer should be..."

"I'm sorry," Harper whispered.

Maggie shook her head. "No," she said, "I am. I thought it should be easy to know what you want. It had been so clear to me that I wanted Indie Lime that I never considered shifting my priorities. But you?

Honestly, Harper, you've had to make that consideration over and over again since your mom got sick. And you're right to be confused and hurt and indecisive. It's impossible. No matter what you choose, someone will think you've made the wrong choice."

"No matter what you choose," Harper admitted, voice cracking, "*you* will think you've made the wrong choice some days."

"Which is why the best any of us can do is to forge a path of least regret, and for me…" She paused and shrugged. "I had never stopped to answer the question of why it might be worth it to be a mother someday. It's why I couldn't talk to you about it after the Christmas party. I knew you had imagined this big, bright, happy future where we could share the experience and grow our families together. Part of me wanted to want that, too. But I wanted to want it because *I* wanted it, not because anyone else told me it was the way it should be. I had to figure out what that big, bright, happy future looked like for me."

Tears slipped silently down Harper's cheeks. "And?"

Maggie smiled. "Do you know when I was happiest cooking? Ever? In my entire life?" Harper shook her head. "When I was at the stove with my grandmother. Ever since then, I've been chasing that feeling through kitchens across the country, but really, nothing has ever compared." She gazed at Harper, and Harper saw true contentment and peace in her chestnut eyes. "Until I started thinking about standing at my own stove, with my own son or daughter, sharing with them what was given to me."

Harper took a ragged breath, choking back the sob that longed to escape her. It was everything she wanted to hear a month ago, the very daydream that had pushed her to the clinic in the first place. It made how everything played out since then hurt that much more.

"I'm so sorry it took losing the restaurant," she managed. Her voice was thick with emotion, and she struggled to clear her throat before she continued. "But I'm also so happy for you and Seth."

Maggie leaned forward on her stool, reaching for Harper, and the two friends embraced, tears spilling onto each other's shoulders. They held each other, sniffling into the silence. As Maggie moved to pull away, Harper kept one hand on her arm. "I need to tell you something," she breathed.

"Tell me something," replied Maggie.

Harper blinked away fresh tears. "There's a chance that big, bright, happy future doesn't include me anymore." She swallowed a rising lump of emotion. "Bryan and I have spent some time at the clinic, and our list of options is shrinking."

Maggie's heartbreak was clear in her expression, and she leaned in, reaching for Harper again. "I am so sorry," she whispered, holding Harper tightly. "Do you want to talk about it?" She pulled back to gauge Harper's reaction.

Harper wiped at her eyes. "I'm not sure what to say," she admitted.

"That's ok. You don't have to say anything." Maggie paused as Harper shook her head.

"The thing is," Harper said slowly, "I *do* want to talk about it. I want someone to validate my confusion, and talk through my questions, and help me rationalize that some days it hurts like hell and other days I'm surprisingly fine that things are playing out the way they are." Her voice rose with emotion. "I want someone to help me make sense of the fact that part of me actually wishes the doctors would tell us we didn't have options–that they would tell us to stop instead of having to make the choice ourselves." Fresh tears streamed down her cheeks. "I need to admit to someone that the thing that hurts most isn't necessarily not having a baby, but being told there's something I'll never be good enough to achieve on my own."

Maggie took Harper's hands. "A baby isn't an achievement, Harper."

"I know," Harper choked.

"Do you?" Maggie looked down at their joined hands, then over at the black-tiled wall of the bar before looking Harper in the eye. "I'm going to ask you a question," she said, voice even. "And I'm one hundred percent sure it is not the question you're supposed to ask your friend who just told you she may not have children. So, I'll apologize in advance, but I'm still going to ask it."

Harper took a deep breath. "Ok."

"Why do you want to be a mom, Harper?"

Harper closed her eyes, thinking back to her list, knowing that, though valid, none of her reasons resonated to the core of who she was the way Maggie talked about someday sharing the kitchen with her child. She wondered if it mattered. How many women felt a vocational call to motherhood, and how many others dove in because circumstances required it, or it seemed like the expected thing to do, or it was 'just time'? She opened her eyes and looked at Maggie. "I don't know," she admitted. She felt instantly lighter for having revealed the truth.

Maggie nodded slowly. "Now, tell me this. Why do you want to be a lawyer?"

The answer came to Harper immediately, and she reached for the stack of papers on the bar. "Because of this," she said, anger flaring again. "Because someone needs to care enough about tiny, buried lines in contracts to make sure people aren't hurt by the consequences of bad transactions. Because people, women especially, need to have advocates in spaces where they're vulnerable." She dropped the contract on the bar. "Because bullshit like that hurts people. And…" The bravado left Harper in a rush. "And I promised her Maggie," she whispered.

Maggie smiled gently. "That promise wasn't about her, Harper. It was about you. And I'm going to guess that some days you're fine and relieved because you can answer one of those questions far easier than the other. But that doesn't have to make it feel any better."

"I just wish that made the other days hurt less," Harper said, silent tears slipping onto her cheeks.

"Me too," Maggie replied, looking around the restaurant. She ran a hand lovingly over the bar. "I can't tell you and Bryan what to decide," she admitted. "But if you're asking for advice, here it is: I think you already have your answer."

Harper looked at her in confusion. "What do you mean?"

Maggie reached into the pocket of her chef's coat and laid a quarter on the bar. Harper's breath caught.

"Would you even need to flip it?" Maggie asked, her voice almost a whisper.

Harper picked up the coin, spinning it slowly between her thumb and forefinger before laying it, heads up, on the knuckle of her thumb. The silver twinkled in the dim light, and Harper stared at it a long moment before flicking it weakly.

Heads. Tails. Heads. Tails.

It clattered onto the bar top.

Maggie was right. She knew. Before she could react, Maggie laid a hand over the coin, looking at Harper with tears in her eyes.

"I want you to know," she said, "you'll always be a part of that big, bright, happy future you imagined. I don't care if we're walking strollers side by side through Grant Park, or I'm walking a stroller through campus to bring you lunch in between your classes."

Harper laughed through the sob that burst from her.

"I'm serious," Maggie insisted. "You're going to be the best damn godmother my kid has ever had, and we're doing this together...whatever *this* ends up being."

"Ok," Harper whispered, and she pulled her best friend tightly to her, relieved to have broken the silence between them, grieved by the losses they both carried, and grateful that though the world had set them on opposite paths, love and friendship had them once again walking side by side.

Chapter 22

The light from the upstairs window was a faint glimmer from the sidewalk below, and Harper stared up at it feeling both the magnetic pull of home and the unwitting desire to put off facing the conversation before her. It wasn't so much that Maggie had given her clarity, but that she finally found the courage to be honest with herself, and being honest with herself now meant being honest with Bryan as well. Her breath fogged the air around her in sparkling clouds, and she sighed heavily, watching the glitter dissipate into the night sky like twinkling stars. She swallowed hard and crossed to the door to swipe herself into the building.

The apartment was dark except for the lamp on the side table next to the sofa, and Bryan sat in its warm glow, his feet propped on the coffee table. He looked up as Harper stepped through the front door.

"How's Maggie?" he asked.

Harper retrieved a hanger from the closet. "All things considered, better than I would have expected." She closed the closet door and moved slowly past the kitchen toward the living room.

"Can she break the contract?" Bryan asked with a trace of hope.

Harper shook her head. "It's bad language. But no. I don't think there's any way around it."

Bryan nodded, slowly rubbing a hand over his face. "I can't believe it can just end like that."

"The odds of everything happening the way they did were infinitesimally small," Harper said, resting her hands on the back of the couch. "I would have told her not to sign it, but it shouldn't have made any difference. If everything had gone as planned, this would just be a setback. She could relaunch."

"It could *still* just be a setback," Bryan said heavily, staring up at the dark ceiling. Harper's hackles rose in Maggie's defense, but before she could respond, Bryan turned to face her. "Not that I think they're making the wrong choice. It's an impossible decision."

Harper moved to her favorite corner of the couch, feeling the conversation creeping toward its ultimate destination. "I can't imagine," she murmured.

Bryan watched as she curled her legs beneath her and pulled the blanket into her lap. "Can't you?" he asked when she finally looked back at him. "Isn't that what we've both been trying to imagine for weeks? How to have it both ways?"

Harper's pulse jumped, and she stared at her hands, waiting for the words to come. "No," she managed. It came out in a whisper. "For me, it's been longer." Bryan's head tipped ever so slightly, his expression equal parts curiosity and confusion. Harper took a steadying breath.

"I've never really been sure about this, not even when we first started," she admitted. Her voice wobbled. "I told myself it was normal to be nervous, and that everyone feels some anxiety around change, and that once we got pregnant the excitement and expectation would gradually replace the apprehension. But then we didn't get pregnant." She looked away, fidgeting with the fringe on the blanket. "And that apprehension turned into sadness and frustration. And when it still didn't happen after that, eventually," she swallowed hard, ashamed. "It turned into relief." She felt Bryan's eyes boring into her, but could not bring herself to look up and meet them.

"If everything had stayed exactly the same, I could probably convince myself that this is something I want," she continued, forcing herself forward. "Maggie and Seth are keeping the baby, and you've finally got tenure, and my work has always been steady but not unreasonable, until recently. I might have even convinced myself it was ok to scale back."

Bryan laughed, a deep, genuine chuckle that made Harper pause. She looked up reflexively. Her eyes locked on Bryan's, the color of a sky before a thunderstorm, but calm and kind. They made Harper's breath catch. "That seems unlikely," he said, his voice a low murmur.

"Maybe," she replied, peeling her gaze away. "But there would have been ways to make it work. Reasons to convince myself that it was worth the time and effort and money to keep trying." Bryan slid toward her corner of the couch, resting a hand on her knee, and it steadied her as she continued.

"When I sit in the waiting room at the clinic, I see the women who will do anything, the ones who have gone all-in to do whatever it takes in the name of growing their family." Her throat tightened with emotion, and she struggled to make the next words come. "And, if I'm being honest with myself," her eyes found his, "I know I'm not one of them." Tears slipped onto her cheeks.

She pulled at the tassel on the corner of the blanket, running her fingers anxiously through the chenille strands until Bryan laid a hand on top of hers. "It's ok," he said, quietly. "I don't need you to be."

Harper tried to force a smile of acknowledgement, but it only made the tears fall faster.

"The thing is," Bryan continued, "I've never been certain either. We had a great life. *Have* a great life. Everyone says that kids make it that much fuller and richer." He raised an eyebrow. "But, really? All the time?" He shook his head. "I don't think we're the only ones who ever jumped in thinking it was the obvious next step, only to reconsider when things didn't just work out as planned." He moved in close, and their knees bumped together as he took both Harper's hands in his own.

"You're not in this decision alone, Harper. I've watched you tie yourself in knots trying to figure out how to make this happen for us and hold on to your personal ambitions at the same time. You try to pretend like everything is ok, and it tears me to pieces not being able to take some of the burden away from you. You don't have to do it anymore. Not for me. I'm not asking you to."

"But this is something you want," Harper said, her voice small. Bryan was responding in as compassionate and measured a manner as she could have hoped for, and she wondered if it was too good to be true. What would happen if he woke up in the morning and realized he agreed to something in a moment of emotion that he desperately regretted? "I can't ask you to walk away from having children."

Bryan leaned in. "Sometimes desire alone isn't enough. You can want something terribly and still decide against it. In fact," he brushed a tear from her cheek with his thumb, "I'd say it's the exact thing you did when you put law school on hold when your mother was sick. You can't tell me you wanted it any less after her diagnosis. You put that desire aside because you weren't willing to give up the alternative."

"It's not the same," Harper lamented.

"Why?" asked Bryan.

"Because that was choosing my family over a job, and this is choosing a job over our family."

"This isn't about a job. This is about *you*."

"No, it's about *us*," Harper insisted. "I can't ask you to not want a family."

"Harper," Bryan's voice was urgent, and he raised a hand to cradle the side of her face, bringing her eyes level with his. "Listen to me right now. *You* are my family. Plain and simple. And if it's only ever us, then so be it. I've questioned and wondered and doubted so many times in the past two years. Are we making the right choices? Is it worth it? Can I ask more of you? But not once did I question, or wonder, or doubt that it was you and me. It's *always* you and me."

Harper's silent tears broke into sobs, and she leaned forward, resting her forehead on his chest. Bryan wrapped his arms around her and held her gently as her shoulders shook. They stayed that way for a long moment, the silence around them interrupted only by sniffles. When she pulled away, Harper found Bryan's face streaked with tears to match her own.

"I guess I just assumed we would do whatever it took," she whispered.

Bryan smiled sadly. "Be honest, though," he said gently. "Did you ever assume that it would take more than we've already done?"

Harper's bottom lip trembled as she shook her head. "What hurts the most," she choked, "is that you would make an amazing dad." Her voice broke as fresh tears flowed.

Bryan's eyes were glassy. He cleared the emotion from his throat. "And you'd be an amazing mom," he admitted. "But that doesn't mean we have to be. We're going to be amazing godparents for Seth and Maggie instead, and we'll be there for your sister and Brady and the twins whenever you want to be."

"What if we regret it? What if you start to resent it?" Harper wiped the back of her hand across her eyes, and Bryan leaned in, resting his forehead against hers.

"Do you think you might?" he asked.

Harper considered, but her certainty was clear, if not painful. She shrugged. "Maybe, a little. But I'm as sure as I've been in a long time."

Bryan squeezed her hand. "Me too," he breathed. "I'm sure there will be things that we both miss, and days that we both mourn, but if you go to law school, and I get to watch you finally fulfill your dream, then I promise I won't regret it a day of our lives, and I don't think you will either."

Harper nodded against him. "I love you," she whispered. It was the only possible response, and yet so plain, so obvious, so simple compared to the complicated, complex emotions rolling through her. Bryan tipped her chin, bringing her mouth to his, and she lost herself in the kind of kiss that they had given up so many months ago when they had traded romance and spontaneity for scheduled, procreative efficiency. It lingered, deliciously, until they both came up gasping for air.

"I love you too," Bryan laughed, unable to wipe the grin from his face. "In fact," he said quietly, leaning forward to kiss her forehead, "I love you so much that I'm going to rain check this obvious opportunity to whisk you to the bedroom in the name of giving you the chance to open your mail." Harper's heart, already racing, hammered against her ribs. Bryan squeezed her hands. "You have some large envelopes at the bottom of the pile," he said, nodding toward the entry table.

"Envelopes?" Harper asked. "Plural."

Bryan smiled, eyes shining. "Plural," he assured her.

Harper untangled herself from the blanket and leapt from the couch. Her hands trembled as she scanned the pile of thin envelopes for any that may contain bad news. Then she landed on the first of the thick, white packets. She slid them from the table and returned to the couch, unable to look away from the red and gold stripe slashed across the front of the first envelope. Lancaster. She shuffled to the next, the clean lines of the familiar stylized, purple N stamped boldly along the left edge of the page. Northwestern. Already knowing what she would find, she flipped to the final envelope, gaze falling to the scarlet embossing of the return address. The University of Chicago.

"All three?" she asked, unbelieving.

"All three," Bryan confirmed. He leapt from the couch and hurried to the kitchen where Harper heard him rummage in the refrigerator before returning to the couch with a bottle of champagne. "Congratulations," he said, eyes shining and voice thick. The cork shot across the living room with a loud pop, ricocheting off the brick wall.

Harper laughed, a giggle at first; then it snowballed to a chuckle, then a chortle, until the real laughter took hold and her shoulders shook and her belly ached and she couldn't stop. It was the crazed laughter of one so caught up in the amazing, momentous, riotous, yet slightly ridiculous joy of a moment that she forgot the hardship that preceded it. It was rare and raw, the same way she laughed with her mother on the shore of Lake Michigan the afternoon she put all her plans on hold. The thought was sobering, and she regained her composure as Bryan handed her a flute of champagne.

"What's wrong?" he asked, returning to his end of the couch.

"Nothing," Harper assured, smiling to herself. She watched the bubbles rising up the sides of the glass. "I was just thinking about the last time I had to make this decision." She glanced at the envelopes fanned out on the cushion between them. "And my mom," she admitted.

"Do you want to flip a coin?" Bryan asked, a playful tease.

"No," Harper said, softly, seriously. "I already have. She told me it would matter someday, and she was right. I just never thought it would happen like this." She raised her glass and took a long sip.

"Well!" Bryan said, eyes wide in expectation. "What's the decision then?"

Harper smiled coyly, pushing the envelopes out of the way as she moved down the couch to her husband. She slid into his lap, arms wrapping around his neck as she kissed the question away.

"You can't distract me with sex, Harper," Bryan insisted, laughing in between kisses. "Where do you want to go?"

Harper pulled back, one hand still threaded through her husband's dark hair. It would have been so easy to blurt the answer. She had waited twelve years to blurt the answer. But the words stuck in her throat, like saying it aloud would jinx it coming to fruition. "It's not a distraction," she insisted, lips brushing lightly against Bryan's. "It's a celebration. And, of course, I'll tell you. I just," she hesitated, suddenly embarrassed by her foolishness. "I just don't want to get too far ahead of myself. The scholarship…"

"Doesn't matter anymore," Bryan said instantly. "Whatever it is," he went on, "*wherever* it is, we're going to make it work."

The tears welled behind Harper's eyes, and she leaned into the kiss to keep from breaking down. Bryan responded automatically, arms sliding around her. A moment later he stood, lifting her off the couch in a swift motion that made her breath catch as she wrapped both arms around his neck. He kicked the bedroom door closed behind them, the question of law school left behind with the envelopes in a soft puddle of lamplight.

Chapter 23

Harper woke hours before the alarm. She showered and dressed, careful not to disturb the deep, even breaths that rose and fell from Bryan's bare chest as she pressed a gentle kiss to his temple and slipped from the bedroom. The lamp in the living room glowed in the gray darkness of predawn, and the envelopes sat in the soft glow, exactly as they had been left the night before. She hadn't even opened them. Harper breathed a deep, contented sigh as she lifted them to the kitchen counter and started the coffee. It gurgled in the background as, one by one, she slid a thumb under the envelope flaps and removed the contents.

Though the opening lines were nearly identical, each sent the same thrill racing through her.

Dear Ms. Andrews,

Congratulations! After thorough consideration and review from the admissions committee, we are delighted to offer you acceptance into the juris doctor program beginning fall term.

They went on in their own ways, outlining the merits of their program as if Harper didn't already know what made each university worthy of consideration and hadn't already spent years of her life waiting to actually accept one of these offers. She laid the pages side by side on the kitchen counter, staring down at the clean, white papers, each one offering her a path forward and a new future. The adrenaline and caffeine coursed through her in equal measure, pushing her out the door and toward the office where she expected there would now be intense speculation and waiting as the committee took however long the committee was going to take to decide her fate.

No, thought Harper. Not fate. This was happening. The most they could influence at this point was how much of her own bank account would be involved in the process. There were glossy pamphlets in each of the envelopes from the university's respective financial aid offices, and she left them on the counter just in case. Then she slid all three letters into one of the mailing envelopes, tucked it into the side pocket of her work bag, retrieved her coat from the hall closet, and stepped quietly from the apartment.

Traffic was light, and the trip to the office was quicker than usual, giving Harper just a brief window to collect her thoughts before arriving at the firm. She was cautiously optimistic, the excitement of her acceptance tempered slightly by her evening with Maggie at Indie Lime. Maggie had built that dream from the ground up, pursued it longer than Harper had even thought about law school, saw everything she wanted come to pass, and then watched it crumble in a heartbeat. Her only mistake had been betting on herself with a little too much fervor. Harper understood how it could happen. As she parked her car a few blocks from the office and strode up La Salle Avenue, she felt invincible. If asked, she would bet on herself twice today.

But it wasn't just the letters that had her floating through the lobby, stepping confidently into the empty elevator, and offering a friendly finger wiggle wave back at the security desk as the doors closed. It was also her night with Bryan, a night they had both needed for months, but had, until now, been unable to get to. As she dozed off under the weight of his arm, she wondered if they had really reached the end of their conversation or if they would both wake up the next morning and begin to walk back their declarations and decisions. Hindsight was, after all, twenty-twenty.

However, as the elevator rose, and Harper replayed the previous night in her mind's eye, it was not with remorse over the decision or regret over the conversation. Instead, her thoughts lingered on the way they had kissed, without pretense or motive beyond being with the other person. The way Bryan had scooped her from the couch. The way they tangled together, needing each other. Only each other. Not because they were told to, or it was on a calendar, or because the test strip suggested that, perhaps, tonight was the night. Rather because that innate, visceral chemistry, dormant and buried under boxes of pregnancy tests and empty pill bottles, still burned. Her relief at finding it still intact was a load off her shoulders she hadn't known she was carrying.

The elevator opened on the twenty-eighth floor, and Harper stepped into the small lobby, heels ticking on the polished tile. The cubicles were empty, and the lights were dim, and her heartbeat skittered as she wondered who would be the first to find her in her office and ask if she had heard about any of her applications. She wondered if she should stop up to see Candace immediately, but a glance at the clock on the wall suggested that 6:30 was early, even for a named partner. Instead, she moved toward her office where, if she was smart, she would get started on an hour of work before the distraction of conversation and anxiety over when and how the committee would decide, upended the rest of the day. It was only then that she noticed the light glowing in Tate's office.

Harper stopped, curiosity flaring. For the briefest moment, she imagined walking the hundred feet between their office doors and sharing the news with Tate first. She thought they had reestablished peace, if not friendship. He had been frank with her about his own letters. She felt like she owed him the same courtesy. But as she took a few steps in his direction, she heard the tinny crackling of a speakerphone, and she lost her nerve. She backtracked to her office, careful not to let her heels click too loudly, and shut the door behind her.

At her desk, Harper opened the thin middle drawer, shifting the pens and post-its around until she found the quarter taped to the bottom. She picked at the edges, pulling up the tape and dislodging the coin into her palm. She set it on the desktop, her index finger pressed to the edge, holding it straight up and down. Turning it slowly, the profile portrait gave way to the stylized eagle. She let it clatter onto the desktop, laying a hand over the top of it. The cool metal warmed beneath her palm. Harper closed her eyes, remembering the same feeling when her mom had pressed it to her hand twelve years before.

Heads. Tails. Heads. Tails.

"I promised, Mom," she whispered, voice catching. She blew out a breath, quickly composing herself before the tears could fall.

A soft rap on the glass door startled Harper out of the moment. Her eyes snapped open, landing on Tate, one hand in his pocket, the other still extended. He gave her a small, apologetic smile and glanced at the door handle. Harper nodded in return. He stepped into the office, letting the door swing closed behind him despite the rest of the floor being empty.

"Andrews."

"Good morning," Harper replied. Tate's eyebrows rose in surprise, and Harper realized it was as cordial a tone as she had taken with him since the competition had started.

"You're in early," he noted.

"Says the man who was already in his office on a call when I got here," she countered, attempting the normal banter that used to come so easily between them. She could hear that her tone was off, slightly accusatory instead of teasing, and she saw Tate shift his weight uncomfortably from one foot to the other.

"It's not that early on the east coast," he said finally.

Harper's brow furrowed as she tried to recall if she knew an east coast client Tate might be working on. "I guess not," she said, lost in thought.

Tate glanced around the room, letting the silence linger between them before taking a step toward the desk and setting the balls in the Newton's cradle clattering against each other. There was something so casual and familiar about the gesture that it both broke Harper's heart. So much had changed, yet here he was trying to pretend as if nothing had. She shifted uneasily in her chair. "Anything I can help with?" she asked.

The corner of Tate's mouth pulled as if he might smile, but there was a sadness to it that Harper couldn't ignore.

"May I?" Tate gestured toward the leather chair by the window where Harper had dropped her bag, and Harper nodded toward it. Tate shifted the bag to the floor where it tipped on its side. The mailing envelope slid from the side pocket. He reached for it reflexively, pulling his hand back as he saw the embossed seal in the return address corner. His eyes flashed to Harper's. "The University of Chicago?" he asked, tone laced with admiration.

Harper nodded.

"That's brilliant," he declared. "Others?"

"Yeah," she said, intensely aware that Tate had yet to experience the joy of receiving even one letter. "Northwestern and Lancaster."

Tate smirked, though it lacked malice. "Lancaster? Bryan's idea or safety school?" he asked.

"Safety school," Harper admitted with a shrug.

Tate nodded slowly. "Wish I had the luxury," he sighed, tucking the envelope back in the bag. He propped an ankle on his knee. "Well, I guess congratulations are in order," he mused. "You're going to make a brilliant lawyer, Andrews."

There was a sadness and sincerity to Tate's tone that didn't match the usual swagger and enthusiasm to which Harper had grown accustomed over the years.

"As for me, I came over because I have news, and I wanted you to hear it from me first," Tate went on. "Seems like keeping things to ourselves is what got us in this mess in the first place."

Harper knew it was a dig, but also felt she deserved it.

"What's up?" she asked, genuinely curious.

"I've just been on the phone with Pollard Frank. I've asked to be reconsidered for a position this spring."

The blood drained from Harper's cheeks. "You're leaving?" she breathed. "Really?"

"Blimey, Andrews." Tate chuckled. "You sound like you're hoping I change my mind."

"You said you had other schools?"

"None of them are the University of Chicago," he scoffed. "So, I can either keep pretending like I deserve this and try to take it from the person who really does, or figure out what I do next."

"I don't understand," Harper interrupted.

"What?"

"Pollard Frank has been on the table for months. Why now?"

"It looks like I'm running away, doesn't it? I know that. And I'm sorry about the mess I made."

"But why do it? Why put yourself through the LSAT…the applications…the scrutiny?" Harper asked.

Tate uncrossed his legs and leaned forward, elbows on his knees. He stared at the floor a long time before looking up at Harper. "I think I just wanted to know if I could," he admitted. "Part of me thought I was supposed to want it. I used to want it, right? Why shouldn't I want it now? It's selfish, I know. I don't expect it to make sense."

Harper sighed sympathetically. "I get it." It should be easier, she thought, to give up what we've been told to want when it means getting what we actually desire. But the weight of expectation was a heavy burden. "Are you?" Harper asked. "Running away, I mean?"

"Maybe," Tate admitted with an easy smile. "Would you have stayed if I had somehow managed to dash your dreams?"

Harper bit her bottom lip. "Fair point. So, Pollard Frank then, paralegal?"

Tate shrugged. "We'll see. I want my options open. If not New York, London perhaps."

"Work for your father?" asked Harper, surprised. "After all this, I figured you would stay well clear."

A smile played at the corners of Tate's mouth. "Would you believe that all these years of defying his wishes has actually somehow endeared me more to the old man?"

"No," Harper laughed. "I wouldn't."

Tate chuckled. "I guess we'll see if it sticks, but he's already talking about when I move to the London office so that he can begin a succession plan."

"Is that what *you* want?"

"I don't know," Tate admitted. He looked wistfully around the office. "But if I go, I will miss this."

Harper rolled her eyes. "You made fun of my office almost once a week."

"Even so." Tate smiled. His gaze drifted to the cubicles, and Harper turned to find the elevator doors sliding open. "That's my cue," he said with a sly grin. "Can't have the office finding out that we are reconciling just moments before your victory is declared."

"I don't think…" Harper started, but Tate held up a hand, nodding toward a pair of curious paralegals glancing between them before quickly ducking into a cubicle where they whispered, heads together.

Tate pushed himself from the chair and buttoned his suit coat.

"Enjoy it, Andrews. They'll all be talking about you in a few hours."

Harper's stomach lurched. "Tate?" Her voice stopped him just as he reached for the door handle, and he turned back. "Is there any chance you stay?"

He took a deep breath and raised both hands, palms up. "Maybe."

"Well," Harper picked up the quarter and laid it flat on the knuckle of her thumb. She flicked it in the air, the silver sparkling in the morning light streaming through the window.

Heads. Tails. Heads. Tails.

She reached up and caught it easily. "When it's time to decide," she offered with a casual shrug, "just flip a coin."

Tate stared at her, eyes flickering between Harper's own and her fist closed around the quarter.

"Is that some lame, old-fashioned American superstition?" he asked with a laugh, breaking the spell of the moment. "Flip a coin, change your life? Bloody hell, Andrews!"

The phone on Harper's desk trilled to life.

Candace.

"Get out," Harper scoffed with a teasing smile, rolling her eyes and reaching for the phone.

"Seriously," Tate chuckled under his breath as he moved to the door.

"Out," Harper demanded, pointing to the door as she answered the call. "Greta, good morning."

Tate shook his head. "You know you missed this," he whispered, letting the door swing closed behind him as he stepped into the hall.

Harper watched him walk back to his office. He was right. She had.

•   •   •

Minutes later, Harper stepped off the elevator on the thirty-second floor and took a hard left toward Candace Walsh's office. Greta looked up as she approached, her gaze hard and assessing. She stood up and hurried from behind the desk, stopping Harper before she was visible through the glass office wall.

"I hope you brought some good news," she said in a tight whisper. "She's in there with Pickett."

Harper had transferred all three acceptance letters to one of the firm's standard pocket folders before leaving her office in an effort to look slightly less conspicuous. She carried it along with the file of case work on embryonic custody from the night before. Greta's gaze slid to where it dangled in her hand. The corners of Harper's mouth flexed automatically in reply, and Greta made an exaggerated sigh of relief.

"In that case," she said, turning on the heel of her practical loafer, "I'll let her know you're here." She rapped lightly on the glass door before stepping into the office. A minute later, Lyle Pickett, looking properly perturbed, pushed past Greta and stepped into the hallway. He glanced at Harper, his gaze momentarily icy, and Harper fought the urge to recoil before forcing a few confident strides toward the door that Greta held open behind him. Pickett sighed as she approached, and his expression softened.

"Andrews," he said in a clipped, yet entirely midwestern accent.

Harper tried to remember if he ever called her that before working so closely with Tate. In twelve years at the firm, he was the named partner she interacted with the least, and she never even had the conversation with him about the scholarship before he became Tate's champion. He had been a specter over the scholarship process the last few months. But now, seeing him in the hallway, angry blotches of color draining from his cheeks, gray hair neatly parted but otherwise slightly disheveled, was a bit more like confronting the man behind the curtain than the great and powerful Oz. He held out a hand as Harper drew near, and she took it, squeezing tightly to match his own, determined, grip.

"Congratulations are in order, I assume," he said, glancing down at the folders in Harper's other hand.

"Thank you, sir," Harper said. "I appreciate the opportunity to have my application reviewed again."

"Bullshit," Pickett laughed. "What's to appreciate? I screwed you over after Candace told you I was considering your application, and as payback, you made a complete ass of me by trouncing my guy in competition."

"In fairness," Harper offered, filled with a sudden boldness that she couldn't ignore, "given the circumstances, you looked like an ass long before these arrived." She raised the folder in her hand.

Pickett pointed an accusatory finger before pursing his lips and shaking his head. "I deserved that. For what it's worth, I never thought you were a lesser applicant than Tate."

"I know," said Harper. "Until Harold Turner called, you probably never thought of him as an applicant at all. Not that it mattered."

Pickett folded his arms and chuckled. "Candace said you were spunky."

Harper's confidence faltered. Is that all Candace considered her?

"Keep that fighting spirit sharp," Pickett continued. "You'll need it."

"Yes, sir," Harper agreed, wondering if his advice was more general or directed specifically to the conversation waiting on the other side of the glass wall.

"Harper!?" Candace called from the office, and Greta cleared her throat in the doorway.

Pickett appraised Harper for a moment before stepping out of the pathway to the door. "Duty calls," he offered, gesturing down the hallway. "Congratulations," he offered again as Harper moved around him to the office.

Greta let the door swing closed behind her.

"What do you have for me?" Candace asked brusquely as soon as they were alone. She held out a hand but did not look up from the file on her desk. Framed by the city skyline behind her, she was entirely the imposing partner that Lyle Pickett had failed to be. Never mind that Candace was supposedly the one on Harper's side. Whereas a moment earlier her confidence had soared, Harper felt the remaining adrenaline melt away as she moved cautiously across the office and offered the folder of case law reports. Candace took it without comment and inspected the pages. "Ok, good. What else?" she asked, glancing at the other folder in Harper's hand.

Harper turned it over, heart in her throat. She watched as Candace flipped it open casually, unsuspectingly. She skimmed the first page. Harper shifted anxiously, waiting for a reaction. Candace's eyes raced over the other documents, and only when Harper saw the corner of her mouth twitch did she dare consider relaxing.

Finally, Candace looked up. "The University of Chicago?" she asked, with what Harper hoped was something akin to pride. "That's a hell of an accomplishment, Harper."

"Thank you," Harper said, wanting to say more, unsure of where to start.

Candace nodded slowly, looking at the other documents. "Not that I'm surprised," she continued. "I could see it written all over your face that day I came down to your office."

"What?" Harper asked, voice small.

Candace chuckled. "How badly you wanted it." Blood rushed to Harper's cheeks. "Just like it's written there now how badly you want to pretend like you haven't given up everything the past few months to be standing here handing me these." She extended the folder back across the desk to Harper. "And that doesn't even include the reason you were at the clinic with Ainsley that day."

Harper hesitated. She knew the conversation would go back to Ainsley and the clinic. How could it not? But she had not expected quite this level of candor. "About that, Candace…"

Candace held up a hand, her expression softening. "It was not ideal, what you did," she admitted. The tightness in Harper's chest loosened ever so slightly. It was a far more tempered response than she had expected, though there could still be fallout left to come, especially if the settlement had fallen apart. "Nevertheless," Candace continued, "I want to apologize."

Harper had to struggle to keep her mouth from dropping open. She followed Candace to the armchairs in front of the desk.

"I put you on the spot yesterday, and not in a way I intended," Candace admitted. "If I would have paid even an iota of attention to the situation beyond my own direct interest, I might have realized the context and responded with, at the very least, some tact." She crossed her legs and folded her hands in her lap. "Better yet, I might have even extended compassion."

Harper picked at the edge of her manicure, uncertain how to respond. "You couldn't have known," she said finally. "There was no reason for you to know, to suspect."

Candace shook her head. "That's the thing, isn't it?" she said, more passing thought than question. "We're women. We shouldn't have to *know*. We shouldn't have to *suspect*. We innately understand the hurt, the struggle, the awkwardness, the desire, the deep, personal, sometimes impossible, nature of it all. We should be sensitive to it, even without all the facts." She looked sadly at Harper. "Whatever your reasons for being at the clinic that afternoon, it's incredibly personal, and if I embarrassed you, I'm sorry."

Harper let the apology hang between them. It was the least likely way she expected the conversation to go, and Candace's genuine remorse had thrown her. She had hoped the acceptance letters would help smooth over any lingering tension, but she was unprepared for sympathy. She was at once relieved, self-conscious, and uncertain of her reply. "If you're worried I won't be able to meet my obligation to the firm with a baby," she began, picking her words carefully.

"I'm not," Candace interrupted immediately. "It's not any of my business, and even if it was, my stance would be the same." She rested an arm on either armrest of the chair and leaned back into the cushions. "You have my vote of confidence, and I trust you to figure it out. Because I think you're going to make a hell of a lawyer."

The knot in Harper's stomach loosened. "Thank you, Candace," she managed. "For what it's worth, I'm sorry, too. I've looked at everything in that custody case, and Ainsley will have a strong precedent to build on."

"No," Candace said quickly, holding up a hand. "She won't. She's agreed to settle."

"You're kidding? Why?"

Candace leveled her gaze at Harper. "Because people have their limits. Knowing you have an option doesn't mean you have to take it. Plus, options are valuable; it's relatively easy to quantify how much it's going to cost to spend three years in a drawn-out legal battle. It's leverage."

"So, the bargaining chip I was supposed to find you turned out to be the winning ticket for Ainsley instead?" lamented Harper.

"Not entirely. I asked for a way to get to an agreement, and you got us there–albeit a bit unorthodoxly."

"I'm sorry I complicated things."

Candace shook her head. "The settlement was always going to be complicated," she said, pulling at a loose thread on the cuff of her blazer. "It's divorce. It was optimistic to think there might be a way to keep things tidy. Unfortunately, separating the parts of an old life is about as complex and unpredictable as trying to create a new one."

"What will happen to them now?" Harper wondered aloud.

"The embryos?" Candace shrugged. "There will be a bunch of legal jockeying to define whether they're a commodity or a child, which will ultimately determine how the settlement proceeds in terms of total monetary compensation. Mark agreed to go ahead with the sale of the company first so that a total financial picture could be drawn before arriving at a final dollar amount."

They sat in thoughtful silence.

"If you had been in the meeting yesterday," Candace said, "how would you have counseled it?"

Harper considered, glancing around the office to buy time. The morning light bounced around the room, reflecting off the polished desktop, the glass walls, and the silver frames lined up along the sideboard. Harper stared at the black and white photos a moment before turning back to Candace. "Hypothetically? I'd advise to delay," she decided.

"Until after the sale?"

Harper shook her head. "Not the settlement, the whole divorce."

Candace scoffed, but Harper pressed on.

"They shouldn't make a big life decision in the middle of two other big life decisions. Losing those pregnancies was life changing. The sale of the company will be life changing. Divorce is life changing, and so are the decisions they're trying to make around the settlement, especially about the embryos."

Slowly, Candace shook her head. "We're not in the business of that kind of counsel, Harper."

"I know," Harper admitted. "I doubt they would take my advice anyway."

"Maybe not," Candace smiled and pushed herself up from the chair. "But it's wise. Keep thinking outside the box. We're going to need that."

Harper hurried to stand, matching Candace. "Yes, ma'am."

Candace smiled appraisingly, glancing at the cream folder that Harper had left lying on the table between them. "I didn't even ask," she said. "It *is* the University of Chicago, isn't it?"

Harper looked past Candace to where her diplomas hung impressively framed on the office wall. She shook her head at the irony. For all she worried about her decision to pursue law school being misunderstood, she forgot that in some circles it was actually her decision *of* law schools that would face the greater scrutiny.

"Is the scholarship contingent on my attending Chicago?" she asked.

Candace's head tipped in confusion. "Of course not," she assured. "But Chicago's a top five program. I would seriously consider..."

"It's Northwestern," Harper interrupted, confident. "I promised my mom."

The furrow in Candace's brow relaxed. "I'm sure your mom would consider acceptance into a more prestigious program keeping that promise."

Harper shook her head. "My mom would know that my mind's been made up for twelve years."

Candace nodded slowly. "I understand. In that case," she awkwardly held up a fist, "go Wildcats."

Harper laughed. "Go Wildcats," she echoed, unable to ignore how her heart swelled to say it.

Chapter 24

The evening was unseasonably warm as Harper and Bryan walked hand-in-hand up Michigan Avenue. The chunks of ice and snow piled along the gutter had thawed to an unseemly, gray sludge that pooled around frozen storm grates and puddled along the curb. They stopped a few feet back from the corner, waiting for the light to change, out of range from the shower of dirty water put up by each passing car whose tires caught the edge of the slushy lake that stretched into the intersection. There was change in the air, the very first hints of the spring to come. Hope for nicer days, better weather, growth, renewal. Harper looked down at her salt encrusted boots. She wished it would hurry up and get here.

The signal changed as a mechanical voice from the box on the light post announced it was clear to walk, and Bryan squeezed her hand as they surged forward with the rest of the evening pedestrian traffic heading toward dinner reservations and theater performances. There was, Harper noticed, not a child among them. Not a stroller or a small hand reaching up for the assurance of their designated adult.

She was doing this more and more recently, paying attention to where she found herself in similar company. It had been so easy to see where she would someday fit as a mother. The picnic tables on the fringes of the neighborhood playground. The drop-off line outside the local elementary school. The clutch of spandex clad moms gripping Starbucks cups along the sidelines of the soccer fields in Nichols Park. In the weeks that followed the decision to stop trying, she had mourned these things, and a part of her knew she always would. And yet, she was beginning to take comfort in the places she now knew she belonged as well. The after-work bar with colleagues. The unexpected weekend away with Bryan on a few hours' notice. The cohort of incoming, non-traditional law students she had been invited to join via social media. The support group for couples at the end of their infertility journey that Dr. Bluffton had recommended at her most recent appointment.

And tonight, the Wednesday night dinner crowd–unconcerned about a babysitter and unhindered by a requisite time to return home. A blessing, really, given the circumstances. Tonight, the only thing, the only person, she wanted to worry about was Maggie.

They turned onto Lake Street, and the green and yellow neon of Indie Lime came into view. There were no velvet ropes along the sidewalk, nor expectant lines of diners crowding around the entrance hoping to nab a table for chef Maggie Evans' final night in the kitchen. Just Seth, waiting with his hands in his pockets, his tweed blazer buttoned over a starched dress shirt and navy sweater vest.

"Very 'dad chic,'" Bryan nodded approvingly as he extended a hand, then pulled his friend into a one-armed embrace.

"Thanks," Seth replied, thumping Bryan on the back once with his free arm. "And here I was going for nutty professor."

"I can snag you a lab coat and goggles next time," Bryan chuckled.

"Thanks for inviting us," Harper said, opening her arms to Seth for a hug. Their dynamic had returned to normal almost immediately after the night that Harper had rushed to the restaurant for Maggie, though Harper still felt a tinge of remorse and embarrassment over the way she had behaved.

Seth returned the embrace without pretense. "Are you kidding?" he said. "You didn't need an invitation. Maggie wants you here." He pulled away, his gaze shifting between them suddenly serious. "She *needs* us here."

Harper nodded. "I know."

Seth smiled tightly before pulling open the door and waving Harper and Bryan through.

The dining room was modestly full, a steady hum in place of the vibrant, whirling energy of the opening. It felt comfortable, familiar. The clatter of ice on metal and the tinkling of glassware punctuating the gentle murmur of conversation. Harper again regretted not having spent more time here, watching how the menu changed with the seasons or which staff members came and went as business rose and fell. It didn't feel like a restaurant on the verge of a relaunch, and Harper couldn't help but wonder if she would have been here more, if she might have helped Maggie fight it. If another set of eyes and ears on the scene might have helped build a compelling argument to save what was left of the vision.

Or, perhaps, it wouldn't have mattered. If there was anything Harper had come to realize in the weeks since that fateful evening, it was that Maggie, remarkably, was at peace. Still, Harper promised herself to spend at least part of her time in future practice as a lawyer making sure clients like Maggie had fair representation and good counsel. They should never have to choose between a career and a family, not if they didn't want to, not because they were forced to.

The host at the station inside the door greeted them warmly and showed them to the same table near the kitchen where they first sat together. Harper took in the room, the impressive light fixture in a dozen shades of green over the bar, the wall of teak slats, backlit with a warm glow. She tried to remember if the plants along the walls and windows were the same. Were they bigger now than they had been in November? A table of Maggie's investors sat in the corner, but beyond that, the smattering of diners here tonight seemed satisfied. The bustle through the narrow window to the kitchen seemed as focused and driven as it had on night one. It didn't seem fair that it hadn't worked. It seemed impossible that she hadn't proven the concept.

Their server arrived with menus and a brief list of chef specials, and one look around the table confirmed what she and Bryan had already decided on the walk over.

"We're ready to order," Bryan assured the server, returning the menus to his outstretched hand. "We'll take one of everything. You can bring the appetizers first."

The waiter looked back, startled. "Of course. Um. Can I start you with something to drink while you wait for your food? Chef recommends the…"

"Mojitos," they answered in unison.

The waiter nodded, his surprise apparent. "I'll get those into the bar right away," he stammered, hurrying from the table.

Harper turned to the kitchen window, watching the sous chefs shifting between stations, occasionally glimpsing Maggie as she passed through to taste and modify the plates coming up for service. Their objective tonight had been simple–give Maggie the opportunity to cook her menu through from start to finish one last time. But what Harper also knew, more than Bryan or Seth could understand, was that in doing so, they were giving Maggie a chance to fully be this version of herself one last time as well. This was everything that Maggie thought she had wanted. This was the person she had dreamed of being. There would be other dinners and maybe even other restaurants, but it would never be the same. It would never be this version of the dream. And even if she had settled into the idea of what came next, she deserved to savor every moment of what was now.

Harper had come to her own such realization two weeks prior as she left the clinic for the last time. Somewhere between the walk to the elevators and her arrival in the waiting room, it occurred to her that she had arrived months ago as a woman trying to start a family and would leave that afternoon as a woman who was, decidedly, not. As she waited to check in and stared at the collage of family photos on the wall, a tight knot of guilt and anxiety and indecision clenched in her stomach. She knew she was certain, but also that her decision likely made little sense to any of the other half-dozen women waiting for their appointments, desperate to have families. Or maybe it did. Maybe there was another woman just like Harper, hoping no one recognized the quiet determination of her own gaze, determination to say enough. I'm done.

And it's ok. Slowly, Harper was coming to understand that there was no script and no right way and no one answer.

For her part, Dr. Bluffton had not once attempted to dissuade Harper's decision. She had presented options, confirmed assumptions, and answered questions dispassionately, until the end of the appointment when the impartial façade cracked ever so slightly. She leaned her elbows onto the desk, folded her hands before her, and peered over her blue plastic frames, giving Harper a tight, sad smile.

"I hate these appointments," she admitted quietly. "I saw you on the schedule this morning, and I've dreaded our conversation ever since. So often people decide to stop trying from a place of defeat, so I'm relieved to find that you actually seem encouraged."

Harper stared at her hands. "I am," she admitted after a moment. "For so long, this has been something that's just happening to me, passively. I have my control back."

Dr. Bluffton sighed, but her smile was genuine. "It's always my goal for my patients to feel like they have agency," she agreed, "even when it's not the outcome I hoped for. Life on your terms again. It's good."

"Sex on my terms again," Harper blurted with a laugh. "It's more than good." And in the weeks since they gave up trying, it undeniably had been.

Dr. Bluffton nodded with a chuckle. "Reproduction and romance are not the same science."

"No," Harper agreed emphatically. "They are not."

Then Dr. Bluffton offered her the pamphlet on the support group, which Harper had not expected to want or need. A week later, however, she found herself checking out their website when she realized that unlike the infertility journey, which had felt intensely private, she wasn't afraid to share this part of her life. She just didn't know how or when to share it.

The waiter returned to the table with three highball glasses and a promise that he would return with their first appetizers momentarily.

Harper raised her glass. "To Indie Lime," she said, "and what it was."

Seth smiled. "And moving on," he added, "and what comes next."

"And all the incredible nights yet to come," Bryan finished. "Cheers."

The glasses clattered together. The waiter returned with a tray piled with food.

"Alright, your first round of appetizers." He propped the tray on the edge of a neighboring table. "Jerk marinated chicken and mango kabobs, Caribbean hot pot broth with Johnny bread, conch ceviche, and the wedge salad with steamed crawfish." He set the dishes in the center of the table as a second server placed a small plate in front of each of them. "Enjoy," he said, as they both stepped away.

"She has a wedge salad?" Harper stared at the nondescript pile of iceberg that Maggie had obviously attempted to deconstruct and make interesting on the platter. "Since when?" she asked, remembering the vibrant and delicately plated fritter that had been presented on opening night. She scooped down into the thick vinaigrette that was sure to be both authentically Maggie and the most interesting thing in the dish, transferring a small pile onto her plate.

Seth shot an icy glance over her shoulder at the table of investors in the corner. "Part of the reworked, less expensive, more approachable relaunch to come," he said glumly.

Harper bit into the lettuce with a watery crunch. It was good, though hardly transcendent, and her heart panged at how Maggie's vision was being diluted. Fortunately, the kabobs and ceviche sang, and they had all but to physically restrain Bryan from licking the remains of the broth from the bowl.

A second round of plates appeared. The plantain lasagna from opening night. A salt encrusted, baked white fish. Stewed lamb over roasted tomatoes and rice. An admittedly docile jambalaya that Seth confirmed was another test item that the management group believed would play to a wider demographic.

By the time the third course arrived, the rest of the dining room was clearing out, just a few stray couples lingering over the end of cocktails and the last few bites of dessert. The server laid out another round of entrée dishes. Roasted oxtail and grits. Curried goat on a bed of black bean fried rice. A lobster, brilliantly red, surrounded by a rainbow of lemon wedges, glazed yams, fried plantains and pickled purple cabbage. A small tray of spicy calamari tacos that seemed both slightly out of place and like Maggie must have at least appreciated the idea enough to apply herself to its execution.

The dining room continued to empty. The friends continued to eat. During the fifth course, the investors in the corner got up and left without a glance toward the kitchen. Harper watched them pass the front windows of the restaurant with relief. She had hoped they could give Maggie a moment at the end of service, and she hadn't wanted to do it in front of an audience of the very people responsible for bringing Maggie's iteration of Indie Lime to an end. They finished the course, and a host of servers, now unoccupied with other tables, came to clear their empty plates.

A long, reflective moment stretched between them as they waited for dessert.

"I never would have guessed that this is how it would all end up." Seth broke the silence, his voice thick. "It kills me to see her have to walk away from it."

Harper spun her straw, stirring the ice cubes melting in her glass. "I think that's why she agreed to start cooking those dishes that aren't hers," she offered. "It's easier to leave something behind when you realize it's not actually what you wanted in the first place." Bryan's knee bumped into Harper's under the table, and she looked up into jade eyes dancing with flickering candlelight. The corner of his mouth twitched.

"Thank you for your patience." The waiter returned to the table, a small tray of three dessert plates balanced over his shoulder on one hand. "In honor of her final service, Chef has prepared what she's calling a 'Ten-K Tiramisu'."

An exchange of weighted glances passed around the table.

"This is a fusion twist on an Italian-style tiramisu, made with cream infused with Caribbean vanilla, allspice and cloves, layered with ladyfingers soaked in Caribbean rum."

"Incredibly expensive Caribbean rum," Bryan muttered under his breath.

"Good for her," Harper murmured. Maggie had asked Harper to inquire about the potential liabilities of using the rare liquor on the menu before she left. Harper had explained the entire situation to Candace, who responded emphatically that, given the circumstances, Maggie shouldn't leave a single drop of rum left in the bottle.

The server lowered the tray on his left hand to serve with his right. He lay a plate in front of Harper, and it took a moment to register what she was looking at–layers of thick, yellow cream in between spongy cake, dark with spiced rum, dusted with cocoa powder and, in the center, neatly stenciled in powdered sugar, the Northwestern "N." Harper swallowed hard around the lump growing in her throat.

The waiter collected the empty glasses from the table, then turned briefly away before snapping back to attention. "Ladies and Gentleman, Chef de Cuisine, Maggie Evans."

Harper, Bryan, and Seth looked up as the staff, servers and sous chefs alike, broke into thunderous applause. Maggie stood at the kitchen door, staring into the near empty dining room, the top button of her chef coat undone, eyes down. Harper, Bryan, and Seth rose to their feet to join in. The ovation continued a full minute before Maggie moved from the doorframe, crossing the dining room to the table in the corner and collapsing onto Seth's shoulder. The applause faded away as the staff returned to their end-of-shift duties, and Maggie sagged into an empty chair.

"That's it," she said, anticlimactically. "I can't believe that's it."

"Dinner was incredible," said Bryan through a mouthful of tiramisu. "And this dessert is…"

"I know," Maggie said with a tired laugh. She looked at Harper and winked. "Thanks for the free counsel on that one."

Harper smiled. "I should have billed it. That free advice just cost me two hundred dollars on tiramisu."

"Worth it!" Bryan exclaimed through another bite.

Harper carved a sliver of the 'N' away with her spoon and took her first bite of Maggie's last dish. It dissolved on her tongue, releasing a burst of rich, spicy rum that warmed Harper from the inside out. It was perfection. "Oh my God!" she said, rolling her eyes dramatically in ecstasy. "This is the best thing I've ever had in my mouth."

Bryan raised an eyebrow. "It's at least the most expensive thing," he corrected. "Seriously, Maggie," he added, laying his spoon to the side. "For everything this has been, congratulations."

Maggie shook her head, tears in her eyes, unable to speak.

They finished their dessert in comfortable, albeit expectant, silence. The staff flitted quietly around the room, clearing the remainder of the dishes and going through the rest of the closing checklist, obviously keen to go home, yet unwilling to interrupt their head chef with her guests. No one at the table seemed to want to be the first to suggest the evening had finally drawn to a close. Only when the team behind the bar turned off the giant chandelier, and the warm glow behind the teak slats dimmed then went dark, did Maggie breathe a heavy sigh and move to stand.

"I'll be just a moment," she said, retreating to the kitchen where her brigade of sous chefs waited for a final word and dismissal. When she returned a few minutes later, her eyes were red, but dry, and she'd traded her chef coat for a gray hoodie with Seth's charter school logo embroidered across the chest. "Ok, I'm ready," she announced, prompting Harper, Bryan, and Seth immediately to their feet.

"Let's go." Seth offered Maggie his arm.

Bryan slipped his arm around Harper's waist, gently guiding her to follow.

They stopped at the door where the host was clearing out old menus and schedules. Maggie dropped a single gold key onto the podium. She held out a hand. "Thank you, Michael."

The man nodded, his expression pained as he accepted the handshake. "My pleasure, Chef. If you ever want to do it again someday, please call." He looked away, his expression suddenly embarrassed.

"You're welcome to run my crews anytime," she assured him. "Take care of the staff."

"Yes, ma'am," he asserted, moving from the podium to the front door, which he held open for the four friends. They stepped into the waiting Chicago night.

As they walked up Lake Street, Harper hooked her elbow through Maggie's free arm.

"You're sure you're still ok about coming to the ultrasound tomorrow?" Maggie asked. "If it's too soon, I understand."

In truth, if it was anyone but Maggie, Harper would not have considered it, but she was determined to be there. She knew that the little part of her mourning over never being the one in the gown in the exam room matched the little part of Maggie mourning over having walked away from Indie Lime.

"I'm not going to miss my first chance to meet my goddaughter," Harper assured her.

"Or god*son*," Seth corrected. "That's the whole point of the ultrasound."

"I'm starting to think I should be offended that I wasn't invited," quipped Bryan.

"You have a class," Harper chided.

"I'm going to be the last to meet the little guy."

"Girl," Harper and Maggie intoned in unison.

The light on the corner of Michigan and Lake changed to yellow, and they stopped clear of the intersection, huddling together to brace against the fresh spring breeze whistling between the skyscrapers.

"We invited everyone to our open houses," Bryan offered in a mock pout.

Maggie laughed. "There's a big difference between browsing through your potential future homes and browsing through my reproductive organs."

"Touché," Bryan nodded. "But you are coming, right?"

"Of course," Maggie replied. "We'll come with Harper right after the appointment. How many are we on the hook for?"

"Seven," offered Bryan, matter-of-factly.

"For what it's worth," Harper said, throwing Bryan a look of exaggerated exasperation, "I've already got it narrowed down to two."

"Which means she knows which one she wants," Bryan teased.

"Does not," Harper insisted.

"Really?" Bryan pressed. "Wanna bet?" He fished in the pocket of his blazer, opening his hand to reveal a quarter lying in the center of his palm.

Harper immediately thought of the red brick townhome down a quiet, one-way street in Ravenswood. Soft gray walls with white crown molding. Two smaller bedrooms featuring original, rainbow-paned stained-glass windows. A spacious master bedroom and bath. Original, dark hardwood floors throughout. Not to mention, halfway between campus and the firm for her, and a mere fifteen minutes to Bryan's office. She had known the minute the listing popped into her inbox that she had to see it. She played along and added to Bryan's growing list as he considered the various virtues of condominiums and single-family homes. But unless something shocked her tomorrow, she wouldn't need to flip the coin. She was already arranging the furniture in her mind.

"I obviously have favorites," she admitted.

"Favorites? Plural?" Maggie teased. Harper rolled her eyes but remained silent, unwilling to rise to the bait.

"We'll make it up to you by going out to dinner after," Bryan offered. "We can celebrate the ultrasound, and by celebrate, I mean I will gamely play along as a one-man gender reveal."

"Such a good sport. In return, we will help you nitpick every detail of your future home." Maggie smiled and patted him playfully on the back.

"What good would it be to bring you along if you didn't?" laughed Bryan. "I'll make reservations. Ideas? Mexican? Thai?" A general murmur of non-preference passed between them. "Helpful guys, thanks."

"How about this?" offered Harper. "Give me the quarter?"

Bryan opened his hand.

"Heads," she pondered, "Thai food." She took the coin from his palm.

"Fine," agreed Bryan.

"Tails, Italian." Harper balanced the quarter on her thumb.

Bryan nodded while Maggie and Seth watched with mild amusement.

"3, 2, 1…" The quarter somersaulted into the air, glinting in the light of the stoplight as it flashed to green.

Heads. Tails. Heads. Tails.

Harper grabbed it as it fell. She looked at Bryan, who laid a hand over her fist closed around the coin. He raised an eyebrow.

Harper smiled. "Thai it is."

Acknowledgements

In many ways, this was a *hard* book: a book that was hard to write; a story that was hard to get my mind wrapped around; characters whom I loved but were hard to like sometimes. Yet, it was also a story that felt important to tell. Therefore, I will be eternally grateful to the people who helped me find both my voice and Harper's.

To the team at Black Rose Writing, who allowed me the space and creative freedom to write real-life characters who aren't always neat and tidy. It is an honor to be part of your community of authors, many of whom were generous with their time and experience and shared perspective on marketing, design, content, and audience.

To Amy, Kelly, Kiett, Kylie, Kim, Kristy, Larissa, Nicole, Sarah K., and Shannon, who graciously offered their thoughts and questions on the various drafts of the manuscript. Every comment and comma was valuable feedback on how to move the story forward.

To Megan and Sarah W., who shared their knowledge and experiences about the IVF process and the contracts involved. Thank you for looking into your own records, reaching out to your clinics, and helping me speculate, even when I texted questions that got strangely specific or entirely hypothetical.

To the team at OMC Women's Health and Dr. Richards– "OBGYN to the stars." Dr. Bluffton is entirely based on the compassion you show women navigating their fertility care. Thank you for your wealth of knowledge.

To the many friends, family members, and acquaintances that have shared parts of their own journeys along the way. It was an impossible task to capture every nuance of every person's experience on the page, but I hope you see yourself represented somewhere in the story and that there is hope and healing in knowing that you're not alone in wrestling through a broken heart or a change of plans.

My family once again waited patiently for this second novel, knowing I would not let them read it and cheering it on just the same. They are unfailing in their support, and I am forever grateful.

Finally, to Josh. You are the one person who knows just how different this story would have been had I stuck with my original idea. You listened to every reinvention and rewrite, never questioning my instincts to move things in completely different directions, and always encouraging me to follow my heart. The thing that every idea and draft had in common was a "really good husband character." Some things are just the easiest to write from personal experience. It's always you and me.

About the Author

Kate Laack is a high school English teacher, theater director, and author. She earned degrees in English and secondary education from the University of Wisconsin–La Crosse, where she got her start in publishing with the university newspaper. Her freelance work has appeared on *Thought Catalog, McSweeney's Internet Tendency, The Comedy Show Show*, and elsewhere. Kate lives in Pine Island, Minnesota, with her husband Josh, and their rescue dog Oakley in a home they built themselves. She is a classically trained pianist, has run four marathons, and is surprisingly good at fantasy football. *While the Coin is in the Air* is her second novel.

Note from Kate Laack

Word-of-mouth is crucial for any author to succeed. If you enjoyed *While the Coin is in the Air*, please leave a review online—anywhere you are able. Even if it's just a sentence or two. It would make all the difference and would be very much appreciated.

Thanks!
Kate Laack

We hope you enjoyed reading this title from:

BLACK✷ROSE
writing™

www.blackrosewriting.com

Subscribe to our mailing list – *The Rosevine* – and receive **FREE** books, daily deals, and stay current with news about upcoming releases and our hottest authors.
Scan the QR code below to sign up.

Already a subscriber? Please accept a sincere thank you for being a fan of Black Rose Writing authors.

View other Black Rose Writing titles at www.blackrosewriting.com/books and use promo code **PRINT** to receive a **20% discount** when purchasing.

www.ingramcontent.com/pod-product-compliance
Lightning Source LLC
LaVergne TN
LVHW041319260225
804617LV00002B/3